LOVE FOR A LIFETIME

A SMALL TOWN CHRISTIAN ROMANCE

LOVE IN BLACKWATER
BOOK 2

MANDI BLAKE

Love for a Lifetime
Love in Blackwater Book 2
By Mandi Blake

Copyright © 2024 Mandi Blake
All Rights Reserved

No part of this book may be used or reproduced in any manner whatsoever without written permission, except in the case of brief quotations embedded in critical articles and reviews. The unauthorized reproduction or distribution of this copyrighted work is illegal. No part of this book may be scanned, uploaded or distributed via the Internet or any other means, electronic or print, without the author's permission.

This book is a work of fiction. The names, characters, places, and incidents are products of the writer's imagination or have been used fictitiously and are not to be construed as real. Any resemblance to persons, living or dead, actual events, locale or organizations is entirely coincidental. The author does not have any control over and does not assume any responsibility for third-party websites or their content.

Published in the United States of America
Cover Designer: Amanda Walker PA & Design Services
Editor: Editing Done Write

CONTENTS

Snack, Food, and Mood List   vii

1. Olivia — 1
2. Dawson — 17
3. Olivia — 36
4. Dawson — 46
5. Olivia — 57
6. Dawson — 68
7. Olivia — 75
8. Olivia — 89
9. Dawson — 109
10. Dawson — 125
11. Olivia — 135
12. Dawson — 151
13. Dawson — 162
14. Olivia — 170
15. Dawson — 188
16. Olivia — 195
17. Dawson — 205
18. Olivia — 215
19. Dawson — 226
20. Olivia — 234
21. Dawson — 251
22. Olivia — 263
23. Dawson — 272
24. Olivia — 287
25. Olivia — 298
26. Dawson — 308
27. Olivia — 322

28. Dawson	330
29. Dawson	346
30. Olivia	353
31. Olivia	365
32. Dawson	371
33. Olivia	383
34. Dawson	390
Epilogue	398
Bonus Epilogue	403
Other Books By Mandi Blake	411
About the Author	415
Love in the Wild	417

Galatians 6:9 (NIV)

Let us not become weary in doing good.

SNACK, FOOD, AND MOOD LIST

Chapter 1 - Eggs (cooked, not smashed)

Chapter 2 - Chicken tenders

Chapter 7 - Shrimp corn chowder (or Skittles, if chowder isn't your taste)

Shrimp Corn Chowder

Ingredients:
3 cans of cream of potato soup
2 cans of milk (measured in empty soup cans)
1 pound of baby frozen shrimp
2 cans of white shoepeg corn
½ cup of green scallions (chopped)
1 stick of margarine

½ tsp of cayenne pepper
8 oz of cream cheese
Salt and pepper to taste

Melt a stick of margarine in a large pan and add scallions.
Sauté until they are slightly brown.
In a slow cooker, combine potato soup and milk. Mix well.
Turn on low.
Add shrimp and corn to soup and milk mixture.
Coat well.
Pour melted margarine and onions into the mixture.
Add cayenne pepper, salt, and pepper.
After the mixture is good and hot, melt the cream cheese into the chowder. Cook for about 2 hours or until cream cheese is melted, stirring occasionally.

Chapter 8 - Bison burger

Chapter 9 - BBQ

Chapters 12-14 - Wedding mints

Chapter 16 - Potato soup or chicken salad

Chapter 17 - Meatloaf and cornbread

Casserole dish cornbread

Cover the bottom of a 13 x 9 casserole dish with vegetable oil.
Heat at 400°F until hot.
Mix ½ of corn meal, 1 egg, and buttermilk until it is very thin.
Pour half of the hot oil into the mixture. Leave the remaining oil in the dish.
Pour the mixture into the casserole dish. Heat at 400°F for at least 20 minutes or until browned on top.

Chapter 19 - Chips, Skittles, Oreos. You know, camping food.

*Okay, if you want something better, Dawson also packed protein bars, granola, and instant oatmeal.

Chapter 20 - Cheeseburgers

Chapter 21 - Beef jerky (It's all we have. Take it or leave it.)

Chapter 23 - Roasted marshmallows

Chapter 26 - Chili

Chapter 27 - Steak

Chapter 32 - Totchos (think nachos, but with tater tots instead of tortilla chips)

Chapter 33 - Fudge brownies

I hope you enjoy the story with these little additions. Thanks again to Jenn (@sweet.cleanreads on Instagram) for this idea!

1

OLIVIA

Olivia's foot slid on the gas pedal, causing her entire vehicle to jerk. "He what?"

"He put eggs in Brett's backpack!" Heather shouted through the speakers of Olivia's trusty old car. "I'm going to have to buy him a new one. It was already starting to smell by the time he got home yesterday. I had to toss it."

Olivia leaned closer to the steering wheel and peered up at the darkening sky. She needed to get home before the rain if she wanted to make the trek to Cluckingham Palace and back without turning into a wet mop.

But seriously? Eggs in a backpack?

Kids were cruel.

"They weren't *my* eggs, were they?" Olivia shouted. The thought of her eggs somehow contributing to a middle-school prank had her ready to riot.

The local news headlines would be epic. *The Chicken Chick Conducts Citizens Arrest Following Egg Misuse.*

On second thought, her Instagram followers would love the scandal. Maybe she'd go viral again with a reel of her exacting revenge on a twelve-year-old bully.

Heather laughed. "Honey, I have no idea, but I consider you innocent in all this. It's a crime to waste your eggs."

Olivia huffed, not at all appeased about the abuse of poultry, but this call wasn't about the prank. It was about Heather's son. "How is Brett?"

Heather sighed. "He's upset. Embarrassed. I mean, kids don't have enough to do these days if they spend their time thinking up new ways to humiliate their peers."

"I'll be praying for him. And you. I know this is hard, mama."

Heather let out a sarcastic chuckle. "So hard. I'm at the end of my rope with these awful kids. I just want Brett to have a decent middle school experience. He can't even focus on his schoolwork because he's terrified to look anyone in the eye."

"You're a good mom. Remind him how special he is. Remind him that middle school and high school are preparing him for something greater.

Brett is a smart kid, and he's going to be a great man one day."

Heather sniffed. "You're right. He's the best. I hope he still remembers that after all this mess. Thanks for talking me off a ledge."

Olivia took a deep breath and stopped at the only stop sign in the tiny town she was driving through. "Anytime. I'm always here if you need me. Only a call away."

"I'll call you Thursday about the bake sale."

"Talk to you soon. Tell Brett I said hi."

Olivia pressed a button on her steering wheel to end the call and looked at the clock on the dash. Heather's need for a chat couldn't have come at a better time. Now, Olivia could pray the entire way home. Anything to keep her mind off the terrible news the doctor had just doled out.

A cold heaviness slid down her back. Why did she think about the appointment? She'd done such a good job of pushing it out of her mind since she left the doctor's office.

Not today, Satan. She was going to pray, not wallow in self-pity.

Olivia's silent pleas to the Lord soon took on a desperate tone. Despite her determination to push the thoughts from her head, thoughts of the impending surgery kept creeping back in. She'd had plenty of bad news about her endometriosis before, but it never got easier.

The panic was rising, and she couldn't turn her thoughts back to Heather and Brett's problems, no matter how hard she tried.

Her phone rang through the speakers, and she pressed the button to answer faster than a contestant on *Family Feud*.

"Hello."

"Hey! Are you busy?" Lyric asked.

The possibility of wedding plans made Olivia sit up straighter. "Not at all. What's up?"

Lyric sighed. "Wendy's having a rough day. Things are slow at the flower shop, and she thinks Julia might let her go soon. Can you say a prayer for her?"

"I'll do one better. Are you free tomorrow afternoon around four?" Olivia asked.

"Yep. As of right now, I'm free as a bird."

"Good. Pencil in some plans with me and Wendy, but for now, I'll definitely say a prayer for her."

"Thanks. I know I can always count on you."

"Every time. Love you."

"Love you too."

Olivia ended the call and asked her incredibly smart vehicle to call Julia's Flower Shop. Was it the car or the phone making the call? Either way, technology was phenomenal.

The robotic voice announced, "Calling Julia's Flower Shop."

Wendy was at the top of Olivia's prayer list with

good reason. The woman was getting pummeled by life lately, and the hits didn't seem to stop coming.

She'd only known Wendy for a few months, but that was another relationship forged by fire. Wendy was a recovering addict who recently lost a friend to the drugs that kept a hold on so many desperate lives. If anyone needed help, it was Wendy, and Olivia never missed a chance to help someone in need. It kept her mind off the soul-crushing fact that she'd probably have another surgery under her belt soon.

Nope. Not going down that road.

"Thanks for calling Julia's Flower Shop. This is Wendy."

"Hey! How are you?"

"Hey! I'm makin' it. How about you?"

And that question would get a quick side-step. "I'm great." (Read: Not great, but I want to assure you that I am absolutely, one hundred percent, great.)

"What can I do for you today?" Wendy asked.

"I was wondering if I could set up a consultation to talk about Lyric's wedding." Asa and Lyric's wedding wouldn't be a massive event, but Olivia and Lyric had already mapped out a small floral budget.

"Oh, of course! That'll be fun. Do you know what colors she wants? I'll put some samples together."

"Navy and chocolate."

"That'll be gorgeous for a fall wedding," Wendy said. "How about tomorrow afternoon."

"Does four work for you?" Olivia asked.

"Of course! When the bride has two jobs, it's usually hard to make plans."

Wasn't that the truth. Thankfully, Lyric's long hours meant she delegated most of the tasks to Olivia, her unofficial wedding planner.

She'd have to add that to her ever-growing resume. If she kept volunteering to help people with things, her credentials were going to look like a trade encyclopedia.

Caterer? Been there.

Moving service? Done that.

Charity event planner? Got the T-shirt.

Snake sitter? Never again.

Face painter for parties and festivals? So many times.

"What time do you get off work tomorrow? Want to have dinner with Lyric and me after?"

"Um, I get off at five, but..."

"My treat," Olivia added. If Wendy was having a hard time, dinner and girl talk might cheer her up.

"Okay. That sounds great. I'll see you tomorrow."

"Talk to you later," Olivia said as she ended the call.

There. Plans were made. Distractions were set in place.

Oh, no. Thinking about distractions only reminded her of the reason why she needed them, which only led her thoughts back to the news that had left her hollow and hopeless less than an hour ago.

Yeah, it was that kind of appointment. Predestined to gut her like an avocado. Doctor Barnes scooped out her insides and spread them on toast.

Her stomach growled at the thought of avocado toast, clearly angry about being left empty all day.

It wasn't Doctor Barnes's fault. She was just the messenger. She'd been on the endometriosis hit list for as long as she could remember. The "treatment" only served to leave her scarred on the inside time after time. Each surgery decreased her chances of ever being able to have children–a family.

No, no, no. That age-old grief was mixing with Olivia's fears to create a gnawing pain in her middle. She tightened her shoulders as she gripped the wheel. She had to avoid the tears at all costs. If she allowed one bit of weakness in, everything would crumble.

The slow whine of a police siren jerked her out of the pressing panic just as blue lights pulsed in her rear-view mirror.

"You've got to be kidding me," Olivia spat through gritted teeth. If she wanted a distraction, here it was in full color.

She pulled over to the side of the road, making sure to keep a good distance from the ditch. Reaching for her purse in the passenger seat, she rummaged for her license and registration.

With credentials in hand, she checked her side mirror. The police officer opened the cruiser door and stepped out.

Dawson. Of course it was Dawson. He would get a good laugh out of this and be sure to tell all of the old ladies at church that she was a menace to society.

The unstable emotions tumbled in her gut. Any other time, she'd be thrilled to see Dawson. He was one of her best friends, and he always knew how to make her smile.

But today was not the day, and now was not the time. Olivia teetered on the verge of not only cracking but breaking open like one of the eggs in Brett's backpack.

Officer Dawson Keller strode confidently toward her. Even in the small mirror, his smooth walk and tall build were suave enough to make any woman between the ages of eighteen and sixty-five break into a nervous sweat. Add a police uniform and you had a delicious recipe for a long-term crush.

Caution: Objects in mirror are hotter than they appear.

Olivia groaned. Going toe-to-toe with her handsome friend required a ton of focus–something she didn't have today.

Dawson approached her car and rested his hands on the open windowsill. His short hair framed playful blue eyes and a strong jaw. Even his slightly crooked nose was cute. Especially since she knew he broke it playing football with the youth at church two years ago and decided against getting it reset because he claimed it gave him "character."

Before she could catch her breath, Dawson Keller smiled, and oh, was it a good one. He had the kind of slow grin that won him dozens of hearts.

Including hers.

But she was completely unarmed and unprepared to protect herself from his charms today.

Dawson bent slightly, leaning on his propped arms to peer into her vehicle. "How's your day going, ma'am?"

"Fine. Yours?"

There. That sounded perfectly grounded. She'd give herself a pat on the back for her performance later.

Dawson crossed his arms on the windowsill and settled in. "Just got a lot better."

"I'm not in the mood, Dawson. Just give me the ticket, and we can go about our days."

Escaping this interaction in the next three minutes was her only chance of getting away without alerting Dawson to her diminished mood.

"It's Officer Keller," he reminded her.

"No, it's not," she said with a laugh. "It's Dawson Theodore Keller."

"Just once," he begged, throwing his head back in an exaggerated plea.

"I'm not playing your fantasy game."

Dawson didn't need the uniform to turn every woman's head. He had personality in spades, making everyone laugh and feel special with one phrase or joke. The uniform only made him lethal. Only when hearts were on the line.

And as far as hearts went–Dawson's was pure gold. He might joke about wanting to be called officer, but he was the epitome of the good cop stereotype. He wanted justice, but he wanted things to be set right. He wanted harmony and fun.

It was too bad his job was a double-edged sword. To right the wrongs, he had to see the darkness in all its many forms.

"Will you call me sir?" he asked in a last-ditch effort to get a rise out of her.

Olivia looked up, ready to keep the sparring match going, until she saw the look on his face. His brows were pulled slightly together, frowning in concern.

Or was it pain?

He already knew something was wrong. She hadn't fooled him for one minute.

"What's wrong, my queen?" he asked softly.

And that stupid nickname he'd given her back when she used to boss him and her brother around when they were kids shattered every gate holding back the tears.

The pressure in her chest expanded until a sob

burst out of her, hard and loud, as she covered her face with her hands. He couldn't see her like this. She was known for keeping it together. It's what she was good at!

She hadn't cried like this since her mom died, and the disappointment crushed her already sagging shoulders.

Her car door opened, and Dawson pulled her to her feet, holding her tight to his chest. His strong arms created a barricade around her as she pressed her face into the hard material of his uniform.

"Who did this to you?" His warm breath brushed against her ear–stern and foreboding. "Who upset you? I'll find them."

Another sob was her only answer. Dawson didn't have a cruel bone in his body, but she had no doubt he'd exact justice on anyone who hurt her.

But this wasn't someone's fault. It was hers. Her own body was attacking her, stealing any hope for the future she wanted.

She should be used to it by now, but she'd keep praying. If it was the Lord's will for her, she'd have to find a way to accept her fate.

That didn't stop the anger from penetrating her every thought. She'd done a good job protecting her heart from Dawson's flirting all these years, because that's all it was–flirting. He flirted with everyone.

She would be thoroughly and completely crushed if she gave in and opened her heart to

Dawson only to have him leave when he found out she had a medical condition that was severe enough to most likely render her unable to have kids.

He wasn't going to find out today, and she was glad she hadn't let Dawson charm his way into her heart. He wanted kids, and he wasn't quiet about it.

She had a reason for keeping everyone at arm's length. Every boyfriend she'd ever had eventually got tired of trying to break through her walls and said a quick goodbye.

No one in town knew about her condition, except her dad and her brother, Beau. She'd been careful not to let the word get out. She couldn't stand it if people started looking at her like she was defective. Lots of people wanted to have kids. It just so happened she was one of them, but that dream would most likely never belong to her.

"Olivia. Tell me what's wrong. I'll fix it."

She sniffed and wiped her tears on the back of her hand. "It's nothing. Just a bad day. Or I guess a lot of bad days hitting me all at once."

"It's not Toby, is it? If he bothers you again–"

"His name was Trey, and I haven't heard from him since he broke up with me. It is *not* Trey."

Trey could go for a dip in the Amazon River for all she cared. She hadn't lost a single night's sleep over that loser.

"What can I do?" Dawson asked.

The hurt in his question hit her right in the

chest. This man would do anything for her, but he couldn't scare this monster away.

"I'm okay. Really." She sniffed and wiped beneath her eyes, thankful she hadn't worn a lot of makeup today.

"Can I help you feed the chicks?" he asked. "I already fed and milked the goats today."

Of course he had already done half the farm chores. Well, it made sense, considering he claimed the goats were his.

They were hers, but she gladly let him take care of them. The chickens were her babies. She only kept the goats because they used to be her mom's favorites, and she hadn't worked up the courage to sell them.

"Nah. I'll be fine. Thanks for letting me water your uniform." She pointed to the dark spot on his chest.

He didn't take his eyes off her. "Are you sure?"

"I'm sure. Totally sure."

Say it one more time, and he'll know you're definitely not sure.

"Will you at least call one of the girls?" he asked, almost pleading.

"No, I don't want to talk. I'm really okay. It's just been a long day."

Dawson nodded, but he didn't look convinced. "Can I follow you home?"

"Nope. I promise I'm okay. I need to feed the

chickens, then I have a long night of making place cards for the wedding. Last I checked, your handwriting was chicken scratch."

Dawson crossed his arms over his chest. "I'll be sure to write very clearly in my report about this incident."

Olivia's eyes widened. "Are you really giving me a ticket?"

"No, but you are getting a nice, official warning. It's a school zone, and even if school isn't in session, the speed limit is still thirty-five miles per hour through here."

Thirty-five? She'd definitely been going faster than that. Olivia tucked her chin to her chest. "I'm sorry, Officer. It won't happen again."

Dawson lifted her chin with one finger and gave her a wicked smile. "Keep your chin up, my queen. Just be careful."

Oh no. The tears were building again. She nodded quickly, desperate to escape before the waterworks came on. "Uh-huh. I'll do that. Thanks for setting me straight." She turned and ducked back into her car and closed the door with a bit too much force.

"Bye," she whispered out the window as she buckled her seatbelt.

Dawson gave her a quick "See you later" and walked off.

Her heart pounded hard and fast like a full

marathon of feet hitting the pavement in rapid succession. She had to get home and find a bunch of things to do to keep her mind busy. Sitting in the car on the long drive back to Blackwater from Cody wasn't doing her any favors.

Dawson reappeared at her window, and a shriek filled the car as she jerked away from the door.

Oh, that was *her* high-pitched shriek. Very smooth.

Dawson chuckled, clearly proud of himself for effectively scaring the life out of her. "I'll call you tomorrow."

"Mhmm," she hummed. "Talk to you tomorrow."

Olivia clamped her mouth shut. If she said one more word, she'd spill the beans and get all woe-is-me about the awful news she got today.

She wanted to tell him. She really did. They shared everything else. Very few topics were off-limits between them. He would be a great listener, and he'd be encouraging. She had no doubt about that.

But Dawson felt things more than other men. He'd be utterly and completely brokenhearted for her, and she couldn't bear seeing the sadness on his face.

He walked back toward his cruiser, and all of her stability left with him. Her moment of bravery was crushing like a paper castle. The urge to cry built again.

Her phone dinged with a text, and she reached for it before getting back on the road.

Karen: Hey, I know this is short notice, but can you work in the morning? Someone called in sick.

Olivia typed out a quick yes and rested her phone in the cupholder. Work was just what she needed to keep her thoughts on the straight and narrow. It also helped to remind her that some people had bigger problems than hers. Working at a senior care facility kept her grateful her disease only rendered her unable to function a couple of times a month.

Her life would go on, at least for now, and she couldn't let the fear keep her from living. The doctor had high hopes for her treatment and recovery, and she had to hold onto that hope. The best thing she could do would be to throw herself into work.

2

DAWSON

Dawson pulled up at the address given by dispatch and shifted the cruiser into park. The basic, two-story house was nestled in the woods just inside the Blackwater town limits.

The call was starting to make sense now. Apparently, a six-year-old boy had climbed out of his upstairs bedroom window, and his mom couldn't get to him. The roof had a steep slant with dormer windows on both sides.

There wasn't a kid in sight, but a woman with dark hair was hanging her top half out of one of the windows.

Dawson radioed to dispatch, "401 on the scene," and stepped out of the vehicle.

As soon as the woman spotted him, she shouted, "Over here!"

Another cruiser pulled into the drive just as Officer Freeman associated herself with the call.

Dawson walked around the side of the house where the woman was still frantically shouting, "He's over there!"

Following where she pointed, Dawson spotted the little boy in a nearby tree.

A *nearby* tree, not the tree nearest the house. The kid had some pretty impressive skills if he'd maneuvered his way from the house to his current location.

Dawson cupped his hands around his mouth and yelled to the woman in the window, "I'm Officer Keller. Do you have a ladder?"

The woman pushed hair from her face and took a series of quick breaths. "I think so."

"Don't panic. We'll help him," Dawson assured her.

Jennifer appeared at Dawson's side, standing half a foot shorter. Officer Freeman had a sweet look about her, but it didn't take long before people saw through her disguise. She was as determined as they came, and no one ever accused her of pulling punches. He had no complaints about handling calls with her. "Where is he?"

Dawson pointed to the tree. "Hanging around."

Jennifer spotted the boy in the tree who was starting to look scared. "We'll be right there. Don't move. We're going to help you."

The woman hanging out of the window seemed

to calm slightly when she saw Jennifer. "I–I think my husband might have a ladder in the shed, but I'm not sure."

"Can I have your permission to check?" Dawson asked.

The woman nodded wildly.

"I need a verbal confirmation, ma'am."

"Yes, please," she said before turning her attention back to her son. "Braxton, stay where you are. They're coming, sweetie!"

Dawson jogged toward the shed, scanning the backyard that housed a climbing dome, a fire pit surrounded by chairs, and a tire swing.

No sign of a pet–thankfully.

The rotting wood of the shed door creaked as he opened it. He pulled his flashlight out of his belt and scanned the dark room.

"Snow shovel, rake, leaf blower…"

A metal ladder rested against the back wall of the shed, but the space between the door and that wall was covered in various supplies and equipment.

Just another day on the job. He started stepping over and around things as he played the live-action game of Frogger through the shed.

With the ladder in hand, he had to navigate his way back through the mess.

"Officer Keller?" Jennifer shouted.

"On my way!" He pushed the ladder out of the doorway where Jennifer pulled it from his hands.

"Don't scare me like that, Keller," Jennifer said in a low voice.

"It'll take more than a pile of junk to keep me down," he said. It wasn't unheard of for officers to respond to a call only to find out it was a trap. It hadn't happened in Blackwater since Dawson had been on the squad, but even tiny towns saw their fair share of twisted criminals.

Jennifer rolled her eyes and hefted the ladder under her arm before walking back to the base of the tree where the boy stood hugging the trunk a good twenty-feet off the ground.

Jennifer set one end of the ladder on the ground beside the tree. Dawson extended it up the side of the trunk and locked it into place.

"You climb. I'll hold," Jennifer said.

Dawson started up the ladder and called out to the boy. "Hey. I'm Officer Keller. What's your name?"

The boy looked from Dawson to his mom–his nostrils flaring as his breathing quickened.

"It's okay, baby. He's here to help!" his mom called.

"Braxton," the boy said as he squatted down on the branch.

"Well, Braxton, this is one story I bet your mom won't forget about any time soon."

The boy tucked his chin, and his shoulders rose to cover his cheeks. "She's gonna be so mad."

Dawson kept climbing, and the pine needles

started to prick his hands and face. "Yeah, but I think she'll just be glad to have you on solid ground again. Just apologize and remind her how cute you are. I'm sure she'll forgive you."

Braxton's small hands clung to the bark as he shifted in his crouch on the branch. "I don't think that'll work this time."

Dawson stopped when he was face-to-face with Braxton. His blond hair had little brown specks in it from the pinecones, and the tear tracks running down his face had dirt smudged in them.

Dawson propped his shoulder on the tree and his other hand on the top of the ladder. "Let me tell you a secret. Mamas don't give up on their kids, even if they're big boys who climb out of windows and get stuck in trees."

Braxton wiped the back of his arm over his face. "Okay."

"But your mom would probably be a lot happier if you didn't go tree hopping again."

Braxton nodded vigorously. "Yes, sir."

"You ever been on a ladder?" Dawson asked.

Braxton peeked down before jerking his head back and clinging to the tree. "No."

"Well, there's a first time for everything. Let me show you how to do this." Dawson wrapped a hand around the far side of the branch and opened his other arm. "Put your feet right here, and I'll stay right behind you. When I step down, you step down. We'll do it together."

Braxton nodded but didn't release his hold on the tree trunk.

"You're gonna have to trust me, Braxton. I'll hold onto you, and my friend, Officer Freeman, is down there holding the ladder steady. We can do this."

Dawson reached his hand out, but Braxton didn't take it.

Man, he could be hanging around here for a while if the kid didn't trust him. Friendliness usually helped forge bonds, but fear sometimes trumped bravery.

This was one of those times he wished Olivia was around. People trusted her. They opened up to her like a faucet. Their secrets spilled out over phone calls and messages. If only people trusted Dawson like they trusted Olivia. His job would be so much easier.

Thoughts of Olivia brought back her crippling sadness when he pulled her over. He'd texted her before bed last night and this morning before his shift. She said she was okay, but he couldn't push the memory of her tears from his mind. It knotted his stomach regularly.

Dawson watched Braxton clinging to the tree. What would Olivia do in this situation?

"Hey, do you know Jesus?" Dawson asked.

Braxton looked up with wide eyes as if they'd just realized they had a mutual friend. "Yeah."

Bingo.

"Then I think we should ask Him for some bravery," Dawson said.

Braxton glanced down, then back up at Dawson. "Yeah. Okay."

Dawson bowed his head and prayed. "Hey, Jesus. I know I just talked to You about an hour ago, but it's me again. I'm here with Braxton, and he's gotten himself into a little bit of a tight spot. I know You told us in the Bible that You'll always be with us, so we'd like to ask You to keep us safe while You're going down this ladder with us."

Dawson peeked one eye open to find Braxton with his head down and eyes closed. His shoulders trembled, but he seemed calm otherwise.

"And maybe hang around for a while after we get down. I know Braxton is worried about what his mom is gonna say. Oh, and thanks for loving us, Jesus. You're awesome, and we love You."

Braxton giggled and squirmed on the branch. That was a hundred times better than tears.

"Amen." Dawson lifted his head and reached his hand out to Braxton. "So, are you with me?"

Braxton took the offered hand, sliding his clammy palm against Dawson's. "Yeah. I think I can do it."

Dawson slowly guided the boy until his feet were

in the right places on the rungs of the ladder. "You know, this isn't my first time on a ladder."

Braxton looked over his shoulder and up at Dawson. "Good because I'm trying really hard not to be scared right now."

Dawson chuckled and placed his hands over Braxton's on the sides of the ladder. "One step at a time."

They slowly descended, until Dawson stepped to the ground and Braxton jumped off the third rung.

Braxton's mom stood by Jennifer, waiting to wrap her son in her arms.

"Mom! I did it!"

His mom smothered him in her embrace. "You did, and I've never been so upset and relieved at the same time in my entire life!"

Braxton's mom didn't let him out of her arms while Dawson and Jennifer completed the reports. The mom wrapped Jennifer in a big hug, and Braxton looked at Dawson.

Dawson extended his fist, then opened his arms. "Fist bump or a hug?" he asked.

Braxton launched himself at Dawson, who barely had time to bend down to the kid's level. With the little arms around his neck, Dawson gave the hug everything he had. "You be good for your mom, okay?"

"I will. Thanks for helping me be brave," Braxton whispered.

Aw, man. The little boy was determined to make Dawson's heart melt. Calls involving kids were either the worst or the best. This was one of the good ones–the kind that reaffirmed his decision to be a part of a force that served and protected.

"Don't forget who helped us," Dawson said, pointing up.

"Jesus. I know," Braxton said quickly.

Mom and son were safely back inside the house ten minutes later. Dawson walked back to the front yard next to Jennifer and playfully shoved her shoulder. "Don't you feel like a real-life hero?"

Jennifer chuckled. "Sometimes. Though, you were great with Braxton. He took to you really quickly."

"Kids love me."

"It's because you're still a kid," Jennifer said.

"Thanks."

Dawson's phone dinged, signaling a text.

Asa: You coming to the garage? Jacob has something to show you.

Dawson typed out a quick reply.

Dawson: Be there in an hour.

"You have big plans this afternoon?" Dawson asked.

Jennifer flipped through her small notebook as she walked. "Nope."

Jennifer was about as introverted as Dawson was extroverted, which meant his mission as her coworker was to slowly fold her into his friend group. If she spent her days home alone because she wanted to, that was fine, but he tried to at least offer her something to do where a few close friends were involved every once in a while.

"I'm heading over to Beau's garage to meet Asa and Jacob. Wanna come?"

"I would, but I don't want to," Jennifer said without looking up.

"Suit yourself." He'd given it a fair shot.

"See you later, Keller," she said with a wave over her shoulder as she slid into her cruiser.

The rest of the workday should have wrapped up quickly, but his worry about Olivia kept jutting into his thoughts like a kid playing peekaboo–always reminding him he could find a million ways to think about her.

He pulled his phone out of his pocket the minute he walked out of the station, pressing the name "Chicken Tender" in his contacts like it was second nature.

Olivia answered on the second ring. "Is this an emergency?"

Her no-nonsense voice was out today, greeting him like a well-meaning mother. "That depends. How is my queen?"

"You have got to stop calling me that. People are going to think we're more than friends."

Dawson hummed. "I see no issue with that."

His relationship with Olivia had grown in interesting ways over the years. She'd gone from his best friend's little sister who wanted to tag along wherever the boys went, to the alluring, beautiful woman he'd give his left pinky toe to spend every second of every day with.

Somehow, she still thought he was joking when he poured his heart out.

Olivia groaned. "I'm fine. You caught me at a bad time yesterday."

Dawson unlocked his truck and got in. "Are you sure?"

"I'm sure you're gonna regret it if you call me during work hours again without a broken bone."

Olivia was a nurse, and she took her work very seriously. She told him once that her friends–as she called the patients–deserved her undivided attention during work hours, and he respected that commitment.

"What about a papercut?" Dawson asked.

"Bye, Dawson," Olivia sang before ending the call.

He pocketed his phone and headed toward Beau's garage, somewhat assured that Olivia was okay.

What could Jacob have to show him? It probably had something to do with the classic car Dawson had basically given him for his eleventh birthday. They'd been fixing it up together for months now, and things were starting to come together.

He pulled up at Blackwater Automotive and parked next to Asa and Beau's trucks. Jacob's excited chatter floated out of the open bay door, but Dawson needed to have a chat with Beau first.

The offices and waiting area were small but surprisingly cozy for a mechanic shop. Olivia deserved a gold medal for all the work she did at her brother's garage. Dawson would bet his last paycheck Beau hadn't asked Olivia to do a single thing around here. She saw a need and took it upon herself to fix it.

He rapped his knuckles on the metal office door before letting himself in. "Hey, boss."

Beau stood next to a filing cabinet rummaging through folders. He didn't look up at the intrusion. "What's up?"

Dawson propped his arm on top of the filing cabinet. "Have you talked to Olivia lately?"

Subtlety was for the weak.

It wasn't anything new that she was first and foremost in his thoughts, but after seeing her cry, she'd basically bought real estate in his head and settled in for the long haul.

Beau looked up from the files. "I talked to her this morning. Why?"

Olivia was Beau's sister, and she looked after him like a mother hen. Since their mom died a few years ago, Olivia made it her mission in life to make sure Beau stayed on the straight and narrow.

"Did she sound okay?" Dawson asked.

"Yeah. Why?"

Beau was about as observant as a stump, but he cared about his sister, whether he acknowledged it or not.

"I ran into her yesterday. Well, I pulled her over."

"Smooth move, Cassanova," Beau said. "Was she really speeding, or were you pestering her?"

Dawson held up a finger. "I'll have you know that I do not pester her. I don't know why you'd think that."

"You do. All the time," Beau confirmed. "All. The. Time."

"For your information, she was speeding. In a school zone."

Beau shut the cabinet and finally gave his attention to the topic. "That doesn't sound like her."

"I know! But the worst part is she started crying while we were talking."

No part of the interaction he had with Olivia yesterday was normal. His usually cool, calm, and collected queen was on edge from the moment he showed up at her window.

Beau tilted his head slightly and narrowed his eyes. "She cried? That doesn't sound like her either. I don't think I've seen her cry since..."

Beau didn't finish the sentence, but Dawson

knew. She hadn't cried since their mom died. At least not publicly.

He'd never forget that awful time. Martha Lawrence had always been a pillar of strength in the Blackwater community. Her sudden death shook the whole county.

"Yeah. But she didn't tell me why she was upset. Just that she had a bad day."

"Maybe she really just had a bad day. She's tough, but she's not a robot," Beau said.

"She cried, dude. She never cries." How could her brother not see the urgency here?

Beau settled into a chair at the desk and stared at the computer screen. The dirty mechanic looked out of place in an office, even if the desk was just as stained as he was. "She's a big girl, but I've heard women have feelings. Tears are normal. And let's be honest, she has a million friends, but Mom was her rock. She doesn't have that anymore."

Martha's death had hit Dawson's life like a brick through a window. She'd been like a second mother to him, and Olivia's relationship with her mom was the stuff of legends. They were cut from the same cloth. As much as he missed Martha, Olivia probably hadn't gotten over the loss, even after all these years.

Could that really be the reason Olivia was upset? Granted, he'd had plenty of nightmares after Martha died where Olivia was distraught and he couldn't get to her.

"Maybe she had a bad day at work," Beau offered.

"She was off work yesterday, and I doubt the chick clique hurt her feelings," Dawson said.

Beau scoffed. "You never know. She didn't speak to anyone for a week when that hen died last year."

"RIP Gemma," Dawson said.

Beau pointed out the office window that looked into the garage. "Jacob has been waiting on you."

"Oh! Right." He'd almost forgotten about the reason he was here. Dashing out into the garage bay, he caught the tail end of what Jacob was saying.

"What do you think? Red or silver?" Jacob asked as he rubbed his smooth chin. If only the kid knew what kind of changes were coming for him in the next few years.

Dawson shuddered, remembering puberty for a second only to shove those embarrassing memories into the back corner of his mind where they belonged.

"Red. Obviously," Dawson answered before jerking to a stop. "Wait. What are we talking about?"

"Dawson!" Jacob turned around and grabbed something off the toolbox. He lifted a model car in both hands–a Porsche 911 in the classic guards red. "What do you think?"

"Whoa. Definitely red," Dawson said as he reached for the model.

"But silver is their signature color," Jacob said.

Dawson lifted the small car. "But have you seen this? That is hot."

Jacob's smile grew, and he clapped his hands. "Yeah. Red looks good on it."

Dawson checked out the life-size Porsche 911 in the bay beside them. It was a far cry from the shiny vision in his hands. The interior was torn out and resting on the garage floor. The dingy white exterior had seen its better days in the last century, and nothing under the hood was operating yet.

"It's gonna be awesome when you finish it," Dawson said as he handed the model back to Jacob.

"Hey, Dad. Can I wear this color in the wedding?" Jacob asked, eyeing the bright red with fascination and wonder.

Asa froze where he leaned under the hood. "That's a little flashy, don't you think?"

Dawson rubbed a hand over his mouth to hide his smile. Asa was getting married in a few weeks, and his son, Jacob, was probably more excited than the bride and groom.

Jacob studied the model again. "Maybe, but it would definitely look cool."

Dawson held up a finger. "Wait, are you taking votes on what the groomsmen get to wear? Because I have ideas."

"Don't let Dawson vote on the suits," Beau said as he made his way over to the Porsche. "I've never been a groomsman before. What else am I supposed to be doing besides playing dress up?"

"Not much," Asa said. "Lyric and Olivia are taking care of everything. I do need to know if you'll be bringing a date. We need a head count."

"That's a no for me," Beau said.

Dawson grabbed Asa's shoulder. "Hold the phone. We get to bring a date?"

Beau shook his head. "Only you would think it's a privilege that you're expected to bring a date."

"Can I have a date too?" Jacob asked.

Asa looked wide-eyed at his kid. "Do you have someone in mind?"

Jacob shrugged one shoulder. "I'm sure I could find someone."

"You bet you can!" Dawson said as he rested an arm around Jacob's shoulders. "You're a catch. The ladies will be lining up to be your date."

Asa glared at Dawson. "He's eleven, not seventeen."

"But he's a gentleman. Women are drawn to those at any age," Dawson explained.

"Pretty sure you mean women are drawn to bad boys," Beau said.

Dawson narrowed his eyes at Beau. "Fight me on it."

Asa pinched the bridge of his nose. "The invitation said you get a plus one. Did you even read it?"

Dawson looked around the garage. "Are you talking to me?"

"Yes, you. Did you read the invitation?"

Dawson assumed he'd hang out with his friends at the wedding. He was a groomsman, so it wasn't as if he could sit with someone during the ceremony.

"No. I looked at the date and threw it away. I know when to show up."

"Well, now you know. You get a plus one," Asa said.

Images of Olivia laughing and dancing in a flowing dress filled his mind. He'd pulled his phone out of his pocket and had his message thread with her open before thinking twice. The name Chicken Tender with a chicken emoji beside it sat at the top of his screen.

He didn't want to ask her to be his official wedding date in a text. Call him old-fashioned, but if he was going to finally get a yes out of the one woman he wanted, seeing the look on her face was a must.

He typed up a message. It was after five, but he wanted her in a good mood for this talk.

Dawson: What are you doing tonight? Want to go to Barn Sour?

He pocketed his phone and tried to ignore the tingling heat under his collar. Did it make him a chicken if he wanted to do the asking in public? Maybe she would let him down easy if her answer was no.

His phone dinged again. Olivia's reply was a photo of her holding Genella up beside her smiling face.

Funny, Olivia would think the chicken was the star of that photo. Oh, how wrong she was. Olivia's dark hair was pulled back into a high ponytail, and her hazel eyes were lighter than usual. They always changed when she was happy, which was any time she was with her chickens.

A text came through right after the photo.

Chicken Tender: I'm just getting to Cluckingham Palace. Want to come see Genella?

That was the wrong question. Did he care about seeing Genella? Sure. Did he want to be wherever Olivia was? Absolutely.

Dawson: I'll be there in ten.

"Change of plans, guys. I gotta run. I'll let you know about my plus one later today."

"You sound pretty sure of yourself," Beau said.

"Here's hoping," Dawson said as he turned and jogged toward his truck.

If all went as planned, Olivia would be his wedding date, and he'd be on the fast track out of the friend zone.

3

OLIVIA

Olivia centered the chicken clique on her phone screen. The trio was positioned on the white-washed chicnic table she'd added to the farm over the summer. "Can you move Ginny about an inch to the right?"

Anna cautiously reached for the hen. She slowly placed her hands on Ginny's sides and lifted her just a little. "Like that?"

"Perfect." Olivia started the video and panned around the trio of chickens. Ginny, Gretta, and Gertie were her Instagram stars, and Olivia's followers went crazy whenever the group made an appearance online.

Who could blame them? The Black Star, Golden Comet, and Leghorn were adorable. It helped that they had plenty of personality too. Ginny was subdued, Gretta was feisty, and Gertie was funny.

Anna chuckled as the hens took turns jumping off the chicnic table, flapping their wings frantically, before trotting off together as if they were headed to ladies' night at the local watering hole.

"They're cute. I'll give you that. But I have no idea how you have a hundred thousand followers on Instagram when all you post about are the chickens."

"Who doesn't love chickens?" Olivia asked as she followed the group toward their play area.

Yes, her hens had a play area. They also had a hotel, a tree house, and a sunning yard. Hence the name, Cluckingham Palace. They were also free to roam, so they often visited the goats or hung out on her dad's front porch.

Olivia's phone dinged and a banner popped up at the top of her screen, reminding her she had an unread message from Dawson.

She clicked it and read his reply. "Dawson is on his way."

Anna straightened. "Now? Why?"

Olivia wasn't gung-ho about seeing him after her embarrassing breakdown yesterday. He'd only hounded her once every hour since then, and she wasn't doing a good job of convincing him that she was as fine as she claimed.

Probably because she wasn't, and it hit her hard that he knew she wasn't, despite her insistence.

"He hasn't seen the goats today."

"Does he come over every day?" Anna asked.

"Pretty much. I mean, I don't think I could go a day without seeing my chicks either."

Anna looked down at her clothes. "I would have worn something different if I'd known Dawson would be here."

Olivia replayed the video and fought the urge to react. It wasn't a secret that Anna had a major crush on Dawson. She'd been trying to get his attention for years, and while he was always friendly to her, he hadn't made the move Anna had been waiting on all this time.

Did that ticking time bomb bother Olivia? Yes and no. She wanted her Anna Banana to be happy, but the thought of losing her best friends to each other made her stomach churn.

She would not be jealous. She would *not* be jealous.

"You look great. Don't worry about it," Olivia said as she moved to the little room outside the palace where she kept treats and equipment. She reached for a plastic cup and handed it to Anna. "Here. Throw these in the sunroom and let me video the feeding frenzy."

Anna took the cup and looked inside. She jerked back with a yelp and shoved the cup back at Olivia. "It's full of worms!"

"They love mealworms. Don't worry. You don't have to touch them. Just toss a few at a time."

Anna frowned at the cup, but even the sour expression couldn't spoil her beautiful features. The woman was model-pretty and with little to no effort. Her straight hair was the perfect shade of sunkissed blonde, and it fell over her shoulders like a golden waterfall. Her blue eyes and easy smile made sure she was never without admirers. Yes, plural. Half the men who came into Blackwater left enamored with her.

As they should because Anna was awesome. They'd been friends long enough for Olivia to know.

Olivia made the motion. "A toss is like this."

Anna took the cup of worms. "I know how to toss." She narrowed her eyes at Olivia. "You owe me for this."

"I have a surprise for you that'll make you love me again," Olivia said, trying to contain her smile.

That got Anna's attention. "Let's toss some worms."

After five minutes of filming the chickens munching on worms, Anna stalked out of the sunning room. "Where's my prize, woman?"

Olivia skipped over to the supply room where she'd stored the box. She cut it open and pulled out the apron she'd ordered. "Look at it!"

Anna's eyes widened, and she let out a hearty laugh. "What is that?"

"It's an egg apron. A new online shop wants me to feature it on Instagram." She held up the apron.

The white material was durable with prints of colorful chickens on it. Small pockets for collecting eggs were attached in straight rows along the front.

"I know that's not for me," Anna said, eyeing the contraption.

"It's for me, but I was hoping you'd help me style it. And maybe take some photos and videos I could use."

Anna rubbed her hands together. "This could be so fun. You definitely need a light-blue blouse and maybe medium wash jeans. And boots. I have the perfect pair."

"Bring them over tomorrow," Olivia said.

"You got it." Anna leaned against the coop wall beside the hen bath. "Remind me again why you don't live here?"

The chickens and goats were on the family farm, and as much as she loved her childhood home and her dad, she didn't want to live here now that her mom was gone.

She'd offered to move back home after her mom passed, but thankfully, her dad declined. She still worried about him, but not as much as right after Mom died.

"Two grieving hearts don't equal a whole. We'd just bring each other down. Plus, I'm in and out so much it would probably annoy him."

Anna sighed and reached for Olivia, wrapping

her arms around her neck. "I love you. I'm always here for you."

Olivia squeezed back. She couldn't be more different from her friend, but they balanced each other out in ways neither of them understood.

Anna loved fashion and made a good living as an online influencer. Clothing designers sent her pieces from all over the world. It helped that Anna looked good in anything. She could wear a towel, and the internet would go wild, scrambling for the exact one she posted on her Instagram and vlog.

Anna was also an attorney working at her dad's firm. She had the brains to back up that beauty.

Olivia, on the other hand, promoted mostly small businesses that made home decor featuring poultry.

"Friend, I ask this with all the love in the world, but how are you going to find a man if you spend all of your extra time volunteering or hanging out with chickens?"

Resting the back of her hand on her forehead, Olivia wailed, "My kingdom for a date!"

Anna swatted Olivia's shoulder. "I'm serious. You never date. It's sad."

Olivia groaned. "I don't need a man. I'm doing what I want to do."

"But who doesn't love love? I mean, you're a strong, independent woman, but we're both getting old, and we need husbands and families."

Olivia closed her eyes and took a deep breath. Anna knew about Olivia's endometriosis, but they'd never talked about Olivia's possible inability to bear children, and it needed to stay that way. "I don't need a man or a baby. I'm fine. Can we talk about something else?"

Anna clapped her hands and flashed a smile so bright it rivaled Times Square. "Yes, let's talk about Dawson. Has he said anything about me lately?"

Not this again. Talking about Dawson always sent her heart racing, and not in a good way like a cardio workout. "He says a lot, but I only listen a little."

Anna tapped a finger against her lips and lifted her chin. "I wonder if he'll ask me to be his date to the wedding."

Ugh. Another topic that needed to be avoided. Dawson would be the perfect wedding date, but there wasn't a chance in the world Olivia would end up with him that night. "Why don't you just ask him?" The words burned her throat as she spoke.

Anna frowned. "Um, no. A woman needs to be pursued."

"Why don't you just tell him how you feel?"

Olivia was one hundred percent guilty of keeping her feelings to herself, but that didn't mean it wasn't good advice. Dawson didn't have a clue Anna was interested in him, despite her obvious attempts to let him know. The guy flirted and joked with everyone. Anna was just another woman who flirted and joked right back.

"I just can't. He needs to make the move. Who are you going with?"

Despite her excitement over Asa and Lyric's wedding, Olivia had zero intentions of bringing a date. "I'm not taking a date. I'm a bridesmaid, and I'm helping with the planning. I have to focus on making sure things go smoothly."

"Too bad things with Trey didn't last a little longer. You could have gone with him."

Olivia furrowed her brows and leveled her friend with a lethal glare. "No, thank you. I'm glad that ship has sailed."

That ship had sailed so far over the horizon, it wasn't even a dot in the distance anymore. She might have been semi-content with their relationship at one point, but he trampled on every good feeling she ever had about him with that epic ending.

Anna sucked in a breath through her teeth. "You're right. I forgot how awful he was."

"He cheated on me, then broke up with me," Olivia reminded her.

"He's a double loser. What about Travis?"

Travis was a good guy. He was a few years older than her, handsome, and had a steady job. "Nah."

"What? Hot and independent isn't your type?" Anna asked.

Olivia didn't want to get into her type, mostly

because it was the same as Anna's–Dawson. "There aren't any sparks there."

"How do you know?"

"I've known him my whole life! If there were sparks, I'd know it by now. No offense to Travis, but he's not my prince charming."

Life would be a lot easier if she was interested in Travis Monroe. Anna was right when she said he was hot. Plus, he had that everyday hero and all-around good guy thing going for him. As a paramedic, he actually saved lives on a regular basis.

Anna crossed her arms over her chest. "Are you being picky?"

Olivia held up a finger. "I am rightfully picky."

"Okay, okay. I'm not trying to get you to settle or anything. Just have some fun with a date."

Olivia walked out of Cluckingham Palace hoping to escape the topic of conversation with the change in scenery. "Besides, pickings are slim in Blackwater, and I don't have time to date."

"You mean you don't want to make time to date," Anna corrected.

"Right. If I wanted to, I would."

Anna stopped following Olivia, and she turned to see what was wrong. "You coming to see the goats?"

Anna's nose crinkled, and she tilted her head slightly. "I forgot about something."

The theatrics meant whatever Anna had to say wasn't good. "Well, spit it out."

To Anna's credit, she really didn't look like she wanted to be the bearer of bad news. "Trey is Lyric's cousin. There's a good chance he'll be at the wedding."

Olivia took a deep breath and pushed the anger deeper into her gut. She'd forgotten about that in her rush to forget him altogether. "Really?"

"Really," Anna whispered.

Fantastic. The guy who cheated on Olivia was going to be at the wedding. Probably with a date. And Olivia would be alone, though, of her own choosing.

Unfortunately, it wasn't the worst news she'd had this week. She'd probably get jury duty before the weekend.

"He's still a creep. Don't think about him one more second," Anna said.

Olivia turned and headed for the goat pens, determined to find some silver lining as the bad news kept coming. "This wedding just keeps getting better by the minute."

4

DAWSON

Dawson pulled up at the Lawrence farm and turned the radio down. Anna's car was parked next to Olivia's.

He'd been hoping for an audience of one this afternoon. Anna was cool, but she wasn't the woman he was here to see. He'd have to hang around until Anna left to ask Olivia about the wedding.

Dawson parked beside Olivia's vehicle and pulled his goat boots out of the backseat.

Yes, goat boots were necessary.

With his boots changed and his speech prepared, he stepped out into Mr. Lawrence's driveway. The chickens were about twenty-five yards behind the house, and the goats were another twenty-five yards past that.

He'd spent more than half his life at the Lawrence house, and somehow he still found himself here every day, even though Beau and Olivia moved out years ago.

He used to come over because Beau was his best friend. Then high school came along, and Dawson's focus was drawn to another Lawrence family member. Olivia went from a little girl to the woman of his dreams. Things changed so gradually that Dawson hadn't known what was happening until he was fully wrapped around her finger.

Beau wasn't the "Stay away from my sister" kind, but he did occasionally remind Dawson to tread lightly. Who in the world knew why? Dawson would fall on his own sword before he'd hurt Olivia.

His phone rang, and he pulled it out of his pocket and answered quickly once he saw the name on the caller ID. "Hey, man. How's it goin'?"

Aaron Harding chuckled. "Pretty good. You?"

"Right as rain." Dawson squatted down as Gertie the chicken waddled over. He reached out a hand to pet her, but she stopped, did a little hop, and ran off as soon as she got to him.

"I'm calling for a favor," Aaron said.

"Consider it done. Whatever you need."

A loud chuckle filtered through from Aaron's end of the line. "You'll want to hear what it is before you agree."

"Way to sell it. Just tell me what you need."

A baby's scream echoed in the background. "Jade and I want to take a trip. Just a couple of days in

Colorado. We have plenty of family who can keep the kids while we're gone, but Levi asked if he could have some cool new babysitters one day."

"Are you saying I'm the cool new babysitter?" Dawson asked.

Aaron chuckled. "Well, you and Olivia. Levi says the two of you promised to take him to the Lawrence Farm."

"That's right," Dawson said. He loved hanging out with Levi, and getting to spend time with Levi, Olivia, the goats, and the chickens at the same time was a win on all fronts.

"Great. I'll text you the dates we'll be gone, and you and Olivia can decide which day works best for both of you."

"You got it. Thanks, man. Tell Levi I'm looking forward to it."

He ended the call, and Genella walked up to him. His chicken friend always greeted him on his way across the farm. She had either developed a true chicken-human connection with him, or she liked getting carted over to the goat pens to see her friends.

"Hey, lady. You keepin' everybody in line around here?"

As soon as he lowered his hands to the ground, Genella hopped in. The old hen was probably his favorite out of all the chickens on the Lawrence farm, but he'd never say the words out loud. The others would definitely be jealous, and the last thing they needed was an uprising when the birds outnumbered Olivia and him seventy to two.

Well, three if Anna was here.

Dawson checked Cluckingham Palace first, but there wasn't any sign of the women. The place was aptly named for the ridiculous amount of time Olivia had put into designing the luxury estate for her chickens. Dawson had built about seventy percent of it based on Olivia's instructions, and he had to admit, the place had class.

He headed for the goat barn and heard the women talking before he reached the entrance. Anna's high-pitched feminine voice carried over the warm August wind.

"Come on. He's got that bad boy vibe going on, and he probably won't be a clinger. Plus, he's handsome in that masculine-rugged way."

"Are you talking about me?" Dawson asked as he walked into the barn.

Anna jerked to face him with bulging eyes like she'd just been caught with her hand in the cookie jar, but Olivia didn't look up from the milking machine.

He got a kick in the chest every time he saw her. No other person in the world did that to him.

"Way to toot your own horn, Keller," Olivia said over her shoulder.

Anna shifted her weight from side to side and

pushed her hair behind her ear. "Um, we were talking about Lincoln North. The guy who works at Wolf Creek Ranch."

Dawson bit the inside of his cheek and made his way over to the milking machine. Lincoln hadn't caused any trouble since coming to town, but Dawson got a good look at his rap sheet when he pulled him over to let him know about a busted taillight last month. Lincoln North had a colorful history that was longer than the Snake River.

"What's wrong with it?" Dawson asked, bending to peer over the side where Olivia worked. Her dark hair was pulled back, leaving the lightly tanned skin on her neck on full display.

Don't look at the pretty woman. Focus on the mechanics.

"Just a leak, but I think I fixed it."

"We were just trying to figure out who Olivia could take to Asa and Lyric's wedding," Anna said.

Dawson grinned, staring at Olivia, who still hadn't looked up from the machine. "Oh, really." Maybe asking her to be his date would be easier than he thought.

"Yeah. Her ex will probably be there, and she needs a hot date."

Dawson stood and turned to Anna. "Troy?"

Genella clucked in Dawson's arms. The hen was right there with him, ready to defend Olivia's honor.

"Trey," Olivia and Anna said at the same time.

"That loser is gonna be there?"

Olivia really picked a winner with her last boyfriend. What guy in their right mind would cheat on Olivia? Or break up with her, for that matter? One who didn't have a clue who Olivia Lawrence really was. She was the total package–smart, funny, confident, and drop-dead gorgeous.

There were some things in this world Dawson would never understand.

"Unfortunately," Anna said. "So, Olivia needs a date. Not just any date. A good one."

Dawson squatted back down beside Olivia. "I'll be your date."

Olivia stood and wiped her greasy hands down her jeans and kept her attention on the dirt floor. "Thanks, but I really don't need a date."

Dawson stood, trying to stay on the same page as Olivia while she kept jumping just out of his grasp. Genella was about to get motion sickness if they kept doing the up-down thing. "Really. I don't have a date either. We could help each other out."

Smooth move. No part of the speech he'd planned mentioned how "convenient" it would be. And the chicken was unexpected too. Olivia should say yes because she *wanted* to be with him, not because it would make her look good in front of her cheating ex.

Olivia looked up with her lips pressed together. She turned to Anna, and the crease between her brows softened. "Actually, Anna needs a date more than I do."

Dawson swallowed a groan. He didn't want to take Anna to the wedding. He wanted Olivia beside him, but he couldn't say that with Anna standing two feet away.

Anna let out a nervous chuckle, but he couldn't tear his gaze away from Olivia. She hadn't looked up at him yet.

"I do need a date," Anna said.

Dawson focused on Olivia. That was one way for her to say, "Thanks, but no thanks." Why was she pushing him off on Anna?

So much for moving out of the friend zone. He'd come up against half a dozen rejections from Olivia in his life, and they never got easier.

Dawson reluctantly turned to Anna. "You want to go together?"

Anna clasped her hands to her chest. "I'd love to!"

Cold dread washed down his neck and back. Being on a date with anyone besides Olivia felt wrong. It was the reason he'd stopped dating over a year ago. His heart was loyal to one woman, even if she didn't know it.

Olivia clapped her hands. "Good. That's settled."

No, nothing felt settled, including Dawson's stomach.

"Oh, no you don't," Anna said as she waved a

finger in the air. "You still need a date. You're not getting out of it."

"I have a lot to do during and after the wedding. I don't need a date."

"And two-timing Trey will probably be there all cuddly with his flavor of the week," Anna said.

"Who cares?" Dawson and Olivia said at the same time.

Okay. Maybe Olivia really didn't need a date. She didn't need to have a man standing beside her to feel like she fit in. Anna was the one who thought the world revolved around romance.

Uh-oh. Was he giving Anna the wrong idea? How'd he get roped into being her date again?

Anna huffed and pulled out her phone. "I swear. If you ever get married, they'll have to wheel me down the aisle as your matron of honor."

"Hey!" Dawson drawled. "I'm only thirty and a quarter years old."

"Not you," Anna said, pointing a finger at Olivia without looking up from her phone. "Miss Independent over there. I think I've found someone."

Dawson was by Anna's side before Olivia even moved. "Who?"

Anna tilted her phone so Dawson could see the social media profile she'd pulled up. "Mark Billings. He's from a few counties over, and his profile says he's been a truck driver for five years. That's a long time to keep a job. Maybe that means he's dependable."

Dawson shook his head. "Nope. It says he's been a truck driver, but it doesn't say he's been with the same company."

"Fair enough, but he doesn't look like a crusty old man with tobacco in his lip," Anna said as she turned her phone around for Olivia to see.

"Way to generalize truckers," Olivia whispered as she grabbed the phone to take a better look.

Was she really considering this? How did she go from "I don't need a date" to checking out this guy's profile in sixty seconds flat?

"He's cute. I'll give him that," Olivia said.

Cute! The guy was cute now. Not only would Dawson not be going to the wedding with Olivia, but some cute guy in a big truck was going to get his girl.

"Do you even know this guy?" Dawson asked.

"No, but my brother commented on one of his photos last week. I'll ask him about Mark," Anna said.

"That's all?" Dawson asked. "Someone you know might know him, and now you're on a first name basis with the guy? We need a background check and his high school transcripts at the very least."

Anna laughed, and the bubbly sound did nothing to dampen his panic. "Don't get so worked up, Grandpa."

"Have you ever heard of stranger danger?"

Anna straightened her shoulders and propped a hand on her hip. "Have you ever heard of live a little?"

"Yeah, you live a little, and then Mark is texting you asking for–"

"Whoa there!" Olivia shouted. "There are little ears around."

Dawson cradled Genella to his chest, covering the little ears in question. "I was gonna say feet pics."

Olivia bit her bottom lip and tilted her head from side to side before letting out a huff. "Let me know what your brother says."

This was not happening. Olivia and Anna both wanted dates to the wedding, but somehow he got paired up with Anna.

Dawson's chest expanded with the building pressure, and Genella was starting to get antsy in his arms. All of the excitement from earlier was gone–flatter than a popped balloon. "Have you seen Herbert?"

Anna looked up from her phone with one raised brow. "Herbert?"

"The goat," Dawson added. He didn't feel like saying much else for the first time in his life.

Olivia looked up without making eye contact. "He's in the west pen."

"Thanks. Genella is ready to be united with her one true love." He held up the chicken and managed a grin at Anna. "Can't stand in the way when it's true love."

Anna smiled wide, showing off her pearly white teeth. "No, that would be a shame."

Dawson jerked his chin over his shoulder as he turned to leave. "Later, ladies."

Anna wasn't the one for him, but they might still have a good time at the wedding.

As long as he could forget about the stranger who just stole his girl.

5

OLIVIA

Anna rounded on Olivia as soon as Dawson was out of sight. "Did you hear that? He asked me to be his date!"

Kinda hard not to hear that since she was an arm's length away. Also difficult to ignore since she'd suggested it.

A hollowness lay gaping in her chest. Going to the wedding with Dawson would be a dream, but she wouldn't be able to enjoy it knowing Anna wanted to be in her place.

"I heard."

"I have to find a dress," Anna said as she pulled out her phone and started typing.

"Just make a post saying you're going to a wedding, and you'll have dozens of boutiques sending you their dresses."

Anna smiled as she looked down at her phone. "I know. This will be epic."

Olivia walked into the goat pen and beckoned Henrietta over. "Come on, girl. You're first."

Dawson wouldn't be happy she was milking his goats, but he'd have to get over it. She needed something to do. Anything to keep her mind off the wedding plans unfolding.

"What about you?" Anna asked.

"I'm the maid of honor. Mine is already being altered."

"No. I mean, what about your date."

Henrietta skipped by, and Olivia followed her into the barn. "That's a problem for future Olivia."

Anna hung back in the barn entry as she tapped on her phone. "I'm asking my brother about Mark now."

"There's no rush. It's not like I'll have much time to hang out. I'm in the wedding, and I'll be up to my ears in coordinating at the reception."

Anna tucked her phone into her back pocket and propped a hand on her slim hip. "You like to play hard to get."

"That's not what I'm doing." At least, it wasn't Olivia's intention. She didn't want to lead someone on, and she had her own issues when it came to dating.

A loud crack sounded from outside the barn, and Olivia jerked her head up at the same time as Anna.

"What was that?" Anna asked.

Olivia strode to the barn opening and stuck her head outside. Dawson was shirtless and reaching for a pile of logs. His broad shoulders were rippled with muscles that ribboned down his back, and his jeans hung low on his hips. Every movement was executed with smooth control.

"Oh my word," Anna whispered just behind Olivia's ear.

Dawson wrapped his arms around a massive log and stood with it against his chest. He set it down on the stump and picked up the ax.

"Does he do this every day?" Anna asked, breathy and dazed.

Chopping wood wasn't an urgent task. It was August, for goodness' sake.

"No, he's putting on a show," Olivia said.

And boy, did he know how to draw a crowd. He wrapped his big hands around the ax handle and held it to his chest as he studied the log. Scars in all shapes and sizes were scattered over his torso.

She knew those scars. She'd been around when he got a few of them. Dawson was attracted to trouble, and he hadn't been easy on his body as a kid. It didn't help that he grew up and chose a dangerous profession either.

Dawson lifted the ax above his head and slung it down until the blade crashed into the log. The thick wood split but not all the way through. He tossed the ax down and pried his fingers into the split. Every muscle in his arms rippled as he pulled the two halves of the log apart.

"Whoa," Anna whispered.

Whoa was the word echoing in Olivia's mind too. Dawson didn't have to show off to catch her attention, but wow.

Dawson lifted his head and locked gazes with Olivia. A rush of heat swept up her neck and face as he gave her a one-sided grin and winked.

"Heaven help me," Anna said.

Olivia straightened her shoulders. "He's ridiculous," she muttered. As if she needed another reason to hyperventilate today.

"Ridiculously hot," Anna added.

A whistled chorus of "Sexy Back" came from outside the barn.

Olivia shook her head and focused on Henrietta, who was patiently waiting by the milking machine. Only Dawson would enjoy a physically demanding activity. "Ignore him."

"That's almost impossible." Anna pulled her phone out and glanced at the screen. "I've gotta run. I told Mom I'd meet her for dinner."

"Tell her I said hey."

"I will. Love you. Call me later," Anna said before blowing Olivia a kiss.

"Love you too."

The barn was quiet after Anna left, except for the

occasional loud crack when Dawson split a log. She'd milked three goats before Dawson's rhythmic footsteps tore into her peaceful awareness.

"I was coming to do the milking," Dawson said beside her.

There wasn't anything to focus on while the machine did its work, but she held off on looking up at him as long as she could. "It's fine. I was finished with my other chores."

Dawson shifted beside her. "Want to talk about what happened earlier?"

Great. He was here to cut to the chase. "I told you, I'm fine."

"I don't mean yesterday. I'm talking about when you pawned me off as Anna's date."

Olivia jerked her chin up. Thankfully, he'd found his shirt, but her neck and face were still scorching. There wasn't an ounce of irritation in Dawson's features, but there wasn't any fondness either. "What do you mean?"

"I asked you if you wanted to go to the wedding with me, but somehow I came out of the conversation as Anna's date. Care to explain?"

Oh no. No, no, no. The quick heartbeats of panic rising flooded her system. "I don't need a date," she said, trying to mask the shakiness in her words.

"But you're thinking about letting a random guy take you. Why is that?"

Dawson tilted his head slightly and rested his

shoulder against the wall, settling in for her explanation.

"I don't need a date. I just said that to appease Anna," Olivia said.

It was the truth. She really had no intention of asking a stranger to be her wedding date.

Dawson bit the inside of his cheek and kept his steely gaze locked on her. His blue eyes probed hers, searching for answers and finding none. "When are you going to give me a chance?"

A heavy grip tightened around her neck. Was he really calling her out? "I–I don't know what you're talking about. Anna is awesome. Everybody loves her. Sounds like you have a good chance of having a great time at the wedding."

He pushed off the wall and took a step toward her. "I don't mean with Anna. I mean–"

Dawson toppled forward and crashed into her with a loud oomph. His arms enveloped her, holding her close as they fell together. She clung to him, floating through the air until they both crashed to the ground in a tangled heap.

Her back struck the ground hard enough to knock the breath out of her lungs, but she tightened her hold on Dawson's shoulders and gasped for air.

"Are you okay?" Dawson quickly asked. "Olivia, talk to me."

He was spread out on top of her–thankfully without the bulk of his weight leaning on her–and she stayed latched onto his shoulders. One of his arms ran up her back and cradled her head while the other was planted on the ground beside her, half caging her in.

"I'm fine," she said on another gasp. "I'm fine."

Dawson jerked his head to the side. An adolescent goat bleated as he walked by.

"Hudson," Dawson grunted.

The menacing goat was gone, but she was still clinging to Dawson's immovable frame. Every inch of her body that was flush against his tingled with awareness. His powerful arm wrapped around her, rendering her almost weightless.

Her body and mind waged war as she hung in his embrace.

No, her two halves were in agreement. She should stay right here forever. Living here wouldn't be so bad. It was safe, and the pounding of her heart had every synapse of her nerve endings firing on all cylinders.

But she had to let him go. She couldn't let her feelings get out of hand or she'd lose more than one person she loved.

She unwrapped one arm and pressed her hand to his chest. The heart beating beneath her palm rushed in a rhythm that rivaled her own.

Lifting the arm that had caught the brunt of their fall, he brushed a hand over her hair as his gaze scanned over her face. His blue eyes were wide, burning dark like shadows had rolled over them. "Are you sure? You hit hard."

The movement brought his whole body closer, and she struggled to form a coherent thought. There wasn't even a hint of his usual lighthearted tone as his intense gaze bore into her.

"Liv, are you sure?" he asked again.

Not even a little. Being this close to Dawson sparked so many feelings she should have gone her entire life without experiencing.

The higher she soared, the harder she'd fall. It was terrifying and thrilling at the same time.

"Yeah. I'm really okay." She patted his chest and relaxed her body. His hold gently released her until her back rested on the straw and dirt.

"Hudson is officially sold. He's headbutted his last behind," Dawson said as he lifted his body from hers.

His absence left a cold void as he moved away. She missed the contact almost immediately. "Don't make rash decisions. You know he's just playing," Olivia said as she sat up and started brushing straw from her arms and hair.

Dawson stood to his full height and offered her a hand. "It's all fun and games until my queen gets hurt."

Olivia took his hand, and he hauled her to her feet. She rolled her eyes and sighed. "I'm fine. We're both fine. No blood, no foul."

His gaze swept over her body and back up to her face. "Are you–"

"I promise! You can stop worrying. I'm not breakable."

Dawson lifted a hand as if to reach out to her but rubbed his jaw with it instead. "Okay. I'll take care of the rest of the chores."

She wanted the chores. She wanted all the responsibilities that would distract her from the swirling turmoil in her middle, but she wasn't going to fight him over it. He liked tending to his goats as much as she loved taking care of her chickens.

With a sigh, she looked around. "I guess I'll head home."

"Be careful. I'll call you tomorrow," Dawson said, still watching her for any signs of injury.

She backed out of the barn one slow step at a time. As soon as the twilight sky came into view, she covered her mouth with a hand. What was she doing? Any feelings for Dawson had to be shut down before they could bloom.

He wasn't the one for her. He was meant to end up with someone sweeter–someone carefree and fun. He deserved a wife who would give him a family, instead of piles of medical bills for a condition that never left well enough alone.

Then there was Anna–the friend who hung half of her hopes and dreams on the man Olivia was sprinting away from as fast as she could.

Olivia broke into a jog, relishing the breeze that cooled her cheeks as she tore across her dad's yard. When she reached her car, she slid inside and panted in the stillness of the cab.

The appointment with her doctor that started the downhill spiral of her week flashed to the forefront of her thoughts. The condition was approaching, whether she was ready to accept it or not. The doctor seemed to think another surgery was in her near future, and she'd known the awful truth before the doctor confirmed it.

Would it be another minor surgery this time? Or would she need a hysterectomy–the sure-fire way to kill any hopes of becoming a mother?

She still hadn't figured out the logistics of disappearing during her recovery. Who would drive her to the hospital and back? Beau was the obvious choice, but he was already neck-deep in work at the garage.

Was she ready to let someone else in yet?

Not Lyric. She was planning a wedding and building a new family with the man she loved.

Not Anna. She wouldn't be quiet about it, and Olivia clung to those rare moments when she could forget about the pain and the appointments and just be normal with her friend.

Not Dawson. He had a way of knowing something was wrong with her before anyone else suspected. He'd ask questions she didn't want to answer. He would worry, even though there wasn't anything to worry about. She would be fine, but Dawson wouldn't believe her.

She didn't want people to think of her health problem every time they saw her, and she didn't want pity stares wherever she went. If no one knew, then she could go about her life and forget about it from time to time. She wanted to be more than a disease or a diagnosis.

No, her life had to be focused on the work she was doing. It was what the Lord had called her to do–be the helping hand that was always needed. Other people had worse problems. Those she could focus on.

She pulled out her phone and scanned the dozens of tasks on her to-do list. There was plenty to keep her distracted. This was the last time she had to think about an impending surgery before her next appointment.

Just the way she wanted it to stay.

6

DAWSON

Dawson wiped the sweat from his brow and went straight back to taking notes. Barry Denson was talking a mile a minute while pointing to the back entrance of his restaurant.

"We have precautions in place. This shouldn't have happened."

Firefighters moved like busy bees around the lot, and a handful of officers milled around. A couple of paramedics waited off to the side in case they were needed.

Barry's jaw moved from side to side as he stared toward the still smoking remains of the kitchen. "We follow codes to the letter, even when it's inconvenient."

"I understand. The fire marshal will have more questions for you about that." The insurance adjuster would be on Barry's case in a hot minute too, but Dawson didn't want to be the one to bring up that unpleasant fact.

Barry hung his head. The Rock had been a popular restaurant for locals and tourists alike since Dawson was in diapers. The place was Barry's pride and joy.

Barry pushed a hand through his thinning gray hair. "I can't believe this. We'll be shut down for months."

Dawson pocketed his notepad and slapped a hand down on Barry's shoulder. "Don't think about the bad. You know people around here are going to be lining up to help get this place back up and running. Where are we gonna watch the games on Saturdays?"

Barry shook his head, but a grin flashed on his face. "You're right. I'm sure it won't take long. The fire was contained to one part of the kitchen."

Dawson added, "I bet Olivia Lawrence will set up a fundraiser as soon as she finds out."

Man, he couldn't even make it through one call without thinking about her. Especially after their little tumble yesterday. Once he got past the concern that she'd hit her head or he'd flattened her into a pancake, the urge to wrap her up and never let go had clouded every thought.

He'd done a decent job of keeping his hands off her for most of his life, but one touch only fueled the fire. She'd fit perfectly against him, snapping into place like two pieces of a puzzle.

He'd been so caught up in the feel of her against him that he'd completely forgotten to continue his questioning about how he'd ended up as Anna's wedding date. Now, it was a little too late to go back and ask for answers.

It wasn't as if he could back out on Anna. He was a man of his word, even if he'd agreed to something under duress.

Enough about his wedding date woes. Barry was in the middle of a crisis, and Dawson needed to figure out a way to help.

Barry straightened his shoulders and let out a deep exhale. "I'd sure appreciate that."

"I'll check in with you later," Dawson said as he headed back toward his cruiser.

Officer Freeman was sitting in the driver's seat of her car with her head down, probably jotting down notes on the call. Dawson rapped his knuckles against the window, and she lowered it.

"What's up, Keller?"

Dawson propped against her door. "You see that Michigan and Washington game last night?"

Jennifer perked up at the mention of one of her favorite teams. "What a nail-biter."

"I don't think I sat down the entire time."

Dawson's phone dinged in his pocket, and he pulled it out. There was a video from Olivia.

His pulse picked up speed. No matter what he was doing, she had the power to drop-kick him in the chest.

He opened the video and watched as Henry, Hudson, and Henderson jumped on the small trampoline he'd put up in the goat pen last week. The kids took turns hopping and jerking their little legs to the sides like snowboarders catching air.

"Look at this!" Dawson turned the phone around so Jennifer could see.

She watched for a moment before giving a single chuckle. "Those goats have about as much energy as you do."

"I'll take that as a compliment," Dawson said as he typed up a response to Olivia.

Dawson: Can I get a video of you on the trampoline now?

Her response made his grin spread even wider.

Chicken Tender: Not a chance.

Dawson and Jennifer's radios chirped to life, alerting them of a domestic disturbance a few miles away.

Jennifer grabbed her radio from her shoulder. "Officer 415 en route."

Dawson pocketed his phone and followed suit, associating himself with the call. "Looks like it's go time again."

Jennifer didn't look over at Dawson as she

started her vehicle. "How much you wanna bet it's the Howards?"

The Howards were trouble. They were either a menace to society or assaulting each other. There was a good chance the call was leading them to the Howards, judging by the address. "I'd take that bet, but I'm not a fan of losing."

Dawson ran through a series of silent prayers as he drove closer to the Howards' property. Jennifer was right, and they parked side-by-side in front of the old house.

"Can we get a premise history on 51 Shades Creek?" Dawson asked as he stepped out of his vehicle.

Nancy from dispatch rattled off a series of recent calls to the residence. None of them were chump change.

Dawson and Jennifer walked up to the single-level, brown house. A rusted, blue pickup truck was parked under a lean-to, and the pressboard front door was slightly ajar. A splintered hole was busted through the bottom half.

Jennifer rested her hand on the gun at her hip as she radioed, "Signs of forced entry. Show us approaching the residence."

Dawson scanned the yard and the woods nearby. Nothing moved–no sign of anyone other than the hole in the door. He stepped up the cinder block steps and knocked on the doorframe. "Blackwater

PD."

Jennifer's attention swung from one side to the other, constantly on alert.

Dawson tried again. "Blackwater PD!"

Muffled shouts came from the back of the house. "You called them?" a man shouted.

A woman snapped back, "I had to!"

There were a few curses thrown both ways before Dawson knocked again, louder this time. "Blackwater PD!"

"I'm coming!" the woman yelled in the same tone she'd used with the man. She stomped through the house and flung the door wide. "It sure took you long enough," she snapped up at Dawson.

The woman was sickly thin with skin that sagged and wrinkled over her bones. Her teeth were half rotten, and her mouse-brown hair was matted on one side. She could have been anywhere from forty to seventy years old.

This call was about to go bad in a hurry. Dawson could feel it in his bones.

Another officer associated himself with the call through the radios.

"We got a call about a domestic disturbance," Jennifer said.

The woman scratched her head and laughed. "Oh sure, if that's what you wanna call it. That man in there has hit me for the last time!"

"What is your name, miss?" Dawson asked as he

pulled his notepad and pencil out of his chest pocket.

The woman frowned up at him. "I don't think you need my name, do you? He's the one you're here for."

She'd just finished the last word when a deep bark echoed through the house.

Dawson's blood ran cold, and his chest tightened. It wasn't the bark of a lapdog. No, that was a full-grown set of chompers pounding through the house.

"10-91V" Jennifer radioed to dispatch.

A tan dog with short hair standing about waist high bounded around the corner behind the woman, sliding over a rug and the slick floor. Jennifer was beside Dawson, and he swept his arm out, pushing her behind him.

The woman yelled and stepped out of the way, opening the door wider as the dog launched at Dawson. He managed to side-step the first attack, but the dog circled back and lunged again, too fast for Dawson to avoid a second time.

The hot, stinging pain wrapped around his leg. You'd think he'd develop an immunity to things like this after repeated exposure, but the familiar ripping in his skin was just as powerful the twenty-fourth time as it had been the first.

7

OLIVIA

Olivia rounded another corner in the old chicken house that had been converted into a flea market. Her arms were overloaded with doilies, glassware, and vases she could use as centerpieces for the wedding.

Lyric stopped a few paces ahead of Olivia and gasped. She pointed to a shelf covered in small, glass figurines. "Look at that!"

Olivia hurried over and immediately spotted the broach. "Oh, you have to get it."

Stepping over the tarnished silver tea set that was displayed on a low table, Lyric reached for the broach and turned it over. "It's twenty-five dollars."

"I don't care if it's fifty. We're getting this broach. It'll look amazing with your bouquet," Olivia said as she adjusted the items in her arms.

Betty stepped up beside Olivia and took a few

things from the pile she carried. "What did you find?"

"This beautiful broach," Lyric said, holding it out to Betty, her future mother-in-law.

"Oh, I love it," Betty said.

Olivia had become friends with Lyric after she started dating Asa, but she'd known Betty since the diaper days. Olivia's diaper days, that is. Her mom had been best friends with Asa's mom, Betty Scott, for as long as the two could remember.

Until Olivia's mom had a heart attack. After that, Betty took it upon herself to be as much of a mom to Olivia as possible. Truth be told, she was still doing a fantastic job all these years later.

Lyric took a few things from Olivia's arms, dropping the broach into a blue-tinted vase. "Are y'all ready for supper? I'm starving."

"Yes, I need food," Olivia said.

Betty fell into step beside Olivia. "I made shrimp chowder last night if you two want leftovers."

Olivia hummed deep in her throat. "I love your shrimp chowder. Count me in."

Lyric gasped and squeezed Olivia's arm. "Oh, I forgot to tell you! I have an interview tomorrow for a dispatch job at the station."

"The police station? Are you serious? That's amazing."

Lyric and Asa first met a long time ago during a

dark time in Lyric's life. Asa arrested her, then asked the judge to give her another chance.

It had taken more than a second chance, but Lyric found her way out of the darkness and met up with Asa again when she was clean and sober.

Talk about a success story. With the help of some friends, Lyric had made the turn-around of the century.

Lyric's smile stretched, and little lines crinkled beside her eyes. "I can't believe they're even considering hiring me. You know, with my record and all."

Olivia wrapped an arm around her friend. "I can believe it. You're not the same person as before, and everyone at the station knows you've proven yourself many times over."

"It still feels like a dream. I'll get to work with Asa and get to help people. I'm scared to hope–"

"None of that," Olivia interrupted. "I'll be praying they see the real you during the interview and you'll stay calm."

"Thanks. I could use all the prayers. If I get the job, I'll have to learn to stay calm in high-stress situations. Nancy already said she'd help me."

"See? You have lots of people in your corner," Olivia said. "This will be awesome. I can't wait to see you whenever I drop off lunch."

Lyric bumped her shoulder against Olivia's. "You're the best. Thanks for always taking care of the department."

"Their job is important. I just hope I can make things a little sweeter for them every now and then."

Dawson always made a scene when she stopped by the station, claiming she needed an excuse to see him. She didn't bring food for the entire police department just because she wanted to see him.

Though, it was definitely a perk. If she could ever catch a glimpse of him before he spotted her, she would see him determined and working hard for a brief moment, and she always got a warm surge of pride seeing her friend being a real-life hero.

Just her friend. And her brother's best friend. And Anna's wedding date.

Soon-to-be Anna's forever date?

"Trust me, Asa appreciates it," Lyric said. "He always tells me when you drop off goodies for them." She let out a deep breath and checked her watch. "I wonder if the guys will be home soon."

"Where are they?" Olivia asked.

Lyric pulled out her phone. "Beau's garage."

"I can take some soup over there if they want to stay," Olivia offered.

"Let me see what they're doing," Lyric said as she lifted the phone to her ear. Her eyes widened as she answered. "Hey. That was fast. The phone didn't even ring."

Lyric was quiet for a few seconds while they walked before saying, "Yeah, she's with me."

Olivia pointed at her chest. "Me?"

Lyric stopped walking and stared straight ahead. "Yeah. Sure. I'll tell her. Where is he again?"

Olivia's legs grew heavy, stopping her in her tracks. Bad news was coming, and she wasn't ready for her good time to take a dark turn.

"Okay, we're leaving now. I love you," Lyric said as she ended the call. "Dawson is at the hospital in Cody."

No, not Dawson. He was the one who kept everyone's hopes up. He was the one who spread joy when things looked grim. "What happened?" Olivia asked as she matched pace with Lyric.

"Dog bite."

"Again?" Olivia asked, a little too high-pitched. Dawson had a long list of dog attacks on his record. Well, one was a horse, and one was a squirrel.

Lyric huffed. "Again. What is that? Twenty-five?"

"Twenty-four by my count. I only remember because the last one was funny, not scary."

Lyric chuckled as they walked toward the checkout counter. "Was that one the pug that got his ankle?"

"I have never in my life heard of a pug attack, but Dawson must have a target on his back for dogs."

Betty started taking things out of Olivia's hands. "You two go on. I'll get this stuff."

"Let me give you some money," Lyric said as she reached for her purse.

Betty waved a hand in the air. "Oh no. It's one of my contributions to the wedding."

Lyric threw her arms around Betty's neck. "You're the best."

"I love you, sweetie," Betty whispered. "And I love you too, Olivia."

"Love you more," Olivia said as she took a step back toward the door. "Thanks for hanging out with us today."

Hopefully, Dawson's condition wasn't critical, but her body hummed with anticipation. She wanted to see for herself that he was okay.

Lyric set a quick pace for the door. "Let's go see your man."

Olivia opened her mouth to protest Lyric's choice of words, but her friend was already marching toward the car.

The sterile air hit Olivia first as she stepped into the hospital, and it made her stomach roll every time. It wasn't the smell that was terrible. It was the awful times she associated with it. You take enough blows in a doctor's office, and even the little things remind you of the times when the world was falling apart.

Lyric pointed to the right. "Asa said take these elevators. Third floor."

Olivia walked straight to the far wall of the small elevator and propped her backside against the rails. Hopefully, Dawson was fine. She tried to convince herself the overabundance of care she had for him was backed by selfishness. Who would feed the goats?

She would. As much as she tried to avoid the goat pens, she'd do all of the chores until he was better.

Who was she kidding? She cared about him, and it had nothing to do with the goats. Worry and fear overcame her every time Dawson was injured. It didn't help that he often found himself prone on a stretcher. It was a part of the job.

One she did not like one single bit, even if she loved him for getting back up after every hit and going back to work.

Olivia's knees buckled, and she slid down the wall a few inches. She loved him. She'd loved him for years. Aside from losing him to an on-the-job injury, her worst fear was Dawson finding out she was ridiculously and hopelessly in love with him.

"Liv, are you okay?" Lyric asked.

Olivia opened her eyes and nodded. "Yep. Just ready to throttle him if we drove all the way over here for a scratch."

Lyric stood beside her. "That'll be fun to watch. Glad I came."

The elevator dinged, and Olivia fell into step

beside Lyric. If Dawson was coherent, he would have some clever comment about how they'd rushed over here to be by his side. Even the thought of the coming jokes had a smile blooming on her face.

Olivia knocked on the door of room 312 and leaned close to it.

"Come in!" said a gravelly voice on the other side of the door.

Olivia opened it and stepped in first. Dawson was lying back on a bed with sheets draped over his large frame. His hair was tousled, and his hand resting on the side of the bed had remnants of blood on it.

Jennifer Freeman sat in a chair by the window, and both of them had blistered red faces.

Swallowing past her constricted throat, Olivia looked back and forth between the police officers. "Are you two okay?"

Dawson pointed to his bloodshot eyes. "I got caught in the pepper spray." He jerked a thumb toward Jennifer. "She's crying because she's terribly worried about me."

"Shut up, Keller," Jennifer snapped. Her voice had the same rasp as Dawson's.

The female officer rested her head back and closed her eyes. Jennifer was the textbook definition of beauty. Blonde hair, green eyes, tall frame, fit build. She'd been at the department for years, and Olivia had never once heard her talk about a boyfriend or a date.

Intrusive thoughts won every once in a while, and Olivia assumed Dawson would fall for Jennifer. What man wouldn't? She was gorgeous, strong, independent, and though she didn't smile much, she was always kind and helpful.

"Thank you all for coming. I always knew I would be surrounded by beautiful women when my time came. I can die a happy man now."

Olivia scoffed. "Did you hit your head too? Where's your mom? Has someone called her yet?"

Dawson tilted his head toward the door. "She went to get coffee. I told her she needs to go home. It's boring sitting here."

"I second that," Jennifer said without lifting her head.

Olivia moved to his side and studied him from head to foot. "So they admitted you? That must mean it was pretty bad."

"Not terrible," Dawson said as he pulled the sheet away from his right leg, revealing bandaging that spread from his knee to his ankle.

The rest of his leg was crisscrossed with scars. Some were different shades of pink while others were pale.

Olivia's shoulders hunched in. She'd seen his scars plenty of times, but the shock never dissipated. Some were from other animal attacks. Some were childhood injuries. Whatever the causes, Dawson had never been easy on his body.

"Not terrible?" Lyric asked from behind Olivia. "It's half your leg."

"They just wanted me to have a few rounds of this antibiotic," Dawson said, pointing at the hanging bag attached to his IV. "I'll go home with some stitches, more meds, and burning eyes."

"Thanks for all the paperwork," Jennifer said.

"Oh, and I should have another nasty battle scar. The ladies are gonna love it."

The ladies. Most women already loved Dawson. He had more friends than Olivia had chickens, which was saying a lot.

But as far as Dawson's girlfriends, Olivia could count them on one hand. She'd gotten a front-row seat to a few of those relationships, and for some reason, he always seemed awkward on dates. It was as if he forgot how to flirt or carry on a casual conversation.

Maybe he got nervous when he liked someone. There were times she'd wondered if he actually liked her in more than a platonic way underneath all the flirting and banter. Then she remembered the way he was with the women he'd dated. He'd never been nervous around her, so that probably meant he only saw her as a friend.

"Whatever," Olivia said as she reached into her back pocket and pulled out the bag of Skittles she'd bought at the gas station on the way over. "Here's your 'congrats on surviving' present."

Dawson caught the bag and ripped it open. "Yes! Finally, some sustenance."

Jennifer lifted her head and frowned. "I offered to get you dinner half an hour ago."

"I know, but I really wanted something better for me." He tipped the bag into his hand and tossed some in his mouth. "I'm watching my figure."

The door opened, and Dawson's mom walked in carrying a coffee cup. Her eyes widened, and she threw her free hand in the air. "It's a party!"

"Hey, Mrs. Keller," Lyric said as she went in for a hug. The two swung from side to side as they squeezed each other.

Dawson got his larger-than-life personality from his mom, and the woman knew how to work a room.

Olivia slid in for her hug next. "It takes a village to raise a kid, doesn't it?"

"That's the truth, and this one has been making me lose sleep for thirty years now." Judy Keller wrapped one arm completely around Olivia's neck, pressing their cheeks together. "I knew you'd be here," she whispered.

"Wild horses couldn't keep me away," Olivia whispered back. Dawson's parents had been like a second family to her growing up, and she'd drop everything in a heartbeat to help the Kellers.

Judy turned back around and grabbed Lyric's arm. "You tell that man of yours I appreciate him calling me so quickly."

A warm hand wrapped around Olivia's arm, and she turned to find Dawson looking up at her with those blue eyes that made her weak in the knees.

"Thanks for coming," Dawson said low. "You didn't have to, but I'm glad you're here."

His hand slid down her arm, leaving a trail of fire on her skin. He was her friend. Her body shouldn't react to his touch this way.

When he reached her hand, he turned it over and poured some Skittles into her palm.

Olivia's chest ached as she remembered the reason she loved the candy so much. They were Dawson's favorite, and he'd offered them to her once. She'd been ten, and Beau, being the typical older brother, didn't want her to play with him and his friends.

Dawson found her sitting on the back porch steps and shared his favorite candy with her.

Nothing had ever tasted as sweet as that candy. It wasn't the taste in her mouth, it was the way her heart recognized Dawson's kindness and wrapped it up in a memory.

She still got a rush every time she ate a Skittle. Dawson had given her a lasting happiness she could relive again and again.

She looked up at Dawson and swallowed past her burning throat. "Is this a bribe? Are you asking me to take care of you?"

"Would you please? I'll love you forever?" Dawson crooned.

Olivia grinned and shook her head. "You're terrible."

"If my mom stays much longer, I'm going to have to beg someone to bail me out. She says she's staying overnight. Spare me."

She chuckled and glanced at Judy Keller. "What's wrong with having your mom waiting on you hand and foot?"

Dawson leaned closer and whispered, "I love her, but she's smothering me."

Olivia covered her mouth to hide her laugh.

"You think I'm kidding, but she likes to watch *General Hospital*, and she talks through the entire thing. I now know Sonny Corinthos's entire life story."

"How are Luke and Laura doing?" Olivia asked with a smile.

"Luke died!" Dawson whisper-screamed.

"No! Not Luke."

Dawson slapped his forehead and let his hand slide slowly down his face. "Please, help me."

Olivia turned around to where Lyric and Judy were talking about the wedding. When there was an opening in the conversation, she stepped up to ask, "When did they say the patient could go home?"

"Probably tomorrow morning," Judy said.

"Why don't you go on home," Olivia said with a

wave of her hand. "I'll stay with him tonight, and you can pick us both up in the morning."

Judy hugged her coffee to her chest. "Oh, I couldn't ask you to do that. I'll stay here with him."

No, but your son didn't have a problem asking.

"I insist," Olivia added. "You'll have all kinds of back problems if you try to sleep in that recliner over there."

All three women looked at the chair in question to find Jennifer lounging with her head back, sound asleep.

"Looks like it's not too bad," Judy said with a chuckle.

"I'll be fine. I'll run to the gift shop and get a toothbrush in a little bit. The goats and chickens are already cared for today. I'm free as a bird."

Judy leaned to the side to look around Olivia at Dawson. "Well, would you be okay with that, hon?"

"I don't need anyone to stay with me, Mom. Go on home."

Olivia tilted her chin down and gave Dawson a side glance. Of course he didn't need anyone, but he'd asked her to stay anyway.

Anyone would get bored sitting in a hospital room for hours on end. He just needed some company. Anyone would do. Why did it have to be her when spending time with him sent her heart into a tailspin?

8

OLIVIA

Olivia waved at Laurie with one finger as she passed the nurse's desk. Dawson had been a patient for almost six hours now, and he'd already won over his nurse's heart. Granted, she was happily married and in her fifties, but Dawson had a way of folding people into his inner circle at record speeds.

"Did you get that boy something good?" Laurie asked.

Olivia held up the bag she carried. "Bison burger."

"And what's that?" the nurse asked as she tilted her chin toward Olivia's other hand.

"Milkshake."

Laurie hummed. "I wish I had a friend like you. Does he know he's lucky?"

Olivia rolled her eyes. "He knows. He's spoiled rotten."

A rolling laugh filled the area as Laurie pressed a hand to her chest. "That's the truth if I ever heard it. Tell him I'll be coming by in a few to give him more pain meds."

"I will," Olivia said as she continued down the hallway. She gave a soft knock on Dawson's door before opening it. "Honey, I'm home."

Dawson scooted up higher in the folded bed and took a long, deep inhale. "It smells amazing. You're an angel."

"You won't be singing my praises when I keep you up all night with my snoring."

Dawson reached for the bag and practically tore it open. "I am unaffected by your snores. The sound of your respiration makes me happy."

Olivia scoffed. "Has that line ever worked for you?"

Stuffing a fry into his mouth, Dawson looked up at her with wide eyes. "What do you mean?"

"I mean..." What did she mean? Sometimes, Dawson joked, but other times, it was easy to misconstrue his honesty for a tease. "Never mind."

He pulled two burgers out of the bag and arranged them on opposite sides of the tray table hovering over his lap. He unfolded the wrapper on her burger before pulling out the fries.

When the food was all laid out, he moved his

injured leg to one side with a slight wince and bent the other to the side under the tray. He gestured to the foot of the bed. "Have a seat."

Olivia slowly lowered to the bed. The juicy burger laid out in front of her had her mouth watering.

Dawson propped his elbows on the table and clasped his hands. "You ready?"

Olivia bowed her head as he went straight into a prayer. She'd eaten dozens of meals with Dawson, and he always took the initiative to pray. She wasn't sure if it was because he enjoyed leading prayer or because he was unable to resist food set in front of him for long.

"Lord, thank You for this food. Thanks for letting me keep my leg today. I'm kinda attached to this one. Thanks for all of the doctors and nurses who are taking care of me and the other patients here. And thanks for sending Olivia. She's probably my favorite person You ever made. Amen."

Olivia lifted her chin and tilted her head to one side. "What was that?"

Dawson lifted the burger to his mouth and took a big bite. "What?" he mumbled around the food he chewed.

"Favorite person?" Olivia asked. "Prayers are supposed to be reverent, not funny."

"There's nothing funny about that. I pray for you all the time. I never joke about talking to the Lord."

Olivia kept her gaze locked on his bright-blue irises, and he didn't back down. There weren't even any laugh lines around his eyes as he chewed the burger.

Something tugged in her middle. Dawson always said sweet things. He always made people feel special. He always went above and beyond to show appreciation.

Anything kind he said to her should not be misconstrued for romantic interest. She wasn't special. She was one of Dawson's many friends. She just happened to be a woman who appreciated his kindness and found him ridiculously attractive.

Olivia turned her attention to her food and dipped a fry in the ketchup running out of the side of her messy burger. Dawson had already torn into his meal like a predator who had to kill to survive. "When was the last time you ate?"

Dawson scrunched one eye closed as he thought. "Yesterday?"

"Yesterday? It's almost seven at night!" Olivia shouted.

Dawson turned back to what little was left of his burger. "I forgot."

"How do you forget to eat? Seriously, no wonder your mom still worries about you."

"I was planning to run by Sticky Sweets for a breakfast sandwich this morning, but Grady called and asked if I'd help him fix his tractor, since he needed it up and running to bale hay as soon as the dew dried. So I ended up running by his store on my way over for some parts, and then I left his place just in time to make it to work. We got a call right as I was going to get some lunch about a fire at The Rock–"

"A fire!" Olivia dropped her burger, sending the top bun going one way and the rest of the burger falling on the other side of her makeshift plate. "Is everyone okay? How is Barry?"

"He's fine. It was a small fire, but the place will be shut down for a bit. I told him you'd probably put a fundraiser together to help with anything insurance didn't cover."

"Of course." She wiped her hands on a napkin and pulled her phone out of her pocket. She needed to come up with a plan as soon as she finished eating.

Dawson rested back against the pillows and shifted to readjust his leg. His nose scrunched up, and his lips pressed into a thin line.

"Are you okay? Laurie said she'd be in soon with more pain meds."

"I hope it's really soon," Dawson said. "It feels like my whole leg is on fire."

Olivia reached for the call button on the remote beside his bed, but Dawson stopped her, wrapping his whole hand around hers. A buzz spread from her fingertips to her chest.

"It's okay. She'll get here when she can."

"I'm a nurse. Trust me, she'd want to know if you were in this kind of pain."

"It's nothing I can't handle. She might be helping someone more important."

Olivia opened her mouth to say something, but the words were stuck–lodged in her larynx, while Dawson's strong hand gripped hers.

Dawson *was* important. While she often had to choose how to divide her time between patients, they were all equally important. Some were just more time-sensitive than others. He was right. Someone else could be in need of immediate help.

There was a quick knock at the door, and Olivia jerked out of the trance of Dawson's gaze. She pulled her hand from his, and he let her go without a fuss.

"So sorry about that," Laurie said as she stormed into the room. "Things always get crazy around shift changes."

"Are you leaving me?" Dawson asked.

"This is where we part ways, dear. Though, I'm leaving you in good hands," Laurie said as she winked at Olivia. "I need to give you more pain meds and change your bandage before I go."

"Try not to rip all of my leg hair off. I work hard to grow it out for the summer," Dawson said as he pulled the sheet back to reveal his bandaged leg.

Laurie clicked a few things on the computer

beside the bed. "Oh, I'll try my best, but no promises."

"Did I tell you about the time I singed my eyebrows off?" Dawson asked Laurie.

"No, but I have a feeling you're gonna," she said as she reached for new gloves.

Dawson leaned back. "It was the summer after eighth grade. I was at a celebratory bonfire after we won the baseball playoffs."

Laurie administered the pain relievers, then Olivia leaned forward to get a better look as the nurse peeled back the bandage. Stitches ran in multiple seams over the side of his leg. The angry red mixed with the black lines.

"Dawson, you didn't tell me it was that bad," Olivia said.

He shrugged. "I've had worse."

"That doesn't mean this isn't serious." No wonder the doctor wanted him to stay overnight. A large wound offered plenty of risks for infection.

"Hey."

Olivia looked up and met Dawson's gaze. How could she not worry?

He gave her a wink that sent her heart into overdrive. "I'll be fine."

He was right. She saw patients every day with worse wounds, but it hit differently when it was someone she knew and cared about.

Dawson grabbed his phone off the tray table and

started tapping on it. "I forgot to tell you. One of my reels went viral on Instagram today."

Olivia took the bait and ran with it. She'd welcome any distraction from her worries right now. "Really? I haven't checked since this morning."

He flipped over to his Instagram page. TheGoatGuy was just as popular as TheChickenChick, but they'd only had a few reels go viral since they started the pages.

He beckoned her over to his side, and she leaned close to him as a video showed him bench pressing two adolescent goats.

"Are you serious?" she asked, stifling a laugh that threatened to escape.

"It gets better," Dawson said, pointing at the screen.

He was curling two kids in the next scene, then a trio of them executed a series of drop-kicks from his back as he did a round of push-ups.

"At least you had your shirt on this time," Olivia said. His last viral video had won over millions of hearts because of the shirtless man instead of the cute goats. Even fully clothed, the fabric of his shirt stretched over his muscular arms.

"It's nice to know I'm loved for more than my body." He turned the phone around to show Laurie. "Have you seen my goats?"

Laurie chuckled as she watched the video.

"You're a riot, boy. Heaven help the woman who ends up with you."

Dawson grunted as Laurie tilted his leg to expose the underside. "I'll take that as a compliment."

"Those meds should be working soon. Just hang tight."

His jaw tensed as he nodded. Olivia had seen more than her fair share of people in pain, but watching Dawson's uneasiness twisted something in her gut. He never complained, despite his many incidents.

Olivia had spent many a night making pointless conversation with Dawson's mom just to keep them both from dwelling on the sneaky fears of what he faced on a daily basis. After Asa was shot in the line of duty a few months ago, the calls became more frequent.

Dawson chatted about the goats until Laurie had finished her administration. She gathered the bandage packaging and dropped it in the trash. "Okay. You're wrapped up and good as new with fresh meds." She gripped the bottom of one glove and asked, "Do you need anything before I go?"

"Nope. You've been perfect. Thanks for taking care of me."

Laurie's cheeks lifted with her smile. "You're a sweetheart. I hope I don't see you again."

They said their goodbyes to the nurse, and Olivia lowered to the chair beside Dawson's bed. She took a deep breath as she released the tension she hadn't realized had tightened throughout her body.

Dawson covered up his newly bandaged leg and grabbed the milkshake from the tray. "You didn't drink this."

"It's for you," she said, still feeling a little queasy after watching Dawson's dressing change.

His brows pinched together. "Are you okay?"

"Yeah. I'm fine. I just wasn't expecting the wound to be so bad."

Dawson shoved the milkshake toward her. "Drink this. You look pale."

How embarrassing. She'd been a nurse for eight years, and she'd never once gotten sick.

Well, there was one time while cleaning a trach tube, but that was something she worked hard to forget.

"It's yours. I'm fine," she said, pushing the drink away.

He put the milkshake down and picked up a foam cup of water. "Olivia Mae, please drink something."

She accepted the cup and took a few slow sips. The uneasiness subsided, and she took a deep breath. "Thanks."

Dawson shifted his position in the bed and picked up the milkshake and took a big gulp. "Let's play truth or dare."

Olivia shook her head. "Nope."

"Why not?" he asked, completely unaware of why she might be against the game.

"I might have been born at night, but it wasn't last night. Nothing is off the table with you."

He held out the milkshake to her. "You say that like it's a bad thing. I just like to be up-front."

She grabbed the offered drink and took a sip. "There's nothing wrong with that, but not everyone is like you. Some of us have filters."

"Are you saying you have secrets from me? I'm hurt."

"I don't have secrets." She blurted her defense before the truth kicked her in the shin. She did have secrets–some she wasn't willing to share with even her best friend.

"Then you don't have anything to worry about."

"How about twenty questions?" She held up a halting finger. "But I reserve the right to refuse any question."

"I'll take it," Dawson said as he rubbed his hands together. "You go first."

Olivia sipped on the milkshake while she thought. She shifted in her seat. "Why did you become a police officer?"

"That's easy. You remember that time my family went to Montana to visit my aunt and uncle?"

Olivia scoured her memories, but nothing was striking a bell. "I don't think so."

"You know, when Uncle Max lost his job, and we spent the summer with them in Livingston?"

"Oh, okay. I remember now." She'd been around six, and Beau had been thoroughly annoyed that his friend was gone for the entire summer.

Truth be told, she'd missed Dawson that summer too.

"We got a flat tire on the way, and I was kind of excited because I knew how to change a tire."

Olivia scoffed. "You couldn't have been more than eight."

"I was, but I watched your dad do it, and I was getting my chance to show Mom what I knew. I had the jack set up under the frame when a police officer stopped to see if we needed help. I told him I had it handled, and he stayed and talked to me and Mom until I had the tire changed."

Olivia smiled, gently pushing the injustice that Dawson's own dad hadn't been the one to teach him that important life skill to the side. "And you wanted to be just like him?"

"No, he told me changing tires for people was part of his job and said I was well on my way to being qualified to serve and protect."

"That is the sweetest story," Olivia said. She could just imagine a little Dawson holding a grown-up conversation with a police officer.

"Plus, Mom always said being an officer was the only way I'd stay out of jail."

Olivia choked on the mouthful of milkshake. She coughed and sputtered past the burning in her throat until she could catch her breath. "You're lying."

"I am not. I never did anything terrible, but I didn't make things easy on her." He rested his head back against the pillow and his eyes fluttered closed for a second. "My leg feels better."

Those pain meds were starting to kick in, and Dawson was looking more relaxed by the second. "Good. You need anything?" she asked.

"No, but it's my turn." He reached out a hand for the milkshake, and she passed it to him.

He took a sip and only hesitated for a second before asking. "What's something about you that I don't know?"

Olivia turned his question over in her mind, trying to decide how to address it. She could go with something as simple as her first crush or something as big and convoluted as her unspoken feelings for him.

One memory stuck out and gnawed at her conscience. "There's something you don't know, but please don't be mad at me."

Dawson shook his head. His eyes glinted with joy as he held her gaze. "I could never be mad at you."

Oh, he might eat those words sooner rather than later. She picked at her fingernails and considered how to tell him. Ripping the bandage off would probably be best.

She looked up at him and sighed. "I didn't vote for you for homecoming king."

Dawson raised his head, eyes wide, and gasped. "Are you serious?"

Olivia hid her eyes behind her hands. "Yes. I'm sorry. I feel terrible. The guilt has been eating me alive for twelve years!"

"Because you have been living a lie! How could you?"

"I said I'm sorry!" Their voices were raised now. Someone would probably burst through the door any minute to break up the fight.

"Who did you vote for?" he asked quickly.

Olivia let her hands fall into her lap. "Micah Harding."

Dawson clenched his hand at his side. "Of course it was Micah. My constant rival."

Olivia humphed. "If the two of you were rivals, Micah had no idea about it."

She'd hung onto a crush on the eldest Harding brother for most of her high school experience. He was the strong, silent type, and she'd been drawn in by his broody, mysterious ways.

The joke was on her. Micah didn't have an ounce of attraction to her, but she'd only figured that out after basically begging him to ask her to the prom.

Now, Olivia was good friends with Micah's wife,

Laney, and it was clear the two of them were made for each other. There might be someone for everyone in this world, but Micah and Olivia weren't meant to be.

Dawson shook his head. "Micah had no chance of winning homecoming king."

"And that's why you won," Olivia pointed out.

"No thanks to you!"

Olivia's smile cracked at Dawson's theatrics. Loyalty was one of his top virtues, but he also didn't hold grudges. That was her only saving grace. "Can you ever forgive me?" she asked.

Olivia's phone rang before Dawson could answer, and she reached for it on the tray table. Any casual comfort she'd built up poured out of her in a rush as she saw Anna's name on the screen.

"I need to answer this. She'll worry if I don't," Olivia said.

Dawson sat back in the bed and crossed his arms over his chest, resting the milkshake straw in front of his lips for easy access.

Olivia answered with as much nonchalance as she could muster. "Hey."

"Hey. What are you up to?" Anna asked.

Olivia played with a seam on the recliner as she spoke. "I'm sitting at the hospital in Cody. Dawson got attacked by a dog today."

"What? Is he okay?"

"Yes, he's fine. They wanted him to stay overnight

to get some antibiotics. He should be discharged in the morning."

"Whew," Anna breathed. "That's a relief. I'll head on over there too."

The bed squeaked as Dawson sat up. He shook his head and waved a hand, mouthing, "No."

Olivia watched him for another few seconds. Could he hear the conversation? "Um, I think he's fine. I'm planning to stay with him tonight. His mom wanted to stay, but we didn't think she should try to sleep in this uncomfortable recliner all night."

"I don't mind! I'll come relieve you. I can be there in forty-five minutes."

Dawson cupped a hand beside his mouth. "We're good. Thanks for the offer though."

"Is that him?" Anna asked.

"Yeah, I'll put you on speaker." Olivia pressed the button and held up the phone between them.

Dawson launched into the conversation. "We're good here, Anna. Thanks for offering to come check on me. These meds are making me drowsy. I'll be asleep in about ten minutes."

"Oh, okay then," Anna said. "Call me if you need anything. I'd be happy to help."

"Thanks. I appreciate it," Dawson said, already relaxing back in his bed.

"Call you tomorrow, Liv," Anna said quietly before ending the call.

Olivia cradled the phone in her lap before looking up at Dawson.

He shifted onto his side and leveled her with an intense stare. "I forgive you. But I also want to know why you wanted me to be Anna's date to the wedding but not yours."

Olivia's chest filled with lead. The organs working to keep her alive jerked to a stop. "What?"

"Why couldn't I be your date?" he asked.

"It's not your turn to ask a question," she whispered.

"This isn't part of the game."

Okay, so he wasn't going to let her get away this time. She put her phone to the side and pressed her fidgeting hands between her knees. "Because Anna needed a date."

"Anna could get a date faster than I could eat a doughnut. Wrong answer."

He was right. Men lined up for Anna's attention. She had a magnetism that few people could ignore. "It would be weird if we went together," she said quickly. "We're friends."

"Our friends are getting married. We're both in the wedding. We'll be hanging out together anyway. What's so bad about being my date?"

Olivia jerked back. It was almost as if she'd been slapped. The last thing she wanted was for Dawson to feel like he wasn't good enough.

"There's nothing wrong with being your date. Any woman would be lucky to be your date."

"But not you."

Each word was a slap in the face.

She opened her mouth, but nothing came out at first. The hurt on his face split her in two. "That's not it at all."

"What is it, Liv?"

"It's not just a date. There are expectations, and–"

Dawson held up a finger. "There are no expectations. I would never expect anything from you or any of my dates."

Olivia waved a hand in front of her face. "That's not what I meant. I mean dates usually lead to more dates and relationships. That's not where we're headed."

The confession left her mouth cottony. A tingle burned behind her eyes.

"That's not where I'm headed with Anna either, but I'm taking her to the wedding. It's okay if you don't want to go to the wedding with me, but reminding me we're just friends would have been a lot easier." He ran a hand over his face, and his eyes half-closed as if they were heavy. "Maybe you're right, but I don't want Anna to have those expectations either."

"I'm sorry. I shouldn't have tried to drive the situation. I just know Anna is looking forward to it now. I think you'll have a great time with her."

Dawson slowly nodded, and his shoulders sank. "I'm sure it'll be fun." His eyelids fluttered closed, then open again. "These meds are making me drowsy."

"Go to sleep. You need to rest."

His eyes closed, and he quietly said, "But I want to spend time with you. Without expectations."

Olivia swallowed past the ache in her throat. Dawson was so good. It was easy to love how much he cared for others. No wonder Anna raved about him all the time.

But if someone had to end up brokenhearted, it had to be Olivia. Anna was the one who picked up the shattered pieces when Olivia's mom died. Anna was the one who encouraged Olivia to get outside of her bubble and do amazing things. Anna was the best friend a woman could ask for–a sister who urged her to look to the Lord when things got tough.

The thought of hurting Anna burned more than missing out on a chance with Dawson. It was only a chance anyway–fifty-fifty at best–that anything could ever work out with Dawson. Those odds were even better than her chances of being able to have kids of her own.

Despite his playful flirting, she had to keep her guard up. In order to pursue anything with Dawson, she'd have to confront Anna, and having that talk would inevitably hurt them all.

Dawson reached out a hand toward Olivia and opened his eyes. "Come here."

She stood and hesitantly placed her hand in his–letting her palm brush against his. He threaded his fingers through the gaps between hers and clasped hard.

He looked up at her with tired eyes. "I'm sorry."

Olivia shook her head. "I'm the one who's sorry."

"You didn't do anything." His eyes fell closed, then slowly opened. "Thanks for staying. I promise I'll wash your car every week for the rest of the year."

Olivia chuckled. Her car was a disaster zone ninety percent of the time. She was usually too busy rushing from one task to the other to clean it out. "You're joking."

"I never joke. I don't know what you're talking about."

Olivia shoved his shoulder with her free hand. "Get some sleep. You're talking crazy."

He let their clasped hands fall to the bed as his head rolled to the side. "Okay."

When his eyes stayed closed, she waited a few more seconds before scooting the recliner closer to the bed so she could keep his hand in hers a little longer.

9

DAWSON

Sitting at home alone was boring. Dawson had flipped through every channel on television and thoroughly lost at half a dozen game shows.

When his phone dinged, he lunged for it on the small table beside the couch. It was a text from Asa.

Asa: Lyric wants to know if you want to have dinner with us tonight.

Dawson's thumbs flew over the screen as he replied.

Dawson: Absolutely.

Asa: You need a ride?

The doctor said to hold off on driving for a few days since the injury was to his right leg, but he could probably manage.

Dawson: I think I can make it. Jeremy is coming by later. He might give me a ride.

Asa: He's invited too.

Dawson: 10-4.

When another response didn't come immediately, Dawson set the phone on the couch beside him and groaned. The short conversation wasn't enough to fend off his boredom.

He could always call his mom again. She never ran out of things to talk about.

The front doorknob jiggled and turned. There was a quick rap against the wood before Olivia sang, "Hello?"

Dawson was on his feet in an instant. The sight of Olivia always sent his pulse into overdrive. "My queen!"

"Your food courier," Olivia quipped, holding up a bag. She was still wearing her purple scrubs and white sneakers from work, and, if anything, the basic outfit brought out her beauty.

Dawson carefully balanced on his good leg. "I don't need food. I need companionship."

"I'm not sure there are any escort agencies around here," Olivia said.

Dawson turned to her and opened his arms. "Come here, woman. I haven't touched another human being since you left yesterday."

Olivia sighed but put the bag on the table and lifted her arms. "I'll bring you a body pillow tomorrow."

Dawson folded Olivia into his frame and inhaled

the sweet smell of her hair. The scent tingled in his nose. "I missed you."

"It's only been a day. Not even twenty-four hours," Olivia said.

"I don't care. I miss you when you're gone."

Olivia pressed her cheek against his chest and squeezed him tight. "I missed you too."

The urge to wrap her up and never let go flared hot inside him. He did more than miss her when she was away. He was half empty without her.

Every moment he was with her was like water racing down his burning throat. When she was gone, the flames were left to rage until he was back in her orbit.

She pulled out of his embrace and pushed her hair out of her face. "Food first, then I'll check on your stitches."

She picked up the bag of food, but Dawson reached for it. "Let me get that for you."

She handed over the bag. "Thanks. It's barbecue."

Dawson inhaled a deep breath of the spicy meat. "You are an angel. I'm starving."

Olivia headed toward the bathroom, and Dawson pulled out the boxes and tubs in the kitchen, sampling onion rings and pickles as he went.

Olivia returned from the bathroom a few minutes later and walked behind him. He held out an onion ring toward her, and she bit off a piece and kept walking toward the cabinets where she pulled out a couple of paper plates.

"You figure out what to do for Barry?" Dawson asked as soon as he blessed the food.

"Oh, we're doing a car wash. Next Saturday at the church."

"I'm off work that day. What time do I need to be there?" Dawson asked.

"Whenever you want to bring your truck by. The youth are doing the work."

"I'll help wash cars. More hands mean quicker service."

"If you could ask everyone at the station to bring their vehicles by, that would be great."

"Consider it done," Dawson said as he tore into another bite of his sandwich. "How are the kids?"

Olivia rolled her eyes. "Giving me fits. Herbert was in the coop-ula this morning with Genella. She didn't seem to mind, but the other hens were bothered."

"He's just looking for friends," Dawson said.

"He's also stressing my laying hens. There's a reason we have the best eggs around, and it isn't because I let my ladies get terrorized."

"I'll have a talk with Herbert. And I'll issue a formal apology to the chicks."

Licking the barbecue sauce from her fingertips,

Olivia eyed him warily. "I'll believe it when I see it. Herbert is a menace."

"He loves you. Just embrace it."

Olivia scooted her chair away from the table and looked down at Dawson's leg. "How are your bandages?"

He pulled up the leg of his sweatpants to show her the small bandage on the side of his calf. It covered the broken skin that hadn't required stitches. "Perfect."

"Does it need changing?" she asked.

"Probably, but I can take care of it."

Olivia stood and headed for the box she'd bought and filled with bandaging supplies. "I'll change it."

Dawson wasn't about to protest. Olivia loved taking care of people, and it was always nice to be on the receiving end of her attention.

Maybe one day she'd let him take care of her.

She gathered the supplies she needed and arranged them on the table.

"Do the patients at work know how lucky they are?" he asked.

Olivia rolled her eyes. "I'm the lucky one. I get to do what I love every day."

Dawson pulled another chair up beside him and rested his leg on the seat. "You know, not many people think your job is fabulous."

She currently worked as a geriatric nurse at an

assisted living facility, but she'd been through the emergency department and a private practice since getting her degree. She made it clear she had no plans to leave geriatric care.

Dawson's chest warmed every time he heard about something Olivia did. Her caring heart was one of the many things he loved about her. She'd been that way since they were kids.

Olivia washed her hands and slipped them into a pair of gloves. "Some people say the same thing about your job."

"Fair enough. But the people I work with don't usually care for me much."

Olivia grinned. "See? At least I chose a career where people are happy to see me."

"I bet those people think you're the sweetest person to walk the planet," Dawson said.

"I am," Olivia said as she worked intently.

"I can't argue with that."

Olivia's phone rang in her pocket, but she didn't lift her head.

"You need to get that?" he asked.

"Not while I'm working," she answered, lifting up her gloved hands.

Dawson reached for the pocket on the side of her pants, and she shifted so he could pull the phone free. Anna Banana was written across the top of the screen with a photo of Olivia and Anna pressed cheek-to-cheek in a hug. He turned the phone around to show her.

Olivia nodded. "Can you answer it on speaker?"

He pressed the buttons and laid the phone on the table.

"Hey, girl," Olivia said as she continued working.

"Hey. So, I talked to my brother about Mark, and–"

"Who?" Olivia asked.

Dawson remembered Mark. The random guy Anna had found on social media who was somehow in the running for Olivia's wedding date. Dawson squirmed just thinking about it, and his hand fisted on the table.

"Your wedding date," Anna said.

Dawson's brows rose as if they had a mind of their own. What did she just say?

"He's not yet," Olivia corrected.

"Well, Drake said he's known him for a while, and he's a good guy."

Olivia sighed low. Dawson couldn't be sure, but she didn't look like she wanted a date.

"He has your number. You two can talk about it," Anna said.

"No, no. Don't do that," Olivia sputtered.

Anna sucked in a breath through her teeth. "I may have already given it to him."

"When?" Olivia asked, looking at the phone on

the table as if Anna could see her glare through the device.

"Just now. Right before I called," Anna muttered.

Olivia's shoulders sank. "Fine, but I can't promise–"

The phone dinged and lit up with a text. A series of numbers showed up on the screen with a message underneath.

"Was that him?" Anna asked.

"It seems so," Olivia said before clenching her jaw. "Why did you give it to him?"

"Because you weren't going to do it. Come on, Liv. I want us to have a good time at the wedding. Our friends are getting married, and that's a great reason to celebrate."

"I can celebrate without a date," Olivia reminded her.

One point for Olivia. Anna was the influential one in their friendship, and Dawson always liked seeing Olivia stand up for herself, even if it was with her own friend.

Baby steps.

"I know, Liv, but you work so hard for everyone but yourself. Don't spend the whole wedding and reception running around checking everybody's work. You're a good planner. Things will fall into place. Plus, you promised to let me help you, so don't try to do it all yourself like I know you want to."

Dawson had to agree. Olivia worked from sunup

to sundown, and she never turned away anyone who needed help.

"Please just relax a little," Anna begged. "Chat with Mark over a meal, dance with him a couple of times, and see where things go. You're a catch, and any man worth his salt would go out of his way to make sure you have a good time at your friend's wedding. It's one night."

Dawson didn't dare breathe as he waited for Olivia's response. Anna was right, again. Olivia deserved someone who would care for her the way she cared for everyone else.

He wanted to be that guy, but it seemed the wedding wasn't going to be his chance to prove it to her.

Olivia stood and gathered the scraps of packaging. "I'll think about it."

"That's all I ask," Anna said. "Let me know how things go with him. I'll see you tomorrow."

"Love you. Bye," Olivia said as she pulled off her gloves and tossed them in the trash.

"Love you more," Anna said before ending the call.

Dawson didn't say anything, and Olivia continued putting things back into the kit and tidying up.

Once everything was back in its place, Olivia turned around but didn't look at him. "I have to go. I'll check on it again tomorrow after work."

Dawson sat up straighter, not ready to let her go. "Where are you going?"

"I have to get back to work."

"What are you doing after?" he asked.

Yes, he was desperately trying to claim some of her time, and he didn't care if he was groveling.

"Cleaning at the church," she said as she put the first-aid kit away and started washing her hands.

Olivia made use of every second of her days. If she wasn't at work, she was at the church or organizing some fundraiser. She sold eggs, goat milk, and butter while she was doing everything else. She dedicated most of her life to serving others.

"Do you ever take time for yourself?" Dawson asked.

Olivia looked over her shoulder at him. Her brows were lowered. "No. Why would I do that?"

"Um, because everyone needs a break."

She turned back to the kit. "People don't help each other anymore. I don't have tons of money to donate to charities and causes, but I have my time, and I choose to give it."

He'd talked to his mom about how Olivia was overworked and underappreciated. His mom claimed Olivia was fine because service was her spiritual gift.

Looking at Olivia now, she didn't seem to be bothered by the work she did. Still, he worried she was stretching herself too thin.

When he didn't say anything, she went on. "The older ladies in our church are getting too old to do everything, and younger people aren't stepping up. We need to be active in the community and taking care of our members, and I won't let those things slip."

Wow. Olivia was quite a motivational speaker when she was fired up about something. "You're absolutely right. Is there anything I can do to help?"

"No, I've got it covered. Thanks for the offer though."

Typical. Olivia never wanted help. He loved her independence, but he wanted her to share the load. In the little time she had left of her days, she took food to Beau and her dad.

"At least let me come to the church with you. I can dust the pulpit. I'm dying to get out of here." He stood on his good leg and took a step toward her, pleading, "Please."

She turned at the exact moment he moved. Olivia crashed into his chest with an "Oof." Dawson tipped back and hit the counter behind him. Olivia toppled off-balance and fell into him.

Dawson wrapped his arms around her until she settled. She looked up at him with wide eyes. Her mouth hung open slightly in surprise.

"We have to stop meeting like this, Liv," Dawson joked with a wide grin. Any chance to have Olivia in his arms was a win.

The knob on the front door jiggled, and the door creaked open.

Olivia jerked back, straightening her shoulders in an instant.

Dawson laughed. "Wow, Liv. Not sure I've ever seen you move that fast."

"Dawson!" Jeremy yelled from the living room.

"Kitchen!" Dawson responded.

Olivia swiped a hand over her hair, looking thoroughly flustered. "Jeremy is in town?"

"Just for a few weeks."

Jeremy walked into the kitchen, and his neutral expression morphed into a mischievous smile when he spotted Olivia. "Chicken chick!"

"Hey, bubba," Olivia said, opening her arms for a hug. Most everyone in Blackwater called Jeremy bubba, and while he disliked the nickname, he never corrected Olivia.

Dawson crossed his arms over his chest. "What am I? Chump change?"

Jeremy released Olivia from the hug, looking a little too happy to see her. "Sorry." He turned to Dawson and wrapped him in a man hug with a few slaps on his back.

"Long time, no see," Dawson said. "Glad you made it home."

Jeremy's grin faltered but only for a second. "You and me both."

"How is Mongolia?" Olivia asked as she pulled out a chair at the table.

Guess Olivia's work could wait now that Jeremy was here. Dawson and Jeremy had always been close, and the nagging pang of jealousy watching Olivia smile up at Dawson's brother was new.

"Pretty calm right now. Though, I don't expect it to last through the winter." Jeremy took a seat beside Olivia and leaned back, stretching his long legs out under the table.

Jeremy and Dawson definitely had the family resemblance. They were both tall and lean, but where Dawson had blue eyes, Jeremy's were green. Jeremy also preferred facial hair.

"Did you get the church finished?" she asked.

"If all goes well, it'll be up and running next month."

"That's exciting! I'll put that in the missions newsletter," Olivia said.

"How did you know he was building a church on the other side of the world?" Dawson asked.

"He sends me a letter every month," Olivia answered. "Haven't you seen them on the bulletin board at church?"

"There are a lot of papers on that board." Dawson looked at his brother. "How come I don't get letters?"

"Olivia is the head of the missions committee."

Okay, that made sense. Maybe Dawson needed to pay more attention.

Olivia looked at her watch and stood. "Oh, I really have to go. We'll talk more soon?" she asked Jeremy.

"Sure. Dinner next week?"

Oh, good gravy. Dawson couldn't watch while his brother asked Olivia out. He already wanted to handcuff Mark to a light pole. He didn't need to be jealous of his own brother.

"Sure. Thursday?" Olivia asked.

Jeremy stood. "Sounds good, and do you have a date to Asa and Lyric's wedding?"

"She does," Dawson blurted.

Olivia narrowed her eyes at him. "I don't, but Anna is trying to get me to go with someone her brother knows."

Jeremy glanced at Dawson with a teasing grin. "Lucky guy."

Olivia huffed. "Considering I'm organizing most of the wedding and reception, he'll be on his own quite a bit."

"Well, if you hear of anyone in need of a date, keep me in mind," Jeremy said.

"Will do. I'll see you two later," she said with a wave.

"I'll walk you out," Jeremy offered, following her from the kitchen.

Drat. Dawson wanted to walk her out. He had some scratches, not a pegleg. "I will too."

"You rest that leg," Olivia said. "I'll check on you tomorrow."

Dawson threw his head back and sighed. Why did Olivia keep dancing just out of his reach? He busied himself unloading the dishwasher and wiping down the countertops that were already spotless.

A few minutes later, Jeremy walked back into the kitchen. He pointed to the spread of food on the table. "Lunch?"

"Help yourself," Dawson said as he tossed the cleaning rag into the sink.

"So, you didn't get to Olivia first?" Jeremy asked.

"Not because I didn't try. I asked Olivia, but somehow I ended up with Anna."

Jeremy was reaching for a plate, but halted when he heard Dawson. "Anna?"

"Yeah. It's a long story."

"Are you two together?" Jeremy asked.

"Nope. And we're not gonna be," Dawson added for good measure. "I like Anna, but not the way you're thinking."

"Does she know that?"

"Surely she does, right? I mean, we've never had any sparks."

"Is that what Olivia thinks about you?" Jeremy asked.

"Way to kill my hopes and dreams," Dawson said. "You really think Olivia doesn't like me at all?"

Jeremy shrugged. "Who knows? It's not like you two haven't had plenty of time to figure it out by now."

"I've tried asking her out plenty of times. She always brushes it off like I'm joking."

"Maybe she needs to know you're serious."

Dawson rubbed his chin. "How do I do that?"

"Beats me."

He couldn't make any major moves until after the wedding. He'd made a promise to take Anna, and he'd follow through with it, but he needed a plan to show Olivia how he felt.

10

DAWSON

Dawson leaned back in Beau's office chair and watched through the large window as Asa and Jacob sanded the paint off the Porsche 911. Jacob was running the sander, and his dad pointed to spots he missed every once in a while.

It was incredibly boring–much like the rest of the longest week of his life.

Adjusting his now-healed leg on the desk, Dawson looked over his shoulder at Beau who was clicking away at a desktop computer on the other side of the small room. "Is David coming for the painting?"

"He'll be here next week," Beau said without taking his attention from the spreadsheet on the screen.

"Jacob is gonna love that."

Lyric's dad loved restoring classic cars as much as Jacob, and the two had bonded over the Porsche Dawson had picked up a few months ago.

Typically, half the fun was in the fix-up, but sitting on the sidelines wasn't so bad when he got to see Jacob enjoying it so much.

It wasn't much fun being commanded to sit and do nothing per the doctor's orders. Dawson let out a sigh and crossed his arms over his chest.

"Will you stop being so loud?" Beau grumbled. "I'm trying to focus, and numbers are hard without distractions."

"I'm so bored. I can't sit anymore."

"When do you get to go back to work?" Beau asked.

"I've been doing light duty all week, but paperwork gets stale in a hurry."

Beau turned around, finally giving up on the spreadsheet. "What about the goats?"

"I think they're actually tired of me. I stayed at the barn all afternoon yesterday. I filmed twenty Instagram reels."

"I can't believe people actually watch your goat videos," Beau said as he stood and checked on the sanding going on in the garage.

"Oh, people love them. Those little guys are hilarious."

Beau kept his attention focused out the window.

"Sometimes, I think I should give up the garage and just make stupid videos for the internet."

Dawson let out a big laugh. "You would suck at social media. There's a reason I manage your Blackwater Auto platforms."

Beau widened his stance. "I need some help."

Dawson threw his hands in the air. "Hello. You have a helper who is willing to do anything to get out of this chair. Put me in, coach. I'm ready to play."

"I need a full-time employee. I have to quit working seventy-hour weeks and paying the other guys so much overtime."

Dawson pointed out the window into the garage. "That's your man, right there."

Beau scoffed. "I'd hire Jacob in a heartbeat if it was legal. He still has at least four years."

"Had any prospects?" Dawson asked.

Beau was a hard worker, but that strength turned into a weakness when he worked himself into the ground on a regular basis.

"Not really. It's hard to find people who want to work these days."

Dawson jerked his thumb toward the garage where Jacob was sweating through his T-shirt. "I still think that guy is your best bet."

"He does more work playing around in the evenings than some of the guys on the payroll," Beau admitted.

"Want me to spread the word you're looking for someone?" Dawson asked.

Beau glared at Dawson. "I'll pass on the criminals, thanks."

"I know a lot of people, not just the ones who get arrested."

Beau rubbed his brow and sighed. "Yeah, that would be great. Let me know if you hear anything."

Dawson stood and gave Beau a stiff salute. "Sir, yes, sir."

Beau jerked a thumb over his shoulder. "Get out of here so I can finish what I was doing."

"I'm leaving, but not because you told me to. I have to pick Levi up in half an hour."

"Oh, yeah. You two have fun grooming goats or whatever it is you do with them."

"We intend to. We'll also be chicken chasing. I'll call you tomorrow with a full update."

"Please don't," Beau said as he sat back down at the computer.

Dawson headed out of the office and stuck his head into the garage to wave at Asa and Jacob. He slipped into the truck and fired off a text to Olivia.

Dawson: Headed to pick up Levi. Be there soon.

He shifted into reverse, and his phone dinged almost immediately.

Chicken Tender: ok

Dawson frowned at the screen. Olivia's messages always held some hint of excitement.

She'd been giddy about having Levi over to the farm for weeks.

He scanned back through their messages. No other two-letter responses.

He tossed the phone into the passenger seat and tried hard to forget about the short text. Maybe she was busy or just didn't have anything else to say.

If he hadn't been texting with her on a regular basis for the last fifteen years, he wouldn't think twice about an "ok" response. Olivia just wasn't an "ok" kinda gal.

He'd thoroughly overanalyzed the text by the time he pulled up at Blackwater Ranch. The rolling hills stretched for miles, and horses grazed in the pasture near the far-off barn.

Aaron said Levi would be at the main house with his grandparents. Silas and Anita Harding were like parents to half the town. Mama Harding had even been Dawson's Sunday School teacher when he was young. He still met up with Silas every week for breakfast with the round table at Deano's. The man had more wisdom than he knew what to do with.

The door of the main house swung open before Dawson parked. Levi stuck his feet in his boots and waved a hand in the air as he barreled toward the truck.

Anita just waved from the doorway with baby Annie on her hip.

Dawson opened the door to go say hello to

Mama Harding, but Levi circled his arm toward the truck. "Let's go! Let's go!"

Mama Harding just shook her head and laughed. "Have fun!"

"Yes, ma'am!" Dawson replied.

Levi hopped into the backseat and bounced. "Where's Miss Olivia?"

"Meeting us there. Buckle up, small fry."

"I'm not a small fry. I'm a...big fry. Or a whole potato," Levi corrected.

Dawson made a show of assessing the kid. Had Levi grown five inches since the last time Dawson saw him? He did look a whole lot bigger. He was starting to look ten instead of eight. "Okay, you can be a potato. As long as I can be a squash."

Levi laughed. "Why would you want to be a squash?"

Dawson shrugged as he pulled out onto the dirt path leading to the main road. "I don't know. I like squash, and they don't get enough representation. What's wrong with squash?"

"Nothing, I guess." Levi stared out the window and rubbed his chin like he was deep in thought. "I haven't thought about squash enough."

"Now's a good time. You want squash for dinner? I bet Olivia would make us some."

"Yeah. That sounds really good, but can I see the goats first?"

"Dude, you spend your days with horses and cattle. Why are you so interested in goats now?"

"That's just it. I don't get to see them a lot, and they're little enough that I can wrap my arms all the way around their necks." Levi acted like he was squeezing the life out of a baby goat's neck, and Dawson winced.

"Easy there. Don't strangle my goats."

Levi chuckled. "I won't. I'm good with Annie. Mom says so."

"I bet you are. She's gonna need a strong big brother to make sure nobody messes with her when she gets older."

Levi scrunched his nose. "Yeah, but right now she just drools a lot. And she cries sometimes."

"I remember when you were little," Dawson said.

"Really?" Levi's eyes widened in excitement.

"Yeah. I wanted to hold you through the church service once. You chewed on the shoulder of my shirt until you fell asleep in your own drool."

"Gross!" Levi exclaimed through a laugh. "Tell me more."

The short drive over to the Lawrence Farm gave Dawson time to tell the story of Levi's first trip to the pumpkin patch. Dawson still had a copy of the photo he took of the Hardings next to a hay bale. Everyone had a smile on their face, except Levi, who was arms and legs flailing in Aaron's arms with his mouth wide open mid-scream.

They parked next to Olivia's car, and Levi jumped out of the truck before it came to a complete stop.

"Good grief, kid," Dawson mumbled as he pulled his goat boots out of the back seat. He made his way around the house to the farm behind it. No sign of Levi or Olivia.

When Dawson got closer to Cluckingham Palace, he heard Levi talking a mile a minute.

"What else do they eat?"

Olivia's response was slow. "Um… Worms. They like bugs. And…"

Dawson stepped into the watering hole area and caught sight of Olivia. Her long hair was pulled back in a ponytail at the nape of her neck, and her brows and nose were scrunched up.

Something was wrong. The simple text he'd worried over was a cry for help.

"Hey, Liv. You okay?" he asked as he stepped up beside her, resting a hand on her back.

"Mmhm," she hummed. "Just not feeling great. Why don't you take Levi to see the goats, and I'll catch up with you in a few minutes?"

Dawson scanned her for any sign of what was going on but found nothing visibly wrong. When she looked up at him, he did his best to silently ask if she needed help.

"I'm really okay," she said. "I just need a minute."

Taking that as the best answer he'd get, he waved Levi over. "Come on, tater. We've got goats to see."

Levi frolicked with the goats, hugging them, petting them, chatting them up like old friends. The kid definitely had a way with animals. He had a herd following him around within the hour. Dawson had sent Aaron and Jade twenty photos and six videos before Levi asked to milk the goats.

Dawson was operating on autopilot as he explained how to manually milk a goat. Then Levi wanted to see what the milking machine could do. Going through the mechanics did little to keep Dawson's thoughts from Olivia. She hadn't shown up yet, and Levi hadn't stopped playing and talking long enough for Dawson to check on her.

They'd milked all of the mama goats and fed the rest before Levi looked around. "Where's Miss Olivia?"

Dawson was on his feet in a split second. "Let's go check on her."

Levi jogged past a few roaming chickens, and Dawson picked up his own pace. He'd been fighting the urge to check on her since the moment he walked away.

"Are you okay, Miss Olivia?" Levi asked.

Dawson rounded the corner into the feed shed and screeched to a halt. Olivia sat doubled over on a crate.

Levi was already by her side, and Dawson fell to his knee at her feet. "What's wrong?"

"Nothing," she said through gritted teeth. "I just need a minute."

"You've had enough minutes. What can I do to help?" The time for waiting was over. Every cell in his body hummed with the need to act.

"Dawson, just–"

"This isn't normal, Liv. Tell me what to do."

Her eyes pressed tightly closed, and deep lines formed between her brows. Her jaw was tense as she tried to stand. "I–"

As soon as she got to her feet, she crumpled. Dawson wrapped her in his arms and pulled her to his chest.

"Miss Olivia!" Levi shouted.

Dawson set her on her feet long enough to readjust his arms to cradle her. With her body held tight against him, he jerked a chin at Levi. "Go tell Mr. Lawrence I'm bringing her to the house."

Levi rushed off at a quick run, eager to help.

"Hang in there, Liv. I'm right here."

11

OLIVIA

The pain gripped Olivia again as Dawson laid her on the couch.

"What's going on?" he asked sternly.

Oh no. Dawson hardly ever used his serious tone. At least not around her. Any of the playfulness she'd come to expect was thoroughly pushed aside to make way for the intimidating man standing over her.

She curled into a ball as another cramp gripped her insides. "My purse."

Dawson looked around. "Where?"

"My car."

"I'll go get it!" Levi said as he ran out the front door.

Olivia's dad stepped out of the room, and the moment she was alone with Dawson he whispered, "What's going on?"

Her cheeks and ears burned, but there wasn't any way to get around telling him about her embarrassing problem.

Her dad came back into the room with a bottle of water in hand. He passed it to Dawson who twisted the top off before handing it to her. Using the moment to figure out how to explain her current situation to him, she took a few extra gulps of the water.

Her dad's mouth pressed into a thin line as he looked down at her. Her hero had aged two decades in the five years since her mom died. The crow's-feet at the corners of his eyes were deeper, and more gray was weaved into his hair and beard.

"She's okay," her dad said. "It's an ongoing issue Olivia has, but it's not dangerous."

Her dad deserved a gold star. He'd repeated the explanation she'd given him to the letter.

"She's in pain!" Dawson insisted, gesturing toward where she lay on the couch.

Levi burst into the room holding up her gray purse. "Found it!"

He handed it to Olivia, and she unzipped the front pocket. She latched onto the pill bottle. Her hand shook as she opened the top. Sweat beaded on her temple, and she wiped it with the back of her hand.

"Levi, can you get her a wet rag?" Dawson asked.

"I'll help," her dad offered as he led Levi into the kitchen.

Dawson knelt down beside her and pinned her with his intense stare. His blue eyes begged for answers, and his words did the same as he whispered, "What's wrong with my queen?"

Olivia's chin quivered as she shook her head. "It's nothing. I have a condition where I have these pains every once in a while. It's nothing serious."

Nothing serious. That description waded into murky waters, depending on which part of the endometriosis she was talking about.

Overall danger to her health? Minimal.

Did it pose a threat to her service to others? Occasionally.

Did it narrow her chances for relationships and a family? Drastically.

Would it quickly become the talk of the town if she let everyone in her life know about it? Most definitely. The last thing she wanted was to have her friends and strangers talking about her feminine problems.

Dawson shook his head. "I'm not convinced, Liv. I need to know how to help you. It's tearing me up to see you in pain, and I *need* to fix it."

Something in this big man's soft expression prodded her to give in. What would it be like to let someone know? Fear and hope warred within her until the pressure was too much to contain.

"It's my time of the month. Every woman goes through this. Mine is just a little worse."

Dawson picked up her hand and squeezed. "I had no idea it was this hard for you. How can I help?"

The tenderness in his voice was a comfort she didn't know she needed. It seeped into her muscles and released all of the tension she'd been carrying.

Levi jogged back into the room with a damp rag in his hand. "Here you go!"

Olivia sat up a little to swallow the pills. Levi gently wiped at her brow with the rag, and a smile broke through the dark storm.

"Thanks, buddy. Sorry I made a scene," she said. "Did you have fun with the goats?"

"I did! Dawson even showed me how to milk them. I didn't know you could do that."

Olivia bit her lips between her teeth to hide a grin. "You learn something new every day."

Dawson was already kneeling at her side, and Levi did the same. Having the two rally around her was heartwarming, and the scene tugged at her heartstrings.

"What else can we do to help? What's making you feel bad?" Levi asked.

Olivia adjusted on the couch. "It's nothing for you to worry about. Sometimes, I get these pains, but it passes pretty quickly."

Dawson stared down at her, clearly still worried despite her assurances.

Levi straightened his shoulders. "What if we cook dinner for you?"

She'd told Aaron that Levi could have dinner with them at her dad's house, but she'd planned to do the cooking. "You know how to cook?"

"I do. Mom and Mama Harding let me help a lot."

Olivia turned to Dawson with a questioning look.

"I can cook too!" Dawson said. "I promise. I'm... decent at it."

Olivia shrugged. "Well, if you really want to. Now that I took my medicine, I should feel better soon and can help finish up."

"No way!" Dawson said confidently. "We've got this."

Levi puffed out his chest. "Yeah. We know what we're doing."

Dawson gave Levi's shoulder a little shove. "We take care of our women. Don't we?"

"Yeah. Dad taught me," Levi said.

The two high-fived and rose to their feet.

"You head on into the kitchen with Mr. Lawrence. I'll be right there," Dawson said.

Levi ran off, and Dawson resumed his position beside her. "Do I need to take you to the hospital?" he whispered.

"No. I promise. It's not an emergency. This is normal for me."

Dawson huffed and shoved his fingers through his hair. "Liv, please let me help."

"The medicine helps. It really does. I just didn't stop and take it like I should have."

"What else helps?" he asked.

"Food would help." She made a shooing motion toward the kitchen.

Dawson wrapped her hand in his and held it. A small smile played on his lips. He leveled her with an intense stare before whispering, "What am I going to do with you?"

The care in his tone sent a powerful jolt straight to her chest. One of her worst fears was being a burden, and she'd not only ruined Levi's play date at the farm, but now they were cooking dinner for her while she sat useless on the couch.

"Nothing. I'm fine," she whispered back.

She would be fine as long as Dawson stopped looking at her as if he could read the secrets of her soul in her eyes. Heat spread over her as she waited to see if he'd press her again.

Dawson laid her hand down on the couch and stood. "Okay. I hope you like squash."

She scrunched her nose. "Squash? Why?"

"I told Levi we could make it for dinner."

"Ooh kay then," she drawled. "I'll be in there in a few minutes to help."

"Nope. No girls allowed in the kitchen. Let the men do the work this time," he said over his shoulder as he walked away.

Olivia rested her head back and closed her eyes as another cramp twisted her insides.

OLIVIA STEPPED out of Dawson's truck into the darkness. She'd spent many evenings at Blackwater Ranch in her life, and the familiar scent called her memories to the forefront of her mind. It wasn't the musty smell of the chickens and goats but a woodsy, leather scent that filled the night.

"Don't forget your eggs," Dawson said as Levi slipped from the truck.

"Oh! Thanks." Levi climbed back in and gathered the eggs he'd chosen. They were all easter eggs–pale green, light pink, and brown.

With eggs in hand, Levi jogged up to Olivia's side and walked so close his shoulder brushed against her hand. "Thanks for these."

"You're very welcome. Be sure to share them."

"I will. Annie is going to love the pink ones."

Olivia chuckled. Annie was too young to care, but it was wonderful seeing Levi excited about the eggs. She'd been afraid her episode had ruined the afternoon, but the kid still had a smile on his face.

Dawson stepped up beside Levi and wrapped an

arm around his shoulder. "And don't forget to tell your mom and dad about the best farm tour guides ever."

"I will."

The porch light was on at the main house, and Mama Harding stepped outside. "You have fun?"

"You bet. Look what I got!" Levi held up the eggs for her to see.

"They're so pretty! Are we having eggs for breakfast?"

"Oh yeah. I want the green ones, please," Levi said.

Mama Harding patted Levi's back. "Say good night to Dawson and Olivia and put those eggs in the kitchen."

Levi turned and snuggled up against Olivia's side, careful to keep his eggs out of the way. "Thanks for everything."

"You're welcome to come hang out anytime," Olivia said. Man, Levi radiated happiness, and she wanted to wrap him up and take him home with her.

This was only a taste of what she'd be missing if she couldn't ever have kids. She swallowed the thought as soon as it climbed up her throat, and it slashed at the sides like razor blades on the way down.

"Can you hold these for a second, please?" he asked Olivia.

"Sure." She took the eggs as he turned to Dawson and held up a fist.

Dawson bumped it with his, and the two dove into a series of hand gestures ending by knocking their forearms together.

"Catch you later, potato," Dawson said.

"Bye, squash!" Levi replied as he gathered his eggs from Olivia and darted inside the house.

"Squash?" Olivia whispered.

"Had to be there," Dawson answered.

Mama Harding clasped her hands together in front of her chest. "Thanks for letting him hang out at the farm. It's all he's talked about lately."

"We really enjoyed having him around," Olivia said.

"See you later, Mama," Dawson said with a wave.

"You two be careful!"

Dawson stepped off the porch and turned back to Mama Harding. "Always. I have precious cargo." He jutted his thumb toward Olivia.

Oh, man. She was in trouble. Did he have to be so sweet all the time? So caring and attentive? So ridiculously thoughtful?

And so good with kids? That one tore her up more than the others.

Dawson followed her to the passenger side of the truck but didn't open the door for her. Instead, he put his hands on her arms and rubbed up and down, soothing the tension she hadn't realized she'd been holding onto.

"Are you feeling better?"

"Yeah. Thanks for taking care of me tonight."

She did feel better compared to earlier, but she'd smiled through the pain a few times.

Dawson let his hands slide down her arms. "Always. I'm here if you need anything."

She pressed her lips together and nodded. Of course he would offer help he didn't understand. There wasn't anything he or anyone else could do to help. The doctors could perform surgery, but it would decrease her chances of having kids.

Life was a double-edged sword.

He opened the passenger door and stepped to the side. She climbed inside the truck, and he waited until she was settled before closing the door and walking around to the other side.

With Dawson in his place behind the wheel, Olivia shoved his shoulder as he backed out. "I knew you were good with kids, but I didn't remember how good. Levi loves you."

Dawson made a clicking noise behind his teeth. "Most people love me, Liv. It's sad you don't notice."

She laughed. "You're so cocky!"

"I'm not cocky. I just love people. Therefore, they love me back."

"Oh, wise one. Teach me your ways," Olivia deadpanned.

"You're loveable too. Don't sell yourself short. Half of the people in Blackwater adore you. They come to you first when they need help or have something to celebrate. That's awesome, Liv."

"I know, and I love all of our friends. I'm just not quite as charismatic as you."

"You're still my favorite," Dawson said.

Olivia chuckled. "I bet you say that to all the ladies, melting hearts along the way."

"No, I only have one favorite." He paused for only a second before asking, "What's your latest service project?"

Way to skate right over that sweet comment. It was getting more difficult to keep her walls up, especially when Dawson was right in front of her, and she hadn't seen Anna in days.

"Um, I'm working on a calendar for Memorial Day. People have been submitting photos of their family members who died in the line of duty, and I'll be pre-selling them to raise money for the Veterans Association in Cody."

"That's awesome. Can I help?" he asked.

"Not really, but thanks for the offer."

The truck was quiet for a minute before Dawson spoke again. "Have you done anything for yourself lately?"

She looked over at him, but she could only make out his profile in the shadows. "I do stuff for myself all the time. I feed the chickens, I'm planning Asa and Lyric's wedding, I'm putting together a gift basket for the volunteer fire department."

"You realize none of those things are for you, right? I know you love to do things for others, but if things are this bad for you every month, maybe you should rest instead of trying to push through. No one is cracking a whip behind you."

He was right, but that didn't change the responsibility she felt after committing to something. She didn't want to miss things or cut back. She wanted to enjoy life.

And she could only do that if she kept having the procedures every so often.

"Maybe you're right, but I don't need anything. I'm happy. I'm…"

Surviving. She was doing what she loved, but half the time, she was barely keeping her head above water. Where was the happy medium? Why hadn't she found it yet?

"I want in on the missions committee at church," Dawson said. "And I want to be a part of any service projects you're working on."

"You don't have to do that," she said, sitting up straighter.

"I don't know what I'm good at, but I guess I'd better get involved in a few things so I can find out."

Olivia sucked in a deep breath of the thick air that had suddenly filled the cab. "You don't have to do that," she repeated. The words were softer this time–not as bold.

"I want to. I love watching you help people. Not only do you make other people happy, but you get this smile on your face that looks like your mouth is about to snap like a rubber band. I'm talking megawatt smile. I love that. It's my favorite thing in the world."

He was treading into the deep end of the pool, and she was having trouble keeping her head above water. "Dawson–"

"Let me do this," he said, cutting her off. "I want to. And when we're working on something together and you need to step back because you're hurting or just not feeling up to it, you can know I'll be there handling things. We can do this together, and you won't have to break your back trying to do it all."

She was still processing everything Dawson had said when he pulled up at her place. The little house was all she could afford, but it was more than enough for her. She barely spent time at home anyway.

Dawson shifted the truck into park and got out. She slid out of the passenger seat as he made his way around. They walked up onto her tiny porch together, and he waited while she pulled out her keys and unlocked the door.

She turned back around to face him, mustering

as much determination as she could. "I'd love to have some help."

Dawson opened his arms. "You got it, my queen."

Olivia fell into his embrace, resting her head against his chest. Lots of people in her life knew she had a passion for service, but Dawson probably understood her reasoning more than anyone else. Her mom had taught her to be the hands and feet of Jesus, and she took that job seriously.

She needed this comfort. She needed a place to rest her head.

"You're not alone," Dawson whispered.

"I know. Thanks for the reminder." She lifted her head and looked up at his waiting smile. "You smell like a goat."

He laughed, and she felt the vibrations from his chest tingle throughout her body. Jerking his chin toward the door, he said, "Go get some rest. I'll call you in the morning."

"I'm going to Brandi's for the catering rehearsal, so don't think anything is wrong if I don't answer."

"Oh, that sounds like something I can do for you. Consider it done. What time do I have to be there?"

Olivia threw her head back and groaned. "You're not going to let me do anything now, are you?"

"Of course I will, but I bet this pain you're having isn't going to go away overnight. You can sleep in and head down there when and if you feel like it."

"Lyric and Asa will be there, so you won't be alone."

"Then why are you worried about it? I'll give my honest opinion on the food, and everything will be a go for the wedding next week."

The wedding. She'd gone through a million little tasks to get to this point, and everything was ready to go.

Why did she feel like someone had dropped her into a rushing river with her arms tied behind her back whenever she thought of the wedding?

Probably because watching Dawson and Anna have fun together was going to be about as confusing as calculus. They were her friends. She should be excited that Anna was finally getting a chance to go out with Dawson.

Except the excitement was doused with lava that burned her insides.

"Okay, you can do it, but I'm coming if I feel better in the morning."

Dawson gave her another squeeze before releasing her. "Sweet dreams, my queen," he said as he backed away from her.

"I'll let Asa and Lyric know you'll be there tomorrow."

He held a thumb up in the air as he headed for his truck. "I've got this."

Of course he did. Olivia wished she had the same

assurance she knew what she was doing every time he was around.

12

DAWSON

The song "Shut Up and Dance" belted through Dawson's bedroom as he struggled with a cuff link. He had a love hate relationship with the tiny things, and he bit back a few choice words.

By the time the chorus hit, the link finally clicked into place, and he joined in, bobbing his head to the beat. His friends were getting married, and Dawson had every intention of dancing the night away.

The song stopped, and his phone dinged with a text. He peeked at the screen on the nightstand before picking it up.

Anna: I'm so sorry. I can't go today. We'll talk soon.

Dawson quirked a brow at the phone. Anna wasn't going to the wedding? That was a curveball if he ever saw one. She'd been giddy about it for weeks.

Before he could text back, an incoming call from Chicken Tender lit up his phone.

"Hey. What's up with Anna?"

"She's sick. Sooo sick," Olivia said. "She wanted me to tell you how sorry she is that she can't make it today."

A traitorous wave of relief seeped from his shoulders. He hadn't figured out the best way to handle the date with Anna, so getting a free pass was a blessing. "Not a problem. She can't help it she's sick. Is she okay?"

"Yes, but it's a stomach virus, and she's miserable. I feel terrible about not being able to be there for her, but her mom is helping."

"Good. Well, I guess that means I'm flying solo tonight. Want me to pick you up on my way to the ranch?"

"Thanks for the offer, but I'm already here. Lyric's parents really went all out and got a nice photographer who wanted some shots of the bridal party getting ready together."

Dawson sat on the bed and settled into the conversation with Olivia. Who knew being dateless could be so freeing? It wasn't that he'd dreaded the day with Anna, but she definitely wasn't on the same page as him.

"Will there be photos of you with your hair in curlers? If so, can I get on the list for one?"

"So sorry. I think I avoided all of those. You'll

have to wait another fifty years for a chance at that sight."

"I'm a patient man. You know, you'd be a cute old lady."

"You're ridiculous, but I have to go. You're supposed to be here in an hour," Olivia reminded him.

"I'll do you one better and see you in forty-five minutes."

"I'm sure the photographer would be happy about that. See you soon."

As soon as the call ended, he checked the time. He could make it to the ranch in half an hour. Maybe Olivia would delegate a few tasks to him.

Silver Falls Ranch was just outside of town, and he passed fewer and fewer vehicles as he drove. The cattle ranch didn't normally host weddings, but their rec center hadn't been used in a while, and the owners, Matthew and Tammie Benson, had offered it to Asa and Lyric at a cheap rate in exchange for some help fixing the place up. Dawson had spent a few weekends painting walls and resealing floors in the last few months.

A sign just before a fork in the road directed him to the bridal suites to the right of the main house. Two small cabins side by side were labeled for bridesmaids and groomsmen.

Dawson parked far enough away so other guests could have the better spots. He walked past a horse pasture and held out his hand to an Appaloosa with dark eyes against a light coat. The horse spooked and ran off in a hurry.

Figured. Apparently, dogs weren't the only ones wary of him. Why didn't they like him? Did he smell?

No, he'd showered this morning. He sniffed the collar of his shirt. Maybe it was the cologne. He didn't always wear it, but the spice was pretty intense.

Inside the groom's cabin, Jacob sat in a corner playing a video game while Asa, Beau, and Lyric's dad watched a football game on a tablet propped up on a table.

"Where's the party?" Dawson asked as he held out a hand to Jacob.

"I don't know, but waiting is boring," the kid said, putting his game aside.

Dawson jerked a thumb over his shoulder. "Want to go check out the horses?"

Jacob was on his feet in an instant. "Please. I've been here for hours."

"We got here half an hour ago," Asa corrected.

"It feels like forever," Jacob muttered.

Outside, Dawson and Jacob approached the fence, and a blue roan stepped up to greet them. She took to the kid like an old friend, and Dawson kept his distance. He'd only scare her off if he tried to get in on the petting.

"What's this one's name?" Jacob asked.

"I don't know. Want to take a guess? We can ask Matthew and Tammie later."

A door creaked behind them, and Olivia stepped out onto the small porch of the bride's cabin. Her dark hair was pinned up in curls, leaving her neck on full display. The navy dress flowed out, brushing against her calves.

"Wow." Dawson's reaction slipped out before he could censor it.

"She's pretty," Jacob said.

"Truer words were never spoken, kid."

Olivia turned their way and waved when she spotted them. Then she stuck her head back inside. A woman with dark hair pulled back into a high ponytail wearing a white blouse and dark dress pants stepped out. Olivia pointed at Dawson and Jacob, and the woman cradled the camera hanging on a strap around her neck close to her chest.

"Oh no. We've been targeted," Dawson said.

"What for?"

"Photos," Dawson whispered ominously.

"Ick," Jacob said. "Dad said I had to smile a lot today.

Dawson bumped Jacob's shoulder. "I'm sure everyone would appreciate that."

Jacob tilted his head from side to side. "Okay. It's just that my cheeks hurt if I smile a lot."

"It's a good thing you're tough."

The woman made her way over and greeted them with handshakes. "Hi. I'm Gloria, one of the photographers. Olivia said Lyric would really like some photos with you two and the horses."

Dawson held up his hands. "I'd love to, but the horses don't like me so much. Jacob, on the other hand, has them wrapped around his finger."

Gloria smiled at Jacob. "Can I take some photos while you play with the horses?" she asked.

"If you want."

Dawson hung around while Jacob made friends with the horses. The kid befriended Gloria too, and he had her laughing the whole time.

A few early guests were starting to arrive, and before long the groomsmen were all accounted for. Gloria ushered Dawson and Jacob back to the groom's cabin where she took a bunch of photos of them pretending to get ready, even though they'd been in their suits for an hour.

"Why are we pretending?" Jacob asked Dawson when the photographer walked a few feet away.

"Because people like to remember their wedding day. Lyric wants to remember that we all knew how to get dressed."

Jacob nodded. "That makes sense."

After pretending to get ready, the men moved outside for a few more photos. Another photographer was standing shoulder-to-shoulder with Olivia near the small chapel where the wedding would take place. She was far enough away that he couldn't see her face, but he'd know Olivia's stance anywhere. She pointed to the camera screen the woman beside her held and said something to the photographer.

A man was walking toward the two women, and Dawson groaned. He hadn't come with a date, but Olivia had. The guy was stocky with a bushy beard, and he wore a dark-green button-down with neon-green swirls all over it.

"What is that guy wearing?" Jacob asked.

The thought could have been pulled straight from Dawson's mind, and it took everything he had to resist making the joke perching on his tongue. He crossed one arm over his chest and covered his mouth with the other.

"He's heading for Olivia. Does she know him?" Jacob asked.

"I hope not," Dawson said, keeping his attention trained on the guy he wanted to squash like a bug.

"He looks like a peacock," Jacob said low.

Dawson swallowed the chuckle that crawled up his throat. He should be the adult here and remind Jacob to be nice, but it was hard to do when Dawson couldn't practice what he preached.

"I'll be right back," Dawson said, already walking toward Olivia.

The guy reached Olivia and the photographer and interrupted the women to introduce himself. Olivia smiled and greeted him warmly before pointing to the chapel where other guests were headed.

Presumably Mark nodded and started toward the chapel, looking back over his shoulder at Olivia.

Keep walkin', peacock.

The photographer stepped back into the bride's cabin, and Olivia brushed a hand over her hair, not quite touching the curls as she looked up and spotted Dawson.

Shoot. What was he doing here?

"Hey," she said, pausing to look him up and down. The glance was almost too quick to pick up, but there was a fleeting look of shock right after her assessment.

"Don't look surprised. I know how to get dressed. Gloria even has photographic evidence."

Olivia swatted his arm. "I knew that. You just look..."

"Handsome?" Dawson offered.

"You look good."

"Just good? Is it because I didn't wear my peacock suit?"

Olivia's eyes widened. "You saw that?"

"Actually, Jacob pointed it out."

She glanced behind Dawson, and her shoulders fell with a sigh.

He looked behind him to see Trey walking across the parking lot. Of course, he had a very overdone blonde woman wearing a short dress on his arm.

No matter who Olivia's ex brought to the wedding, he was still a loser.

"Don't worry about him. It's his loss. He probably cries himself to sleep at night because he was dumb enough to let you slip away."

Olivia shook her head and tucked her chin to her chest. "Not quite."

"I'm sure your exotic pheasant will make him jealous," Dawson added.

She didn't even look up. Not even a grin at his bird joke.

"Did you really like him?" he asked, unsure if he wanted to hear the answer.

Her head jerked up. "No. I didn't, but rejection hurts just the same." She swiped her hands down her sides and over her waist.

Dawson reached for one of her hands and lifted the knuckles to his lips. "You're gorgeous. He can eat his heart out."

Olivia pressed her lips together and looked up at him. She thought he was joking, but that couldn't be further from the truth.

"Let's both make a promise to be nice tonight," she said.

"Are you afraid I'll make a scene?" Dawson asked.

"Should I be worried?"

"Possibly. I can't make any promises."

"Trey deserves a cold shoulder, but Mark is an unassuming stranger. Please be nice," she begged.

Dawson narrowed his eyes. "I'll think about it, but I don't have to like him."

"You haven't even met him," Olivia said.

Dawson shrugged. He didn't have to meet the guy. He probably wouldn't like anyone Olivia dated, but he'd keep his mouth shut for her.

Unless speaking up was necessary.

What determined "necessary?"

"Dawson!"

He turned, looking for the source of the shout, and spotted Bethany heading his way in a tight pink dress and outrageously high heels that reminded him of stilts.

Walking in those things probably took skill. Bethany practically bounced with each step, sending her long, strawberry-blonde hair flowing behind her.

"What are you doing here?" Bethany asked as she stepped up to his side, stopping a little too close for comfort.

He'd met Bethany at a barn dance at Wolf Creek over the summer. She was working at the front office there and very much in her wild and crazy era.

"It's my best friend's wedding," Dawson said. "Have you met Olivia Lawrence?"

He turned back to Olivia who had a very fake smile plastered on her face. She gave a small wave.

"I haven't. Sorry, you must be Dawson's date," Bethany said.

"Oh no. My date is inside."

Bethany looked around. "Oh, where's your date?" she asked, looking up at Dawson without as much innocence as she intended.

"She got sick and couldn't make it," Dawson reluctantly admitted.

Bethany gasped and slid her arm around his. "You can be my date!"

He pulled his arm away and desperately looked around for a distraction. "Um, I really have a lot to do today. You know, groomsmen duties." He started backing toward the groom's cabin. "I'll catch up with you at the reception, but I... I think the photographer is waiting on me."

"Okay! Save me a bunch of dances!" Bethany said as he backed away.

He waved at the women, and Bethany waved back ecstatically.

Olivia, however, covered her mouth to hide her chuckles.

Dawson turned and headed toward the cabin. Bethany was pretty, but it was hard to even see her when the only woman he wanted was standing three feet away.

So close, but just out of reach.

13

DAWSON

Dawson stepped up to his spot at the front of the church and settled in. He clasped his hands in front of him just like Olivia had instructed him to do.

Now, how long did they have to stand here before things got started?

He scanned the familiar faces in the small chapel. The pews were filled from one end to the other. He waved when he spotted his mom and Jeremy in the crowd.

"Dad, is it time yet?" Jacob asked.

"Almost," Asa whispered back.

Seconds later, the music started. Lyric's mom walked down the aisle first. A few seconds later, Asa's mom made her way toward them. Betty Scott's smile was wide, and the crow's-feet beside her eyes were deep as she beamed at her son standing at the altar.

The next person to appear at the end of the aisle was Olivia. The sight of her in a dress, holding a bouquet, and walking toward him stole his breath.

He'd give anything to have a chance with her–a chance to show her how much he loved her. He would protect her with his life, provide for her every need and want, and never miss a chance to adore her.

Would that be enough? If she couldn't love him in a romantic way, would anything change her mind?

Olivia walked slowly to the front of the chapel. When she glanced up at him, he gave her a quick wink. She smiled and turned to take her place on the other side of the officiant.

Finally, Lyric and her dad made their way into the chapel. There were whispered awes above the music, and everyone's attention was on the bride. Lyric's dad looked happier than a kid in a candy store as he gave her away at the altar.

It had been a while since Dawson had attended a wedding ceremony, but Olivia assured him it would be a quick thing. He'd missed the rehearsal dinner last night because of work, so he tried to listen for the cues Olivia had given him this morning.

"These two have come here today in front of their family, friends, witnesses, and God to pledge a renewal. A renewal in Christ, and a coming together as one."

Man, Asa and Lyric were perfect for each other. Seriously, no one could tear those two apart. And a renewal in Christ? Dawson wanted to sign up for that kind of commitment. He wanted a life with a woman who was just as adamant in her faith as him.

But not with just anyone. Only the woman standing on the other side of the chapel. It had to be Olivia. No doubt about it.

His attention drifted to her again, and her gaze slipped to him. Her eyes darted toward the couple, urging him to pay attention.

He was paying attention, but what kind of trouble would he get in if he kept this up just to see Olivia make funny faces at him in front of a church full of people?

The officiant read from 1 Corinthians 13, and Dawson pictured that kind of love. A love for a lifetime with his best friend. It was actually a clear vision–easy to imagine.

He glanced out at the crowd, and shifting caught his attention. Trey rested his arm behind his date. The woman was nothing like Olivia. What screws had to be loose in a guy's head to make him think cheating was a good idea?

Then the flamboyant shirt he'd seen earlier stood out. Dawson wasn't looking forward to making small talk with Olivia's date for the evening.

Just as Olivia promised, the service was over quickly, and the newlywed couple kissed to cheers, whistles, and hoots. The music started up again as Asa and Lyric made their way out as a married couple.

Dawson walked down a couple of steps and held out an arm for Olivia. Any unease inside him settled when she took her place at his side. He tucked her close and imagined walking the aisle in a church with her again one day. They might be years from it right now, but he had plenty of hope left.

After the ceremony, Gloria led the bridal party outside for some group photos with Asa and Lyric. Dawson stood where he was told, which was usually beside Olivia, and smiled when prompted.

Jacob was right. Dawson's cheeks were already twitching. He should be conditioned for this. He smiled all the time.

The reception was held in an old barn at Silver Falls Ranch that the Bensons were hoping to get up and going for more events. The place was plenty big enough, and the twinkle lights and drapes Olivia had hung from the rafters gave it a romantic feel.

Once the bride and groom had been introduced, everyone was free to get food and move around. Asa and Lyric hadn't assigned seats, but Dawson made a point to claim his spot at Olivia's table.

Of course, that meant he had to share air space with the peacock. Thankfully, his friends Asher and Haley had claimed two other seats, and Lauren had another.

Lauren had been involved in an abduction and assault a few months back, and the sweet librarian had been on the Blackwater police force radar ever since. The tiny town was generally safe, but Lauren had brushed a little too close to death that night.

Dawson still had flashbacks about that gunshot–the one that hit Asa but was meant for Lauren. The Wilson brothers who'd held her against her will were up for trial soon, and hopefully, justice would be served.

Haley Harding set a plate on the table and took the seat on the other side of Lauren. "Hey, girl. How's the remodel going?"

Lauren's eyes lifted at the corners. The woman always lit up at the mention of the local library or the kids in her Sunday School classes.

"It's going great. I've been ready to get that old carpet from the seventies out of the library since I started. It was threadbare in some places."

Haley's husband, Asher, appeared at the table, bouncing their son, Caleb, on his hip.

"Hey, man. How's life?"

"Any better and I'd be you," Dawson said as he stood to shake hands. "How are your folks?"

"Good as gold." Asher jerked his head toward Lauren and leaned in to whisper, "You got any good news on the Wilsons?"

Lauren's abduction had rattled the whole county. She was the hometown sweetheart–the last person anyone expected to be targeted by criminals. Unfortunately, her cousin owed the brothers money, and they'd seen her as their bartering tool.

"Trial coming up. I imagine they'll be locked up for a while."

Asher shook his head. "No sign of Rome?"

"Not yet, but I'm hoping Zach will talk." Zach and Bobby Wilson had been tight-lipped about their brother's whereabouts since the incident, but Asa and Dawson had made their own opinions about what had gone on that night.

Bobby would have shot Lauren had Zach not interfered. That gave plenty of room for questions. The brothers were partners in crime, but it seemed they weren't on the same page when it came to murder.

"I'll sleep better at night knowing they're off the streets," Asher said.

Olivia marched over to the table with a plate in one hand and a punch cup in the other. Her eyes were wide, and she avoided eye contact until she plopped down in a seat next to Dawson.

Mark was right behind her and took the seat next to Asher. The conversation about the Wilsons would have to wait for another time.

Olivia spread her napkin in her lap. The smile on her face was completely fake. Dawson had seen it plenty of times before.

"Olivia! This wedding is gorgeous," Haley

gushed. "Everly has been admiring your planning work all afternoon. You know she's one of the wedding planners at Wolf Creek Ranch."

"I heard about that." Now Olivia was truly smiling.

The women talked about the beautiful decorations and Lyric's dress, while the men tried to make baby Caleb laugh with ridiculous faces.

Well, that's what Asher and Dawson were doing. Mark was doing everything he could to sneak into the ladies' conversation. Dawson was focused on Caleb, but he kept one ear open for everything else happening around him. The guy was plain rude, and Olivia kept giving Lauren and Haley apologetic looks.

The guy hadn't even said anything about how beautiful Olivia was. He could have mentioned something while in line getting food, but since they'd been at the table, he hadn't said a word about anyone but himself.

Dawson glanced over at Olivia just as Mark reached his hand toward her under the table. Olivia kept her attention on Lauren, but her jaw tightened. Her arm slid toward him, clearly moving the guy's hand back into his own lap.

Dawson's neck heated as his hand fisted on the table. The guy definitely had a death wish. He had no idea how close he was to having that hand pinned behind his back.

Now, Dawson wasn't paying enough attention to baby Caleb, who started to cry. Asher stood and picked up a light-green backpack. "Duty calls."

Soon, everyone was milling around and dancing. Dawson took a few turns around the floor with some ladies, while keeping one eye on Olivia and Mark. The guy was definitely too touchy-feely.

After a few dances, Olivia stepped away from Mark and pointed toward the exit. Mark made a move to follow her, but she held up a hand, shooing him back with a plastered-on smile.

Dude, she's trying to get away from you. Back off.

Dawson was about to saddle up to the peacock to give a stern but gentle warning when Beau intercepted Mark first. He'd probably noticed Olivia trying to shed her date for a while, and Beau's warning wouldn't be easily dismissed. If Dawson hadn't known him since they were kids, he'd assume Beau was more bark than bite.

Perfect. Mark was getting spoon-fed the hint, Trey was brooding at a table in the corner while his date cha-cha'd a little too hard on the dance floor, and Dawson was overdue for some punch.

14

OLIVIA

Sweat beaded on the back of Olivia's neck as she took her sweet, precious time washing her hands. Of all the ways she'd imagined the night going, hiding in the bathroom wasn't one of them.

The nerve of that guy. She'd known him for two seconds–barely spoken to him before–and he was trying to lock lips and touch her sacred place before dessert.

No, thank you, Mr. Peacock.

Checking herself in the mirror, she wiped the back of her neck with a towel, pulled the tube of lipstick out of her cleavage, and fixed her makeup. She would not let an inappropriate date ruin the evening.

Olivia pushed open the bathroom door and nearly collided with the wall of green waiting in the hallway. Backing up, she pressed a hand to her chest where her heart beat double-time.

"Mark, what are you doing?"

"Looking for you." His gaze slid up and down her body, washing a sticky chill over her skin. He probably thought he looked brooding, but the expression was just creepy.

"I told you I was going to the bathroom." Maybe she should have just made a stealthy escape.

Mark looked over both shoulders before turning that icky look toward her. "Let's get outta here."

Olivia sidestepped Mark and started backing toward the main room. "Um, no. It's my friends' wedding, and I'm not going anywhere with you."

Good grief. Did he really think she'd just leave with him?

A deep ridge formed between Mark's brows, and his gaze slid down her body, then back up. He scoffed. "What a prude."

She'd been called worse things, and he could call her Cookie Monster for all she cared. This guy didn't deserve another ounce of her time. Waving a hand above her head, she turned toward the doors leading to the reception. "Have a nice life."

Olivia let out a sigh of relief as soon as she stepped into the main room. At least one of her problems was solved. She snaked through the crowd to the table where she'd left her clutch. She pulled out her phone and sent a quick text to Anna.

Olivia: How are you?

She didn't expect a quick response, so she tucked the phone away and scanned the room. The party had really amped up in the minutes she'd been gone.

A gentle hand rested on her shoulder. "Hey, where's your date?" Lauren asked.

Olivia sagged onto a chair. "Gone."

Lauren took the seat beside her. "I hate to say it, but I'm glad. He was–"

"Intense? Rude? Forward?" Olivia offered.

Lauren chuckled. "I was going to say creepy."

"You nailed it. Anna set me up with him, and she's getting an ear full tomorrow."

"A good man is hard to find," Lauren said. "But it looks like Asa and Lyric were made for each other."

Olivia looked over her shoulder to see the happy couple swaying in a slow dance. A smile bloomed on Lyric's face as Asa whispered in her ear.

"They are. I'm so glad those two found each other."

Lauren inhaled a deep breath and looked down to brush her hands over her hunter-green dress. "I'm just glad he's okay. After...what happened."

Olivia reached out to Lauren. They'd talked many times since the night Lauren was abducted by the Wilson brothers. She'd suffered from a few bumps and bruises that were no small thing, but Asa had taken a bullet to the shoulder.

"Hey, none of it was your fault," Olivia whispered.

"I know, but that doesn't stop the nightmares. I've had dreams where the bullet hit his chest instead of his shoulder." Lauren looked at the happy couple, but she wasn't smiling.

Olivia squeezed Lauren's hand. "I'm glad you're both here. Your work isn't finished. The Lord still has a plan for you. Asa too, it seems."

Lauren's smile reappeared. "Thanks. You're right. I needed to hear that."

"Miss Lauren!"

Olivia turned to see Levi bounding toward them. Aaron and Jade followed behind him. The kid barreled into Lauren's arms, wrapping her in a tight hug.

"Oh, hey. Didn't see you there, Miss Olivia," Levi said as he gave her the same excited greeting.

Jade stepped up beside them with baby Annie resting on her chest. "I swear, this is Levi's dream come true. All of his favorite people are together in one place."

"It's awesome, isn't it?" Olivia asked.

Levi looked around. "Yeah, but where's Dawson?"

That was just what she'd been wondering. Well, Dawson hardly ever left her thoughts, but tonight, he'd been a real distraction. She had a wedding to manage, and the man was impossible to ignore.

"I can help you look for him," Lauren said.

Levi bounced on his toes. "Okay!"

Olivia turned to Aaron and Jade as Lauren and Levi slipped into the crowd. "He's such a good kid."

Jade patted baby Annie's back. "He's the sweetest, but he's a mess sometimes. I've been meaning to ask how you're doing. Levi said you were hurting when he was at the farm."

"Oh, I'm fine. It wasn't anything major. I'm sorry I worried him." Olivia rubbed the back of Annie's little head as she slept soundly on Jade's shoulder. "He adores Annie."

"He's proud to be a big brother," Aaron said.

"Would you like to hold her?" Jade asked.

"You don't have to ask me twice," Olivia said, reaching for the baby. Annie settled in her arms without opening her eyes. She was the epitome of peace and comfort, surrounded by the people she loved and trusted.

A twinge of longing pierced Olivia's chest, and the happiness faded to a cold dread. Baby fever was a real thing, and she'd been struck by the bug. It made innocent moments like this almost gut-wrenching.

"She's adorable!"

Olivia looked up to see Trey's date clasping her hands with a wide, open-mouthed smile. Trey was right behind the woman, caught off guard. He clearly hadn't expected Olivia to be the one holding the baby, and it seemed he hadn't filled the woman in on his connection to her.

"How old is she?" Trey's date asked.

Olivia stood frozen, unable to speak through the warring emotions. Of course, her cheating ex would catch her at a moment when she was lamenting the things she couldn't have.

"She's seven months," Jade said.

Trey's date said something else about Annie, but the roaring in Olivia's ears obstructed her hearing. Trey was staring at her with an expression she couldn't decipher. Was that pity?

Oh, no. Her breaths were coming quicker, and the thin air barely registered in her lungs.

"Liv, are you okay?" Jade asked.

"Um, yeah. I just need to get some air." She quickly passed Annie back to Jade and headed for the door without looking back. She'd apologize to Aaron and Jade later for the hasty exit, but she had precious few seconds to get away from the crowd before the panic attack reached its peak.

The chill in the night air stuck to the sweat beading down her back, but she could breathe again. The full, deep breaths spread a tingling over her skin as she scanned the vehicles parked at the ranch. The music from inside was muffled to a small hum.

Low blades of grass tickled her feet around her strappy heels as she walked over to the wall of the reception building. She rested her back against the wood and closed her eyes.

"Lord, help me. Help me," Olivia pleaded over and over. What was she even asking Him to do? What would it take to get rid of the irrational emotions?

She didn't care about Trey. Why did it bother her to see him? She was happy for Aaron and Jade. Why couldn't she look at a baby without wanting that life for herself?

She wasn't even in a relationship. Her wants didn't make any sense. Her overreaction seemed silly now that she was away from the triggers. Her breaths came easier, and her muscles relaxed.

The door opened, and an older couple stepped out into the darkness. The woman wrapped her arm around the man's, and they walked through the darkness and the parked cars that filled the hillside.

With a deep breath, Olivia headed back into the building. It took a moment for her vision to adjust to the bright lights. The entryway was empty, as well as the hallway leading around the outside of the main room.

"Liv."

Dawson strode down the hallway toward her. His tall frame and powerful stride matched his intense expression. He was usually the funniest guy in the room, but not right now.

They met halfway down the hallway, and he ducked his head to look into her eyes.

"Are you okay? I've been looking all over for you."

His piercing blue gaze bore into her. Why did her best friend have to be everything she ever wanted in a man? He made her laugh, he watched over her, and he protected her.

"I'm fine. I just stepped outside to get some air."

He inched closer and brushed a hand down her arm, leaving her skin tingling where he touched her. "Jade said you ran out of there pretty quickly. She thought something was wrong. Did that guy bother you?"

Olivia rolled her eyes. "No, Mark is long gone. He was a piece of work."

Dawson nodded once. "You said it."

"But you were thinking it," she added.

"You caught me. It took everything I had to keep from showing him to the door when he was rattling on and on about himself at dinner."

"Did you hear the part where he said he's been driving trucks for fifteen years?"

"Yeah. It's like he wants an award for it," Dawson said.

"Well, he told me yesterday that he's twenty-nine."

Dawson scrunched his nose. "That math ain't mathin', babe."

"Exactly. Plus, he was way too touchy."

Dawson's jaw clenched. "I was about half a second away from introducing him to my fist when you moved his hand."

Olivia covered her eyes. "Oh my goodness. You saw that?" Lingering embarrassment heated her face.

"Seriously, I'm glad he's gone. I didn't want to end up in jail tonight."

Olivia chuckled and lowered her hand, but there wasn't a trace of a smile on Dawson's face.

Oh. He was serious. Olivia wasn't a fan of unwanted touches, but what would she have done if Mark had been the slightest bit more forceful? She'd like to think she could take care of herself, but it was nice to know Dawson was always in her corner.

"No one needs to go to jail. He's gone."

Dawson's shoulders relaxed the slightest bit, and he leaned his side against the wall. "On another note, Levi asked Jade if you could be his teacher sometimes."

Olivia chuckled. Jade homeschooled Levi, and they used all of Blackwater Ranch as their classroom. "How did that go over?"

"Not well. You could tell Jade's feelings were hurt, but Levi said, 'I only meant like two days a week or something.'"

"Oh no," Olivia whispered.

"Yeah. At least he didn't ask for three out of five. Jade might have cried."

"He knows he has the perfect teacher. They both love learning. He'd miss her if he had a different teacher."

"That's what I told him." Dawson glanced over Olivia's head and whispered, "Don't look now, but Trey just walked out."

Olivia tucked her chin at the mention of her ex. Between her awful date and Trey, Olivia was officially maxed out on awkward social situations.

She lifted her chin to let Dawson know she didn't care, but his usually friendly expression turned intense. He stepped closer, and she turned, resting her back against the wall.

"Want to make him jealous?" Dawson whispered.

Jealous? Who? She didn't have one thought in her head for anyone except Dawson–the man currently looking at her as if he wanted to consume her. His inviting eyes begged her to fall into the rush waiting mere inches away.

Dawson leaned closer and brushed his lips over her cheek, sending a tingling dancing over her skin. She inhaled an audible breath, but there wasn't anything she could do to stop her reaction. A second later, his rough fingertips grazed up her neck before resting at her nape. The pad of his thumb swept the sensitive skin below her ear.

The whole world fell away. The only thought in

her head was the man adoring her with every touch. She was grounded to Dawson. Right here. Right now. Everything within her shifted, reaching for Dawson as if they were two magnets searching for their counterparts. Her carefully packaged mind came untied.

Dawson breathed her name in the hollow of her neck, and the vibration of his voice ran through her veins. His broad body shielded her as his hand rested on the wall beside her.

Heat rose from her middle, spreading throughout her body. The tension from her initial shock subsided, flowing out of her as she melted beneath his affection.

She lifted her hand to reach for him–to touch him the way he touched her.

Before her fingertips touched his back, his chin rose. He inhaled a deep breath and whispered, "Mission accomplished."

"What?" The question held all of the confusion blocking her thoughts.

"You should have seen the look on his face." Dawson pulled away, letting his hand slide down her arm as he retreated. The movement was like a sweep of the second hand past a number–holding on one second and gone the next.

Oh, her ex. If he'd seen Dawson mere centimeters from kissing her and clearly adoring her, he'd definitely gotten a show. The look on Trey's face probably mirrored the shock in her own expression.

Staring up at her friend, she forced her chest to expand and contract. Her feelings had taken on a mind of their own, growing and twisting into a tangled web that held her captive. Every muscle in her body begged to reach for him–to link his heart to hers in irreversible ways.

When she didn't look away, Dawson stared back at her. His head tilted slightly, silently asking what she wanted.

She wanted so much. Too much. There was a gaping hole in her chest that only Dawson could fill.

A door opened down the hallway, and both of them looked up in an instant. Mark and Bethany came out of a room with their arms wrapped around each other.

Olivia gasped as Dawson chuckled. The couple started toward them, and Dawson leaned his shoulder against the wall, blocking her from the couple's view. Pressing a finger against his lips, he waited for Mark and Bethany to stumble past.

Dawson and Olivia might as well have been invisible. Neither Mark nor Bethany could tear their attention away from each other to notice anything around them.

When the couple was out of sight, Olivia pressed a hand over her mouth and stared wide-eyed at Dawson.

"That was unexpected," he said.

Yeah. That and everything else about this night. Mark ending up with Bethany wasn't nearly as surprising as Olivia's desire to pull Dawson close and kiss him the way she wanted.

Olivia let out a breath and stared at the door where her awful date had just disappeared. "Wow."

"Those two are perfect for each other," he said.

"I thought he left," Olivia breathed as she lowered her hand.

"Looks like he found a reason to stick around."

The doors to the reception hall opened, and Asher and Haley appeared. Haley spotted them down the hallway and waved a friendly goodbye.

Dawson and Olivia waved back. If the Hardings had walked out a minute sooner, they would have seen Dawson nuzzling Olivia's neck.

Don't think about that.

Yeah, as if she'd be able to forget it. The lines he drew on her skin would be tingling for a while.

Olivia straightened her shoulders and brushed her hands down the sides of her silky dress. "I should get back in there. People will be leaving soon, and I need to stay and help clean up."

Dawson nodded. "I'll help."

"You don't have to. I can handle it."

"I know you can, but I want to. I don't have a date waiting on me."

Right. Anna was meant to be his date tonight. A

cold chill dampened any fire Dawson had kindled inside her.

Anna was her friend–her friend who was completely infatuated with her other friend. How could she ever tell Anna about what happened with Dawson?

Technically, nothing happened. Olivia just had feelings for Dawson that were bubbling over–sure to be obvious to everyone if she didn't get them under control.

"Okay. If you're sure you don't have anything better to do on a Saturday night."

"There's no place I'd rather be."

Olivia rolled her eyes, but a traitorous smile played on her lips. It was much easier to think Dawson was joking when he said incredibly sweet things than to give in to the hope that his words held truth. "Of course."

She took the first step toward the reception, but Dawson grabbed her hand, holding it like a lifeline for a man lost at sea.

He lifted her chin with a gentle finger. When she looked at him, his playful smirk greeted her.

"Keep your chin up, my queen. You're the most beautiful woman in any room."

She couldn't play it off like his kindness didn't affect her anymore. Looks weren't her primary focus or even near the top of her list, but his assurances touched a soft part in her heart she'd forgotten to nurture.

"Thank you."

His hand dropped from her chin, and he flashed her a playful wink. "Let's finish up this night on a good note."

Nodding, she fell into step beside him as they made their way back to the reception. The dances were dying down, and guests congregated in groups to say their goodbyes.

When the crowd thinned, Olivia began working. The Bensons had generously offered their building for cheap, and she intended to leave it in better shape than before.

Once the happy couple were off, Dawson and a few other friends pitched in. Before long, everything was packed away, and the entire building was spotless.

Olivia tied up a large trash bag, but when she went to move it, the thing was so heavy it dragged on the ground.

"Got it!" Dawson said beside her before relieving her of the weight. Then he was off without another word.

Maybe he was right. Many hands did make light work.

Olivia finished sweeping the floor when Dawson walked back into the reception hall. The place looked bigger when it was empty.

"You ready to head out?" he asked.

Olivia looked around. She rode with Lyric to the ranch with the intention of asking Mark for a ride home, but that plan bit the dust a long time ago. "I think so."

Dawson jerked his chin toward the door. "Let me take you home."

Turning off lights and locking doors as she went, she followed Dawson out of the building. Stars hid behind clouds, leaving the night pitch black as soon as she turned off the exterior lights.

Dawson reached for her, wrapping his big hand around hers. The touch tightened her muscles at first, but she quickly relaxed as he guided her past the cabins to his truck.

The ride to her house was short and quiet. Getting up before the sun and working till well after dark wasn't out of the ordinary for either of them, but the emotional toil of the day had Olivia's shoulders sagging.

He pulled up in front of her small house and turned off the engine. Without a word, he got out and made his way around the truck to her. He could have just dropped her off in the driveway, but Dawson had never been that way. She stepped out of the truck, careful to watch her footing in the heels as she navigated the darkness.

She unlocked the door and turned to Dawson. Shadows covered his features, but she could easily make out the lines of his jaw and the heat in his eyes.

He took a step toward her, but she kept her place. A fire burned in her middle as he lifted a hand and brushed a stray curl behind her ear.

"You're so beautiful," he whispered. "I should have been your date."

Her small gasp was the only sound in the night. His words wound around her, tightening until she couldn't breathe. What could she say? How could she even respond to that?

One response fought for attention. She would have loved nothing more than to have been by his side tonight.

But another reply dampened the fire. He was meant to be her friend's date. Anna was already upset about missing her chance with Dawson. How could Olivia give in to the sweet hope Dawson offered her with a clear conscience?

She couldn't.

Dawson leaned in and pressed a kiss to her forehead. The connection was swift, but it seared her skin like a brand.

As if sensing the turmoil boiling inside her, he pulled back. "I'll call you tomorrow."

The only thing she could do was nod. Words were so far away, she couldn't even reach for them in the far recesses of her mind.

Olivia walked inside and closed the door as if she could keep out the ghost that was chasing her.

Her feelings weren't ghosts. They were tangible.

They were dangerous. They were irritatingly persistent and cruel.

She rested her back against the door and sucked in breath after breath, fighting off the panic that had followed her inside.

Her breaths started to hitch, and she closed her eyes, pushing the moisture out. "God, why? Why am I so confused?" She covered her face and tucked her chin to her chest. "I want to be happy where I am. Don't tempt me with things I can't have!"

But Dawson would always be there–in her life and begging her to give in to the happiness he offered.

So would Anna. Her friend wasn't going anywhere, and neither were those feelings that were just as important as any Olivia had grown.

The phone in Olivia's purse dinged, and she searched for it. Her friend's name lit up the screen with a reply to her earlier message.

No, she couldn't have Dawson, no matter how much she wanted him.

15

DAWSON

Dawson eyed Bobby Wilson from across the small courtroom. Blackwater didn't have a formal courthouse like in TV shows. Judge Gentry's chambers were set up as needed in the town municipal building. Her stand was a fold-out table with a rolling chair beside her for the witness. The jury sat in metal chairs against one wall, and rows of pop-up chairs made up the rest of the seating.

Half of the people in the room waited for their own hearing, while the other half were ready to see justice served to the Wilsons.

Lauren sat beside Jade with her hands clasped in her lap and hadn't looked up since she arrived an hour ago.

And Bobby Wilson? He was staring a hole through the innocent woman he'd almost killed in cold blood. His greasy dark hair stuck to his forehead, and his fat nose scrunched every few seconds, twitching with his irritation.

Dawson knew evil existed. He saw the devil's work every day, but even after eleven years on the Blackwater Police force, he still couldn't understand it. The things people did were so twisted and dark that he couldn't piece the messed-up puzzle together.

Lauren was innocent in all this. She'd been leaving work at the library when Bobby and Zach Wilson took her, holding her against her will and beating her when she hadn't given them the information they wanted.

Dawson swallowed the acid rising up his throat. He'd been involved in his share of fights, in high school and on the clock, but he could say with all honesty that every move he made was in defense of himself or someone else.

On days like today, he wanted to change that. The Wilsons deserved more punishment than Dawson's well-aimed punches could inflict.

Asa elbowed Dawson in the side and whispered, "Get it together. You look like you want to murder someone."

Dawson turned his attention to the judge at the front of the room and forced a deep breath. The judge better knock this one out of the park.

Judge Gentry entered, and everyone stood. As

soon as she took her seat, everyone in the room did the same. She went through the case list, detailing the timeline she expected while asking any representation if they had any ideas about how long their case should take.

Dawson half listened to some of the cases. He was the investigating officer in some, but they were minor compared to the one everyone around was waiting for with bated breath.

The wild card in the room was Zach Wilson. Dawson remembered the night Lauren had been abducted like it was yesterday, and he'd questioned Zach enough to know there was more to the story than he was disclosing. There was a chance–a slight one–that Zach could become an informant.

If Zach flipped, this whole trial could go a different direction. Alliances were thin, and betrayal was a death sentence for one or both of the brothers. Zach had been adamant that he wouldn't rat on Bobby, but Dawson wasn't ready to give up. There were half a dozen felonies they could attach to Bobby if they had a shred of supporting evidence.

The trial was long. Voir Dire, striking a jury, and opening remarks took all morning. Dawson, Asa, and Detective Morrow had lunch at Saul's Grill, but Dawson had little to nothing to say. Cases hardly ever got him down, but this one was hanging on. Lauren could have been killed right in front of him.

Asa almost died. He had more than a little skin in the game.

The trial resumed after lunch, and Judge Gentry was known for running an efficient courtroom. She didn't spare a second for trivial things and stayed focused on moving the case along.

Bobby and Zach both pled guilty to a grocery list of misdemeanors and felonies. It was enough to send both of them away for a while.

Why didn't it feel like a win?

The other Wilson brother was still MIA, Bobby and Zach were sentenced to ten years with a possibility of parole, and something told Dawson Lauren wasn't any safer with only two out of three brothers behind bars. Her cousin, who provoked the Wilson's retaliation, was still out there without a care in the world that his kin had taken the fall for him.

Justice was served, but cynicism clouded Dawson's mood today. After dozens of conversations with Zach in the last few months, Dawson had reason to believe the guy's bark was worse than his bite. Zach had a hard look, but looks could be deceiving, and Dawson had a hunch that Zach was capable of coming back from the dark side.

Officer Guthrie led Bobby Wilson toward the exit, while Officer Freeman did the same to Zach.

Unable to resist, Dawson made a comment as Zach passed by. "You could have made a difference."

Zach lifted his head, finding Lauren in an instant amongst the crowd. "Nah. That's not how this works."

Dawson crossed his arms over his chest. This guy didn't get it. "How does this work? The setup is you do the crime, you do the time, but we offered you a way out. It was the right thing to do, but you didn't take it."

Zach shook his head. "This road was paved for me."

"Yeah, and anything else would have been a little bit of a struggle. I'd hoped you were better," Asa said.

Zach scoffed. "Sorry to disappoint you, Pop. Better luck next time."

Dawson exhaled a deep breath. Was it stupid to hope Zach would have a change of heart? Once an outlaw, always an outlaw?

No. Dawson had been there when Zach pushed that gun away from Lauren. He hadn't wanted to hurt her or even Asa by accident.

Stepping out of the way, Dawson said, "See you on the other side."

Zach didn't spare him a second glance as Jennifer led him from the chambers. Lauren's quiet sobs were the only sound in the room as she walked out with Jade.

Asa slapped a hand on Dawson's shoulder. "Another time."

"He'll be up for parole in five years," Dawson said. "The jail is crowded as it is."

"When did you become such a downer? Two criminals–guilty criminals–are behind bars for attempted murder. That sounds like a win," Asa said.

Dawson rubbed a hand over his face. "Yeah. I just had a feeling Zach would have a change of heart."

Asa clicked his tongue behind his teeth. "Not today. You ready to get outta here?"

"Yeah, I need to head to the farm." He pulled his phone out of his chest pocket to text Olivia.

Dawson: You at the farm?

Chicken Tender: Yes. I'll take care of the goats today.

Not on his watch. He needed to see Olivia after the long day, and some goat snuggles would do him good too.

Dawson: I'm heading over.

Chicken Tender: No! I've got it.

Dawson stopped walking as he read the message. Pressing the button, he called her instead. Something was up.

"Hey, I can take care of the goats today," Olivia said in greeting.

What was up with her? "I need to see them. And you. It's been a long day."

There was scuffling on Olivia's end of the line. "Um. Okay."

Dawson lowered his voice to ask, "Are you in pain? Do I need to bring you something?"

"No. I'm fine. Promise," she said hastily.

Something was up, and he wouldn't be satisfied with a quick brush-off. At least until he'd seen her with his own two eyes. "I'll be right there."

16

OLIVIA

Olivia propped her back against the goat feed shed and stared at her new foster. The terrier mix lay on the blanket she'd used to dry it off after the second bath, snapping and biting at it like the piece of cloth would attack at any second.

"Dawson is going to flip when he sees you." She threaded her hands into her hair and tugged. Pacing the small yard outside the goat barn, she tried to think of something to say to him when he showed up. She was running out of time to figure it out.

She didn't plan to keep the dog, but when a friend called and asked if she could foster, she couldn't say no.

Dawson would understand, right?

Probably not. You don't get burned–or bitten–

twenty-four times and still get excited about meeting another dog.

"This is only temporary," Olivia told the dog. "But you have got to be nice to him. For the love of all things good, please don't bite him."

"Liv!" Dawson called from the other side of the barn.

Olivia tugged the blanket from the snipping dog and got down on her level. "Please. I'm begging you. I'll give you all the treats you want. Just don't bite him."

Dawson's footsteps rounded the corner...and halted. Olivia looked up to see him frozen, staring at her and the dog.

Busted. She might as well have "Traitor" stamped on her forehead.

"Cheese and crackers, Liv. What did I ever do to you?"

The dog hopped up and lunged at Dawson, but Olivia had expected the move. She grabbed the little beast out of the air and plastered it to her chest.

"What did we talk about, Betsy?" Olivia asked, infusing every ounce of calm she possessed into her words.

"Betsy?" Dawson asked, eyes wider than a saucer.

Olivia shrugged. "I thought it was cute."

A low scoff escaped Dawson's throat. "You can give it a cute name all you want, but she'll still want to tear the skin off my bones."

Olivia cuddled her new friend. Well, Betsy would be her new friend if she could learn how to get along with her other friend. "She just needs some love. For a little while. I'm fostering."

Dawson crossed his arms over his chest, but the hardness in his eyes was melting away. "Twenty-four bites, Liv," he reminded her.

"I'm sorry, but I couldn't say no. She needs a home. Just until the shelter finds someone else."

Dawson's jaw relaxed, and his eyes softened. "I know you wouldn't turn her away. You're right. She needs help, and you're the best person for the job."

Olivia perked up at his unexpected compliment. "Thanks."

Dawson took a tentative step forward. Betsy lowered her head and growled at him, not letting up.

"What do I do? She already hates me."

"She's been mistreated. It's not you. I'm sure you'll like her eventually. Once you get to know her." Olivia grasped at every straw within her reach. They all just needed to get along for a little while.

Dawson stared down at the dog. "That's not the problem. She has to like me first."

The little fireball in Olivia's arms wasn't making this easy. What could she do when Betsy had been hurt by men and Dawson had been bitten by dogs? Trust wasn't even in the distant future for these two.

Dawson's shoulders slumped. "You're doing a good thing. I'll just...keep my distance."

"I'm going to work with her. She's not really fond of anyone at this point."

"Except you," Dawson pointed out. "Well, who can blame her? Instinct probably tells her you're a good woman."

Why did he have to say such sweet things? As if she needed another reason to be hung up on Dawson. He'd hardly left her thoughts since the wedding reception. Memories of his fingers tangling in her hair and the warmth of his breath on her neck still sent shivers up her spine.

Olivia ducked her chin and nuzzled the dog's fur. The rotten smell from earlier was almost gone. "I'm just asking for patience."

Dawson rubbed his chin. "Do you need any help with her?"

A grin quirked up the corners of Olivia's lips. What exactly did he think he could do to help her care for his nemesis?

"I think I've got it."

The phone in Olivia's pocket rang, and she adjusted her hold on the dog to answer it.

Dawson jerked a thumb over his shoulder. "I'm going to get started on the milking."

Olivia gave him a single nod before checking the screen. Anna.

"Hey. How are you?" Olivia asked in greeting.

Anna cleared her throat, and her words had a rough edge to them. "Back in the land of the living.

That stomach virus is no joke. My throat is sore from throwing up."

"Yikes," Olivia said. "Did the electrolyte drinks I dropped off help?"

"I'm happy to report that I'm not in danger of dehydration."

One of the newest kids hopped over to Olivia's side, and she bent to let Betsy down. She'd taken to the goats a lot quicker than humans. "What about the crackers?"

"They were gross, but I kept three of them down yesterday."

"You're on the road to recovery," Olivia said.

Anna groaned. "I just hope Mom doesn't get this after being around me so much. I wouldn't wish it on my worst enemy."

"Give her some of those vitamins I dropped off the other day."

"She already took some. And she said to tell you that the potato soup was amazing."

Olivia watched Betsy and Hank dart around as they played. When she was convinced Betsy wasn't going to attack the baby goat, she started toward Cluckingham Palace. "Thanks. I'll send her the recipe."

There was rustling on Anna's end of the line, and she sighed. "You're so good to me. Have I told you how much I love you?"

Olivia swallowed hard past the swelling of her

throat. Anna was a constant in her life. When Olivia's mom died, Anna didn't leave her side. When she had to stay in because the endometriosis pain was too much, Anna stayed in too. Through boyfriends, breakups, and broken hearts, Anna was always there. "I love you too."

"Any news I've missed? I feel like I've been hidden under a rock for three days."

Olivia looked over her shoulder toward the goat barn. Betsy wasn't following her, but she'd be fine as long as she played well with Hank. "I'm fostering a dog. Her name is Betsy."

"Aww, that's adorable. I can't wait to see her. If I'm feeling better, can I come over tomorrow?"

Bending to turn on the hose, Olivia pressed the phone between her shoulder and ear. "Of course."

"How is Dawson? I haven't seen him since before the wedding."

How was Dawson? Just being ridiculously hot and directing all of his flirtatious charm at Olivia, making him impossible to resist.

No biggie.

"He's fine, I guess. Just hanging out with his four-legged friends."

"Is he there? Shoot, Liv. You get to see him all the time. I'm so jealous."

There was the guilt. Right on schedule. "He's with the goats. I'm feeding the chickens. We're not actually here together."

"You know what I mean. You see him a lot more than I do."

"We just run into each other at the farm a lot." And at Beau's garage. And at the station. And at church.

No sense in mentioning those things to Anna.

"Yeah. He did call yesterday to check on me. That was sweet."

Olivia got a call or text from Dawson at least once a day. Sometimes, there were many in a twenty-four hour period. As far as she knew, he didn't call Anna that much, and they didn't make plans to hang out together the way he and Olivia did.

The comparisons were enough to both worry and excite her. Did Anna notice that Dawson called Olivia more? Did it bother her more than she was letting on?

Safely steering the conversation to Anna's job at her dad's law firm, Olivia fed the chickens, refilled their water stations, and gathered eggs.

Anna's words started to get lower and lower until she huffed a deep breath. "Okay, I can't talk anymore. I need a nap."

"Get some rest. I'll swing by Sticky Sweets later and grab you some chicken salad."

Anna hummed. "You're the best. Love you."

"Love you too."

Olivia slipped the eggs into containers and looked around. She hadn't heard a peep out of Betsy in a while. The pup was cute as a button now that she was clean, but they'd have to have a come to Jesus meeting if Betsy sank her teeth into Dawson.

The sun was starting to set as she trekked back to the goat barn. Only a few of the goats milled around outside, which meant Dawson was probably milking inside.

She raised her hand to rap her knuckles against the wooden door frame when she stopped. Dawson's baritone voice reached her just in time, and she leaned to peek inside the barn.

Dawson was crouched in front of Betsy with a hand extended toward the dog. Betsy was crouched with her head low to the ground. Her teeth were bared at him with a soft, continuous growl.

"Come on, Betsy. We have to get along."

Betsy's growl died, but she didn't change her stance. She stayed poised for battle as Olivia held her breath.

"Come on," Dawson whispered. "I promise I'm a good guy. Olivia likes me. I think."

Covering her mouth, Olivia waited to see how the meeting would go. She did like Dawson. A lot. Way more than she should.

Dawson left his hand hovering in the air. "Come on, girl. I promise I'll be good to you too. Just give me a chance."

Betsy's head bobbed up and down as her attention jerked from his hand to his face.

Dawson turned his hand over and opened it. "Olivia is my girl. If you're gonna be in her life, you have to make room for me. I'm not going anywhere."

Olivia bit her lips between her teeth. If Dawson was going to stay in her life, she had to figure out a way to manage her feelings. She couldn't pinpoint the moment when her crush on her brother's best friend turned into love. It snuck up on her when she wasn't looking.

Now, she needed to do damage control. After years of letting everything Dawson did burrow into her heart, he'd broken down her walls without setting off the alarms.

Betsy leaned forward, sniffed Dawson's hand, then darted away.

Olivia brushed her hands over her shirt and stepped into the barn. "Hey."

Dawson stood and flashed her a grin. "Hey."

She shoved her hands into the back pockets of her jeans. Ever since their moment at the wedding, the urge to reach for him had been building. "I'm gonna head out. You need anything?"

Dawson's jaw worked one way, then the other. He was giving the simple question a lot of thought. "I'm good. See you tomorrow?"

"Probably. I'll be around." They ran into each other often–sometimes planned, and sometimes not. Even in the times they weren't together, she was thinking about him.

They'd worn a path in this routine. Why did it suddenly feel dangerous?

"Do you know where Betsy went?" she asked.

Dawson pointed to the back of the barn. "Probably playing with Hank and Henry."

"Did she bother you?"

Dawson adjusted his stance and crossed his arms over his chest. "Nah. I think she'll warm up to me. No worries."

"I'm not worried. Women can't help but love you."

Dawson's grin dipped a fraction of an inch before perking back up. "If you say so."

"Thanks for understanding."

He winked and started stepping back toward the exit. "Anything for you, my queen."

That nickname sent her stomach tumbling every single time. Dawson was the king of making her feel special. Was he like that for everyone? Was she silly to think she was special?

Olivia turned to look for Betsy. She needed to put distance between Dawson and herself before she did something stupid, like run after him.

17

DAWSON

Dawson parked his truck next to Olivia's car at Beau's garage. Asa's truck and another he didn't recognize were parked in the side lot.

Twelve hours in his uniform was about all Dawson could stand, but when Olivia texted promising meatloaf at the garage, he couldn't say no. No matter what Olivia was offering, his answer was always yes.

Pizza? Yes.

Spaghetti? Yes.

A lifetime of love? Absolutely.

Okay, he was getting ahead of himself, but he'd settle for meatloaf today.

He walked in and headed straight for the break room, the scent of spiced meat leading the way.

Olivia, Asa, Lyric, and Jacob sat at the table with half-eaten plates in front of them.

Betsy stood from the dog bed by the wall. Of course, the newest crew member already had her own place at the garage.

Dawson crouched and held out a hand to Betsy. "Come on, girl."

She trotted over and pressed her head to Dawson's hand. She'd warmed up to him over the last few days, and he liked to think they were already thick as thieves.

"Miracles happen every day," Asa said.

Dawson could make friends with a fence post. He could handle a dog the size of his left shin. "Betsy should hold a press conference and let her furry friends know how awesome I am," Dawson joked. "Where's Beau?"

Asa looked up at Lyric before turning his attention back to his food. Olivia hesitated before answering. "Interviewing someone in his office."

"Good," Dawson said as he pulled up a chair at the table. "He needs some better help around here. Business is booming."

"They said you know him," Jacob piped up. "It's Gage Howard."

Dawson stopped with his hand hanging in the air above the corn bread. "Gage? Are you kidding me?"

"Wish we were," Asa said without looking up.

Gage Howard. Everyone in town knew the Howards, and there wasn't a good one of them in the bunch. Dawson himself had arrested eighty percent of them at some point in time.

Gage? He wasn't the worst one. In fact, he was the lesser of many evils, but that didn't mean he was Dawson's favorite person.

Dawson picked up a piece of cornbread. "Does Beau actually think he'd be a good hire?"

Asa shrugged. "He knows his way around a machine. He's been working at his uncle's shop for a decade or more."

"Why does he want to work here then? Sounds like he's getting a piece of the family pie."

"He said business is slow over there," Asa answered before stuffing his face with a bite of meatloaf.

Dawson scoffed. "That's what happens when you overcharge and don't have a clue what you're doing under the hood of a vehicle."

"Beau thinks Gage knows what he's doing," Olivia added.

Dawson looked around the room. "Whose side are you on?"

Lyric spoke up. "She's right. People can change."

He didn't have a retort for that. Lyric was living proof that people were capable of change in a good way, but Gage Howard was a different story.

"Weren't you hoping just last week that Zach would turn over a new leaf?" Asa asked.

Dawson let his fork fall to the table. Nothing like getting taught a lesson over lunch.

Beau walked into the break room and picked up a plate. Everyone watched as he loaded up some meatloaf and green beans. He didn't notice that all the attention was on him until he looked up.

"Um, everything okay?" Beau asked warily.

"What happened?" Jacob asked.

Beau narrowed his eyes. "When?"

"In the interview, genius," Olivia quipped. "Are you hiring Gage?"

Beau shrugged and loaded his fork with meatloaf. "Probably."

"What did he say about his criminal history?" Dawson asked.

"Said he's trying to distance himself from his family. He knows they're a sinking ship, and he wants off before things go south."

Dawson scoffed. "Should'a jumped ship a while ago then." The Howards knew how to do two things: Get away with murder and train up-and-coming criminals.

Olivia dropped her fist onto the table with a thud and stared at Dawson with fire in her eyes. "I've heard enough. Gage might be serious, and it would be nice if you gave him a shot."

The room got quiet as Olivia's outburst sank in.

She was right, and her flaming arrow hit him straight in the chest.

"I'm sorry. I'll give him a chance," Dawson said quietly.

Olivia ducked her chin and moved her food around her plate with her fork.

Great. The last thing he wanted to do was upset Olivia. Or anyone. He'd been talking faster than he was thinking.

Normal talk resumed for the rest of the meal, but Betsy snuck over to Olivia's side and whined until she picked the dog up and cradled her to her chest.

So much for forming alliances today.

When everyone had finished eating, Olivia started cleaning up. Lyric jumped into action with her, but Dawson caught her attention.

"You mind if I have a minute alone with Olivia? I'll clean up."

Lyric gave him a bright smile and glanced at her friend. "She's not mad at you," she whispered back.

"How do you know?"

Lyric patted his arm. "She'll forgive you."

"Do *you* forgive me?" he asked. Lyric turned her back on her old life and was a different and better person. Her change wasn't anything to scoff at. She'd worked hard and earned mountains of trust she didn't have before. She'd knit her family back together and become a good wife to Asa.

She was right. People could make drastic changes.

Shaking her head, Lyric waved a hand. "Water under the bridge."

Dawson bumped her arm with his elbow. "Thanks. Wish me luck." His eyes shifted to Olivia packing up the leftover food.

Lyric slipped out with a quick goodbye to Olivia. Betsy stood at Olivia's feet, looking up and waiting patiently for attention.

Dawson scooped up the pup and held her to his chest. His vest probably wasn't comfortable, but the dog didn't seem to mind. Her eager tongue swiped over his jaw. He approached Olivia's side, and she paused what she was doing to look up at him.

He moved Betsy's paw in a waving gesture. "Hey, I'm your friend who messed up, and I come with a cute puppy to beg for your forgiveness."

Olivia's lips thinned and stretched. It didn't take long for her frown to disappear. "How can I resist the puppy dog eyes?"

"She's too cute to resist. And she likes me now, so I'm hoping you will too."

Olivia propped her hip against the counter. "I was talking about *your* puppy dog eyes."

Dawson let out a deep exhale. "I shouldn't have said what I did. You're right about everything, and I shouldn't be so cynical. If Gage is making a decision to change, I should support it."

Reaching out, Olivia brushed her hand over Betsy's head and ears. "I appreciate it. I hate to think that people who make mistakes have to stay stuck in that trap. Seeing what Lyric and Wendy have gone through gives me a better appreciation for what it takes to dig yourself out of a hole."

"You're right. I'm sorry," Dawson said.

Olivia continued petting Betsy, showering the pup with attention. They hadn't heard anything about a family who wanted the dog. Was it wrong to hope Olivia would get to keep Betsy? He liked having a dog that let him get close enough to touch.

Dawson tilted his head to the side. "Can I get some of that attention?"

Olivia laughed and reached up to brush a hand over Dawson's hair. Her soft touch was barely more than a breeze as her hand swept behind his ear and down his neck.

His entire body lit on fire when she made contact with his skin. His chest expanded, his hands tingled with the need to touch her. It took all of his willpower not to groan and lean into her delicate palm.

Her gaze traveled lazily over his features as her thumb traced the edge of his jaw. "You're a good man. I never doubt that."

"I'll be anything for you," Dawson said, leaning in and lowering his voice. "I'll be whatever you want me to be."

Olivia's eyes widened, and he realized what he'd said. There he went again, talking faster than his brain could filter. The truth he'd laid out on the line was a little bold, but it wasn't wrong. He was honest, and hiding anything from Olivia didn't sit well with him.

Her head tilted slightly to the side, and her brows pulled together. "You don't have to be anything for me."

The truth he'd been holding back was taut, but he was tired of pushing his feelings for her back like they needed to be hidden. "Olivia, I–"

"Don't," she said quickly, lifting a hand between them. "Don't say anything."

That spring inside him was ready to fly, and now that he'd made the decision to act, he didn't want to hold back. "Why not?"

"Because... because I can't..."

"You can't? You can't what?"

She fisted her hands at her chest, and her eyes narrowed in pleading. "I can't say what you want me to say."

"You can't, or you won't?"

What were they even talking about? He hadn't even gotten the words out yet, and she was already telling him she couldn't return his feelings?

"Both," she said, dropping her hands to her sides in defeat.

Dawson took half a step forward and locked his

gaze with hers. He wanted answers, and she was dancing around the truth just enough to give him hints. "Do you feel it even though you tell me you won't say it?"

Olivia's gaze bore into his as she contemplated her answer. He held his breath as her teeth pressed into her bottom lip.

"Come on, Liv. Do you feel it? Not what I feel for you. I'm talking about what *you* feel."

Olivia opened her mouth to speak, then closed it again. The words were right on the tip of her tongue. She had something big to say, and he had a feeling it wasn't a flat-out "No."

"Dawson!" Jacob shouted from the hallway.

"In here!" Dawson shouted back without breaking his eye contact with Olivia.

Two seconds later, Jacob was at the door. "Come see this. The seats for the Shelby came!"

"I'll be there in just a sec," Dawson said.

When Jacob disappeared as quickly as he'd appeared, Dawson handed Betsy over to Olivia. "Listen, I know you're not in the same place I am, but I want to talk about…something. Anything. Chances, possibilities, the future? I don't mean a define-the-relationship talk, but I want to know where things are going. Or not going."

Man, it killed him to add that last part.

Olivia swept her hand over Betsy's ears. "Okay.

I'll be home later this afternoon. Can you come by the house?"

Well, that progressed quickly. He'd expected "eventually" or a non-descriptive "sure."

She wanted to talk *tonight*. Which meant she was ready to say something.

No big deal. Today would be the beginning or the end of his more-than-platonic relationship with Olivia.

Please don't let it be the end before we even get started.

"Four okay?" he asked.

Olivia nodded–a little too emphatically for the simple response. "Four is great."

"Dawson!" Jacob shouted again.

Olivia looked at her watch and rested Betsy on the floor. "I need to get this put up. I have to be at Anna's in fifteen minutes."

Dawson rested a hand on her shoulder. "I'll take care of it. Tell Jacob I'm cleaning up the kitchen and I'll be out in a minute."

She looked around at the leftovers on the table and counter. "Are you sure?"

"Positive. Go hang out with your friend."

A small grin jumped on Olivia's lips before disappearing again. "Thanks."

"See you at four."

Four couldn't come soon enough.

18

OLIVIA

Olivia held up a button-up blouse and gasped. Each quadrant had a different material and pattern. Rhinestones were splattered over the entire piece, and fringe hung from the bottom. "Are you kidding me? Is this in style?"

Anna stopped shifting hangers of clothes in her closet long enough to look over her shoulder and laugh. "It's not, but a boutique in New Orleans was trying to make it happen last fall. Toss that one into the donation pile, will you?"

Picking up the next one, Olivia chuckled. It was a tight-fitting sequined tank top that only belonged in a dance club. She held it up in front of her chest. "Does this one say 'I'm a crazy chicken lady?'"

"No, but this one does." Anna held out a fitted,

pink flannel shirt with blue accents. "It'll look great. Try it on."

Olivia caught the top when Anna tossed it to her and laid it on the bed. "I can't believe you have so many clothes. How could you possibly wear all of this?"

"Sometimes, I wear more than one outfit in a day," Anna admitted, like it was the most normal thing in the world to go through so many expensive outfits.

Granted, her upbringing wasn't the same as Olivia's. Anna's parents were a power couple, heading up one of the state's biggest law firms. They'd won thousands of cases and had dozens of associate attorneys working alongside them.

Olivia? She was a farmer's daughter. While Anna spent her childhood in piano lessons and country club parties, Olivia woke up with the chickens and sold vegetables at the local farmer's market.

Their differences hadn't kept them apart. They'd both decided in third grade to be best friends for life, and neither had wavered on that promise.

At least, not yet. Guilt tightened its rope around her throat every time she let her feelings for Dawson bubble up to the surface.

With the flannel on, Olivia held out her arms and did a slow turn. "What do you think?"

"Perfect," Anna said as she reached for a camisole on a different hanging rack. "Wear this one under it, and pair it with your pink-and-brown boots."

Olivia pulled off the flannel and folded it into the neat pile she'd started. Her chicken-lover Instagram was a fun side project, and while she didn't make any money sharing cute and funny videos of her chickens to the world, Anna's second job title was influencer. She'd made a great living before becoming an attorney.

Olivia's Instagram wasn't about her. It was about the cute chickens and the laughs. She barely showed her face. Still, Anna enjoyed sharing the mountains of clothes the high-end boutiques sent her. She picked out the more casual ones for Olivia to wear in the small moments when she made an appearance in her videos with the chickens.

"What about the olive pants from a couple of weeks ago? Can I wear something else with those?"

Anna perked up. "Those were so comfortable."

"The softest pants I've ever worn. I want them in every color."

"They're two-hundred and fifty dollars a pop."

Olivia gasped. "Are you serious? And I wore them to dance with my chicks!"

Laughing, Anna pulled her phone out of her pocket. "Don't worry about it. They were excited when I asked if you could wear them to post on your page."

Olivia pressed a hand to her stomach as a weak

cramp gripped her insides. "Okay. I think this is plenty."

Anna fell back onto her bed, sinking into the downy-white comforter. "Wait a minute. I have an idea, but I need to check to see if you've already worn an outfit like it."

"You remember every outfit," Olivia pointed out.

"Yeah, but I think I remember..." Anna sat up, still staring at her phone. "What's this?"

Olivia peeked over Anna's shoulder to see the Instagram collaboration she'd done with Dawson earlier in the week. He'd lined up her hens on Henry's back, then coaxed the chickens to jump off the goat's head into his arms.

It was ridiculous, but the reel had gotten over seven hundred thousand views. Dawson turned the women of the internet into mush, and everything he touched turned to gold.

"Dawson's idea," Olivia said.

Continuing to stare at the screen with longing, Anna whispered, "I wish he'd look at me with that smile. I mean, look at him. He's got those birds free falling into his arms. And those aren't the only chicks who would jump off a cliff for him."

Olivia snorted. "Don't go jumping off any cliffs. There isn't a man in the world worth that risk."

"Look at those arms. Solid muscle," Anna said, turning her phone around so Olivia could see the muscles in question.

Shielding her eyes, Olivia turned back to the clothes she'd picked out. "I try not to ogle my friends."

Anna sat up on the bed, sending her blonde hair flying around her. "You can't tell me he's not hotter than a blue flame. The man is masculine perfection. He's tall, dark, and handsome, but his personality is light and funny. How am I supposed to resist that combination?"

Olivia pressed her hands to her flaming cheeks. Yes, she noticed all of those things about Dawson, but she spent most of her time trying to stomp her attraction back into the dirt.

Anna, on the other hand, wanted to talk about her feelings for Dawson on a continual loop, which didn't help Olivia hide hers at all.

Olivia hadn't breathed a word about her close encounter with Dawson a few hours ago. His promise to come by her house later to "talk" held the weight of a deceitful lie as it sat in the back of her throat.

She'd stopped him from confessing some kind of feelings earlier. If he let a true confession see the light of day, she wouldn't be able to lie and say she didn't feel the same.

The impending "talk" waiting for her in just a few hours was twisting her insides like a vise.

"What am I gonna do!" Anna howled.

Betsy jerked up from her little bed in the corner

of Anna's room and yipped.

Recoiling, Anna lowered her voice. "Sorry. Didn't mean to wake you." She turned to Olivia with her shoulders sagging. "She doesn't like me."

"It's not that she doesn't like you," Olivia said, reaching for Betsy. "People haven't always been good to her. It took a while before she warmed up to Dawson too."

Anna scoffed. "I don't believe a word of that. Dawson could charm the bark off a tree." She rubbed her hands over her arms like the chill in Betsy's bark had permeated the room. "I've never had a dog. Mom and Dad hate pets. Maybe that's another reason I should get my own place."

Olivia gritted her teeth. Anna's Mom had intense separation anxiety. She'd suffered from panic attacks when Derek went to college, but Anna's brother hadn't let that stop him.

Anna, on the other hand, sympathized with her mom a little too much. So much so that she was still living at home in her twenties. She stayed the night at Olivia's a few times a month, but so far she hadn't made any moves to venture out.

Olivia bent at the waist as another pain seized her middle. She forced measured breaths in through her nose and out through her mouth as the stabbing lingered.

"You okay?" Anna said, scooting closer to Olivia on the bed.

Betsy trotted over to Olivia's feet and whimpered. After all the little dog had been through, it was a curse that she was so perceptive to her pain.

Olivia reached for Betsy, who nuzzled her face into the hollow of Olivia's neck as soon as she was close enough.

"Liv, are you okay? Do you need me to get you some medicine?"

"No. It's not as bad as yesterday. This is the tail end of it." She sat on the bed and fell back, letting the tension go as she closed her eyes.

"Just one more week, and this might be over," Anna whispered.

Olivia laughed. "It's never over. The surgery helps, but it'll come right back. The only way to get rid of it is to get rid of half of my reproductive system."

Anna froze, knowing the heartache that came with that thought. Sure, Olivia had said the words like they didn't land like a round-house kick to the face, but it tore her up to consider the hysterectomy. She was young. She should be having babies, not heading into her golden years.

She squeezed Betsy, but Anna scooted across the bed and tucked herself against Olivia's side. With an arm around both Olivia and Betsy, Anna whispered, "I'm always here for you. I wish I could make this go away without taking something so precious from you."

Olivia inhaled a deep breath and squeezed her eyes closed. "I know," she whispered. "But this is just the way it is for me. I'm not doing a very good job accepting it."

"It's not a lost cause. Don't give up hope."

Olivia rested her cheek against Anna's head. "I know. Don't stop praying," she begged.

"Every day, my friend," Anna said.

Olivia lifted Betsy from her chest. "I need to get home. Thanks for all the clothes."

"You're welcome to them anytime. My closet is your closet," Anna said, sitting up and stretching her arms.

They said their goodbyes, and Betsy behaved, even giving Anna a few licks on her jaw. The ride home had Olivia's nerves flaring up again. What did Dawson want to talk about? She thought she knew, but what was he really going to say? Was it really a love confession like she thought?

When she got home, she went straight to the bedroom and changed into the most comfortable and unflattering sleep pants and T-shirt she owned before taking her makeup off and tying her hair into a ponytail.

If Dawson had some big revelation of feelings to share, he needed to know exactly what he was getting into–flaws and all.

She started a load of laundry and sat on the couch with a book. She wasn't a big reader, but she liked to dip into a wholesome romance every once in a while.

The knock on the door startled her, and Betsy jumped out of her lap. It hadn't taken long for Olivia to get engrossed in the book. She hadn't even heard Dawson's truck.

"Coming!" She opened the door to find Dawson propping one arm against the frame, wearing a playful grin.

Oh no. That handsome grin that lifted one side of his mouth more than the other was her kryptonite. There wasn't a chance in northern Wyoming she'd be able to withstand anything he said.

"Let's go," he said with a quirk of his brow.

Okay, there were limits to his charm. Olivia rested her hands on her pajama-clad hips and lifted her chin. "I'm not going anywhere."

Dawson just chuckled. She had to admit, he made the spontaneous life look appealing.

"Why don't we put the serious talk on hold and do something together instead?"

She was all in favor of putting the "Define-the-relationship" talk on hold, but at what cost? They'd have to address the elephant in the room at some point.

But running off into the night with Dawson was too tempting to resist. They could just be themselves for a little longer.

Olivia propped her shoulder against the other side of the door frame. "Where?"

"It's a secret," Dawson whispered.

Great. Any adventure she agreed to this afternoon would require full trust in him.

"Is this a secret that will require any energy? Because I'm not planning on doing anything for the rest of the day."

Dawson let his head fall back and sighed. "I'll do all the heavy lifting. I'll even carry you if you don't want to walk."

"So I *will* have to burn more calories today. This doesn't sound like fun."

Dawson pointed to the driveway, nearly laughing at her attempt to put him off. "Stop being stubborn and get in the truck."

Olivia straightened her backbone, rising to his bait like a starving fish. "Did you just boss me?"

Dawson took a step toward her, and her entire body heated like a torch. His jaw tensed as his eyes danced in the shadows of the afternoon sun sinking behind her house. "Stop it. You like it when I surprise you," he whispered, barely hiding his grin.

Okay, so she did like it when he made her break out of her shell, and she could usually admit to having fun once she got past the initial decision. "Fair enough."

Dawson's arms wrapped around her, lifting her

off her feet and swinging her in a circle before she'd even finished the last word.

Laughing, she squealed, "Dawson!" as he set her back on her feet.

Once she had her balance again, she pointed a finger at him. "But I'm bringing a book."

Dawson grabbed her hand, pulling her with him into the house. "No need. I promise to keep you entertained."

"Why are you dragging me inside if we're going somewhere?"

Dawson stopped in front of her bedroom door and propped his hands on his hips. "Your chariot awaits, my queen." He gestured to her room. "Pack a bag. Three days, max."

Olivia's eyes widened. "Nu-uh. I have to work on Tuesday."

Dawson tilted his head from side to side. "Compromise. Make it two."

With a controlled inhale, Olivia nodded. "Fine. Two days. But I better have my own bed."

Dawson shook his head. "No beds, but you won't have to sleep with me." He pointed toward the kitchen. "I'll pack snacks. Your chariot leaves in fifteen minutes."

Staring after him, Olivia pressed a hand to her chest to settle the war drum beating inside it. What had she just agreed to?

19

DAWSON

Walking away from Olivia was never easy. The only thing propelling his steps forward was the promise of spending the next few days with her.

And nights.

It didn't matter that he hadn't had a full night's sleep all week. As soon as Lucas called and said camping, Dawson kicked up dust on his way out to Silver Falls.

He wouldn't be alone with Olivia, but spending time in the wilderness hit differently. It also helped that there were cabins on the ridge, and he wouldn't have to sleep right outside her tent to ward off critters.

Okay, camping was a loose term. Really, the Bensons needed help renovating the cabins on the mountain, so they'd called in reinforcements.

Work a little, play a little. A winning combination.

And deep down, Dawson was a chicken. Not the cute birds Olivia adored. He was scared of rejection, and admitting it stung his pride.

For once, he couldn't read Olivia's mind. He'd been so close to laying it all on the line earlier, but something in her expression held him back.

He could see it now.

"I'm in love with you. Pretty much obsessed. Please be my queen, and I'll adore you forever."

Yeah, he couldn't see her mirroring those feelings back. If she did, they would have moved past the friends stage by now.

Walking into her kitchen, he went straight for the pantry. Protein bars, granola, oatmeal. He gathered a few of each and set them on the counter.

Now, where did she hide the good stuff? He opened cabinets two at a time until he found a stash of potato chips, Skittles, and Oreos.

Bingo.

With the potato chips tucked under his arm, he settled on the couch to wait for Olivia to pack. The book on the end table caught his eye, and he opened to the first page. He read through the prologue, shoving chips into his mouth like he was on a timer.

Olivia stepped into the living room and tossed a backpack onto the floor. "What are you doing?"

"Getting sucked in. Now I need to know if Liz and Ian are going to get back together."

Olivia tipped her chin. "Toss that in my bag. I'll grab a cooler."

"No need. Drinks are provided," Dawson said as he tucked the book into the outer pocket of her backpack.

"So, I think it's safe to say this isn't a road trip. Are these the snacks you want?" Olivia shouted from the kitchen.

Dawson was right behind her, stuck in her orbit like a satellite. "You want anything else?"

"Nope. Looks good to me. I'll get a bag. Grab me a soda, please."

Dawson pulled on the handle of the refrigerator, but it bent where the screws were loose, only opening the door as an afterthought. Squatting to grab a screwdriver from where he'd seen it in his snack search earlier, he tightened the handle.

"You need new appliances," Dawson said over his shoulder.

Olivia strode back into the kitchen and started tossing snacks into a bag. "Stop saying mean things about my refrigerator. This is the longest loyal relationship I've ever had."

Dawson rounded on her. "That's not true! Does my devotion mean nothing to you?"

She crossed her arms over her gray sweater and grinned up at him. That almost imperceptible move of her lips made him want to brush his own against them.

He swallowed hard and tore his attention from her curving lips. Her eyes narrowed, silently teasing that she'd noticed his stare.

And she liked it. That much, he could tell.

Peas and carrots, it was going to be hard to resist her on this trip.

She'd redone her hair into a high ponytail, but she hadn't put on any makeup. For some reason, her natural self made his love burn even hotter. It was like she was giving him a peek at a side of her she didn't show to the world–like she was his to admire in private places.

Nope. No private places with Olivia. Way too tempting.

She took a step toward him and tilted her head, looking up at him with a confidence that said she knew exactly what she was doing to him.

If she didn't cut it out, they'd be spending the rest of the evening in the kitchen instead of camping with friends.

Witnesses. They definitely needed witnesses.

"Thank you for fixing the handle. I've been meaning to do that for a while," she said.

What was she talking about? He must have looked like a lost ball in high weeds because she pointed to the refrigerator.

"Oh. No problem."

She let her arms fall to her sides, revealing the brown chicken on her sweater. "Did you get my soda?"

"Soda? Oh, I'll do that." He turned and grabbed a can before handing it to her.

Smooth move. Now, pay attention!

Betsy trotted up to Olivia, and she lifted the little shaggy-haired pup into her arms. "Can Betsy come?"

Dawson reached out and brushed his big hand over the dog's tiny head. "Sure. We'll need to bring some food for her. And make sure she doesn't get eaten by wolves."

Olivia's jaw dropped, and her eyes widened. "Where exactly are we going?"

Shaking his head, he reached for Betsy. "It's a surprise. At least until we get in the truck and you can't back out."

"But–"

"You take care of the food, and I'll catch up with my friend." Dawson lifted Betsy a little as she squirmed and rapidly licked his chin.

Olivia let out a contented sigh. "I can't believe she loves you."

Dawson gasped. "Is it so hard to believe that a female would love me? I'll have you know I am super lovable."

Giggling, Olivia swatted his arm. "No. I can't believe she trusts you so soon." Her smile faded as she watched the dog love on Dawson. "She was abused, so she was really timid when I got her."

Man, he couldn't imagine hurting a dog, but he came face-to-face with those people on a regular basis. "She knows she's safe with us."

Olivia looked up at him, and her smile returned. "I'll get her food."

Dawson found Betsy's leash by the door and let her lead him outside. She stayed within a few feet of the porch until Olivia stepped outside carrying a backpack, the snack bag, and another small bag of dog food.

Hurrying to Olivia's side, Dawson took the bags and handed over Betsy's leash. "I think she's ready to ride."

"Come on, girl," Olivia said in the high-pitched voice she reserved for Betsy. "Dawson is taking us to some undisclosed location, but we are hoping it's not because he wants to kill us and hide the bodies."

Dawson tossed her bags into the backseat and scoffed. "You have never been safer than when you're with me, my queen."

Olivia and Betsy settled into the passenger seat, and the truck was quiet until he turned left at the end of her road, leading farther from town.

"I'm not worried or anything, but can you tell me where we're going now?" Olivia asked.

"The Bensons have some cabins out on the ridge

they want fixed up. Some of us volunteered to spend a weekend out here doing some renovation."

"So, you tricked me into working on my weekend off. I see how it is," Olivia said.

"Actually, I believe I said you wouldn't have to do anything. I know at least a couple of women are coming. It's not like you'll be alone."

"Wait, you said no beds," Olivia reminded him.

"Well, there are two cabins, but the mattresses are old and have to be tossed. Beau is bringing the new ones tomorrow when he gets off work. So, tonight, we're on the floor."

Olivia looked over her shoulder at the road falling away behind them. "Bye warm bed!"

"Come on, it'll be fun."

She sighed, letting him know she was resigned to her fate for the next few days. "Who's coming?"

Dawson listed off the people he knew were waiting at the campsite. Olivia spent the rest of the ride to Silver Falls Ranch telling Betsy everything she knew about their friends–introducing each one as if Betsy needed all the details before meeting anyone.

In between hurried words, she poured Skittles into her hand, occasionally offering him a few without missing a beat.

What more could a man want? Olivia was the most beautiful woman he'd ever laid eyes on, she spent all of her free time helping others, she was nurturing a formerly abused dog, she'd agreed to go on this crazy ride with him before even knowing where they were going, and she shared her snacks with him.

Yeah, Olivia was the perfect woman. Hands down.

Turning into the maintenance entrance on the eastern side of the ranch, they made their way around a pasture that spanned a dozen acres. When the fence line took a sharp turn to the left, Dawson kept to the washed-out path leading up the mountain.

"Are you sure this is the way?" Olivia asked, sitting on the edge of her seat.

"Promise. I was out here earlier today. Almost there."

Soon, the dense forest cleared, and three trucks came into view. Olivia sat straight and tall in the seat beside him with Betsy clutched to her chest. Her gaze scanned the woods with an excited glint in her eyes.

Dawson parked behind the other trucks and killed the engine. "Are you ready for this?" he asked.

Olivia jumped out of the vehicle before he got the last word out. "Let's go, slow poke!"

Dawson let the laughter bubbling in his chest out in the cold night. Olivia might act reserved sometimes, but she was just as wild as the wind.

20

OLIVIA

Olivia gripped Betsy to her chest as she stepped over a fallen tree. They'd been walking for ten minutes, and the dog was starting to get antsy, wiggling in Olivia's grip and letting out soft whimpers every so often.

"Just a little longer, babe," Dawson called over his shoulder as he led them through the woods.

"Babe?" Olivia said as she held Betsy up until they were face-to-face. "He gets me out of the house one night, and he's already calling me babe."

"I was talking to Betsy," Dawson said over the crunch of the dried leaves covering the forest floor. "You'll always be my queen."

Olivia pulled Betsy back in to nuzzle against her neck. It was a good thing Dawson was walking ahead of them or else he'd see the color blooming on her face.

He had no idea that her heart thudded against the walls of her chest every time he called her his queen. She might be able to gloss over it and convince herself he was just teasing, but he always said the words with such care. They were never hastily tacked onto a sentence.

She wanted to wrap up in those words and live there–safely surrounded by Dawson's affection.

Let's not get started on the crazy excitement she'd been keeping a lid on since he showed up at her door with an invitation and a smile.

They walked for a few more minutes in silence before voices drifted over the crunching of leaves.

"Are you kidding me?" Dawson said.

"What's wrong?" Olivia leaned to the side to see what was in front of him.

A small creek that had carefully dug out its own trench in the rock and dirt wound down the mountain. The gorge was about four feet wide.

Olivia clicked her tongue behind her teeth. They were close enough to hear their friends laughing on the ridge, but the chasm in front of them was a little too deep and wide for her taste.

"I told them to bring some boards down here to make a bridge." He tossed the snack bag and Betsy's food across the gap and turned to her. "Give me your bag."

She let the backpack fall from one shoulder, then the other, as Dawson lifted its weight.

"Anything fragile in here?" he asked.

She glanced at the bags on the other side of the creek. "No."

He hefted the bag into the air as if it hadn't been giving her back pain since they started walking.

"You're not tossing Betsy over there," Olivia said, holding the dog close to her chest.

Dawson wrapped an arm around her waist and pressed her close to his side until she was flush against him. She held onto the dog with one arm and wrapped the other around his back just in time.

"Dawson!"

The exclamation burst from her as he lifted her. He took one massive step across the creek and set her down on the other side.

The roaring in her ears was loud enough to wake up all woodland creatures within a half-mile radius. Clutching Betsy, she stayed plastered to his side, all too aware of the hard planes of his muscular back.

"You gonna dig your fingernails out of my back, Liv?"

She jolted, looking up at him with her mouth gaping open. What did he say?

Oh, she was still holding onto him as if he could save her from herself.

Disentangling her arm from around him, she cleared her throat and stepped back. "Thanks for the lift." She looked back at the trench. She couldn't have crossed over it the way he had. Even a running jump might have sent her to the bottom.

"Anytime," Dawson said as he bent to pick up their bags. When he hefted her backpack over his shoulder, she didn't protest. Her knees were still quaking from the unexpected flight, and they didn't have far left to walk.

Dawson grabbed her hand and led her up the incline to the clearing where their friends waited, and the contact seared her palm. She'd touched Dawson before. It was no big deal.

Except, the adrenaline coursing through her body hadn't gotten the memo to stand down. Friends held hands sometimes, right?

When they reached the top of the hill, Dawson released her hand and stepped aside, letting her walk into the clearing first. A handful of people she knew were huddled around the fire pit.

"Miss Olivia!" Levi shouted. He jumped from the stump where he'd been sitting and darted toward her.

"Hold up," Dawson said, extending a hand to stop Levi's charge. "Betsy here gets scared easily."

Levi's mouth opened as he noticed the dog in Olivia's arms. "Oh! You got a dog?"

"I'm fostering her."

"What's that?" Levi asked as he tiptoed toward her.

"I'm taking care of her until someone wants to make her part of their family."

Levi held out a hand, letting Betsy sniff it. "Why don't you keep her?"

Olivia glanced at Dawson. She'd agreed to only foster when she was afraid her friend wouldn't like the new pet. Now that Dawson and Betsy were friends, there wasn't a reason to cut her time with Betsy short. "I might."

Some of the others made their way over, giving hugs to Olivia and slaps on the back to Dawson. Maddie Harding stood beside Levi and gushed over Betsy.

"She's adorable," Maddie said. "If she wasn't so small, I'd say we could take her."

Levi looked up at Maddie. "What does that matter?"

"We have Dixie, and she's a big border collie. She can take care of herself most of the time. But this girl," Maddie said, tentatively brushing a hand over Betsy's side. "She'd probably have to stay inside. A predator might gobble her up."

"Yeah. We wouldn't want that," Levi said with a scrunch of his nose.

Lauren worked her way into the circle of Betsy's adoring fans. "I'm so glad you came. Now we have four ladies for our cabin."

"Four? There are three," Levi said. "You, Maddie, and Olivia."

"And Betsy," Lauren pointed out.

Levi's shoulders sank. "Aww. I was hoping Betsy could sleep with me."

The dog was already licking Levi's hand. "We'll see how she does before bedtime. She might want to sleep with you."

A hand rested on her shoulder, and Dawson leaned in to whisper, "I'll put your bags in your cabin."

"Thanks." It didn't seem like she'd be able to get away from Betsy's fans anytime soon.

Levi showed Olivia around, pointing out everything they'd been doing at the campsite that day. A grill was set up near the fire pit, logs were stacked by the cabins, and brush had been cleared from the area and put into piles around the tree line.

Lucas Harding was busy grilling hamburger patties, and his wife, Maddie, set out buns and condiments on a picnic table.

Sometime around twilight, everyone sat down to eat. Betsy roamed on a leash near the stump where Olivia sat. Everyone huddled around the fire for warmth and light. The conversation died for a bit as everyone scarfed down the food after a long workday, but Levi told everyone exactly how he and Lucas had built the picnic table.

After dinner, Olivia and Dawson cleaned up while Lucas tended the fire and whittled points on sticks for roasting marshmallows.

"I put an air mattress in your cabin," Dawson said as he stashed the condiments in a cooler.

"I thought you said no beds."

Dawson shrugged. "Well, I didn't like the idea of you sleeping on the floor, even if it's only one night."

Olivia didn't need to read too much into his care. He would have probably brought an air mattress for the women even if she hadn't come.

Putting away the last of the food, she wiped her cold hands on her pants. Gloves would be necessary for the rest of the night. The temperatures had really dropped since the sun sank beneath the trees.

Olivia checked to see that Betsy was well taken care of with Levi and Lauren. "I guess I'd better blow up the air mattress."

"I'll get the fire going in your cabin," Dawson said as he gestured for her to lead.

Betsy was sprawled out on her back getting tons of attention. The night had fully settled in, making it impossible to do any real work.

There were no excuses to get out of this one, and she didn't want any. Hanging out with their friends was great, but the selfish part of her wanted Dawson all to herself.

It was ridiculous. He didn't belong to her in name or in secret. He was just her friend and nothing more.

But that didn't stop her from wanting. Every time he did something sweet, every time he innocently touched her, every time he looked at her, she fell a little harder for him.

The sharp whisper in the back of her mind said she should squash the feelings before they had a chance to grow, but she didn't want to. She was here with Dawson, and she wanted him all to herself.

Dawson slowed his steps to walk beside her on the way to the cabin. His pinky brushed against hers before wrapping around it. The connection was so small, so imperceptible to anyone around, but it sent her heart racing. She should pull away, but it was impossible.

He pushed the door open and let her enter first. The cabin was dark, but Dawson walked straight to a lantern and lit it. He walked back outside and reappeared a few seconds later with firewood stacked in his arms.

Olivia unrolled the air mattress and spread it out on the floor. It took up most of the room, so she slid it against the wall. She found the battery-powered pump and got things going. Once it was started, she sat back on her heels and let the machine do its job.

She stood and inspected her bag. Pajamas? Check. Toothbrush? Check. Retainer? Check (unfortunately).

There was one thing she couldn't find, but she couldn't remember taking it out of her purse and putting it in her bag.

"Shoot," she whispered.

"What's wrong?"

Dawson was right behind her as she turned. "I forgot my medicine in the truck. It's to prevent migraines."

Stupid migraines had been interfering in her life for a few years now. She still had breakthrough migraines every once in a while, but the preventative meds certainly kept them manageable.

Dawson looked out the window into the black night. "I'll go get it."

"I'll go with you. This is my fault. I should have remembered it."

"I'd rather you stay here. Quite a few predators come out at night."

Okay, that didn't sound great, but she was the one responsible for leaving it in the first place. "Now I don't want you out there by yourself either."

Dawson lifted the hem of his hoodie to reveal a pistol in its holster on his waist. "I'll be fine."

Sometimes she forgot that Dawson carried a gun as part of his job. He could also use it effectively. Why was competence so attractive? Why did it make him more appealing knowing he could protect her if necessary, with or without a gun?

"Good. Then I'll be fine too. It's not that far. We can bring some boards to put over the creek on our way."

Dawson grinned down at her, and his eyes were

shadowed in mischief. "You didn't like being carried?"

"I didn't say that."

The words were out before her brain filtered them. What was she thinking?

Stepping closer, Dawson brushed the pad of his thumb over her jaw. Every muscle in her body froze, then melted at his touch.

"I'd carry you anywhere," Dawson whispered.

Oh, wow. That was definitely not a friendly declaration, and a magnetic force pulled her toward Dawson. She wanted him to carry her, hold her, and shower her with the pretty words he used to adore her.

Why was it so wrong to give in? Why did being with the man she wanted have to come at the consequence of her friend's broken heart?

There was another secret holding her back. She likely couldn't give Dawson the future he wanted with a wife. He would never be content with just her. He'd want a family–kids who shared his last name and his sea-blue eyes.

Snared by his gaze, she studied his face. They were on the same page now, but this wasn't the story with a happily ever after. If they took the leap, someone would get hurt.

Dawson let his hand fall from her cheek to grasp her hand. "We need flashlights, and we can leave Betsy with Lauren and Maddie."

Right. A plan to get her medicine from his truck. The words made sense, but she was having a hard time focusing on anything except his hand gripping hers.

When they walked outside, a deep darkness had set over the camp, and the fire cast long shadows behind their friends huddled around it. The crackle and pop of the burning wood played a soundtrack behind the talking.

Dawson grabbed a flashlight from the ground beside the stump Lucas was sitting on. "Gotta make a trip to the truck. We'll be back in a few."

"Everything okay?" Lauren asked.

Olivia waved a hand in the air, the one that wasn't gripped tightly in Dawson's. "I left my medicine in the truck."

"We'll play with Betsy while you're gone!" Levi said as the dog lapped at his face.

"Thanks. I think she likes you," Olivia said. It warmed her heart to see Betsy so happy and comfortable around her friends.

Dawson gently tugged on her hand, and she followed him to the path that snaked into the woods. They walked down the hill in silence before stopping at the creek.

"We forgot the wood," Olivia said, turning back toward the camp.

"I'll do it in the morning when I can see better."

He turned to her and handed over the flashlight. "You ready?"

She couldn't see his face, but she could tell by the lilt in his voice that he was smiling. Her stomach flipped before he wrapped his arm around her. She knew what was coming, and her body's instinctual reaction was a bubbly celebration.

This time, she was ready. When he settled his hold around her, she did the same, wrapping her arms around his neck and reveling in the closeness. Taking a chance, she rested her head against his shoulder as he leaped over the creek.

The moment in the air was fleeting, but her heart kept flying long after he rested her feet back on the ground. He was her anchor, and her gravitational force had shifted.

It was Dawson–the man who would walk out into the night for her, show up at her door with an adventure, and protect her heart like he protected her body.

When her heels met the dirt, she didn't let go, and Dawson only hesitated a second before pulling her closer.

"Liv?"

"Yeah?" she whispered. Anticipation buzzed over her skin as her fingers slid into his hair.

"You okay?"

That was a loaded question. She was flying and falling, freezing and burning, weightless and heavy.

Was she okay? She couldn't even take a full breath.

"I think so."

Dawson brushed the tip of his nose along the side of hers, and all of the air around them rushed into her lungs. Tilting her chin up, she waited for him to make the first move. Had she been imagining the special treatment he gave her? Was she reading too much into his flirting?

She needed him to show her. He wouldn't risk their friendship if he wasn't serious. They were already playing with fire, and there was no going back.

He shifted his hold on her, bringing them closer together. His fingertips trailed from her temple to her jaw before framing her face. "Did you do all this so you could get me alone?"

A laugh burst from her chest, and it was pure freedom. Freedom to be herself. Freedom to play Dawson's game that drew the fear from her bones. "Did I?" she asked.

His breath was warm against her cheek as his mouth hovered a mere inch from her skin. "If you wanted to kiss me, you should have just asked."

Oh, now her skin was burning–tingling as if fire danced over it. She opened her mouth to say something, but the words wouldn't come out.

Brushing his thumb over her lower lip, he whispered, "May I have this kiss, my queen?"

"Uh-huh." It was the most ungraceful response, but it was all her mind could conjure at the moment. She was wrapped up in Dawson's affections–too lost in the fog to find her way out.

His mouth captured hers, stampeding all of her senses. She breathed him in as his lips brushed over hers. Softly, then harder. Trying and failing to contain the years of longing pouring out of them.

He dropped the flashlight and tightened his hold around her waist, dragging her to him as if he could meld them together into one being.

Her hands trailed down his face, over the scruff on his jaw, memorizing the features she'd known for thousands of days. The fear seeped out of her as his lips danced over hers.

This was her Dawson. He always had been.

A knowing settled in her middle as she matched his kiss. This was *right*, Dawson was different, and everything was about to change. Her world went from black and white to screaming color, and the shadows turned to highlights.

His heavy breaths mingled with the night air as he broke the kiss, only to pepper her with smaller ones–punctuating every one with a silent promise.

He chuckled, and the sound vibrated against her chest. "I thought we were supposed to talk first," he whispered.

"I don't know that we're doing a lot of thinking," she whispered back.

His thumb brushed over her brow, smoothing the frown lines he couldn't see in the dark but knew would be there. "Don't overthink it before you give me a chance, Liv."

"No, I'm not doing that. It's just... we do have a lot to talk about."

He let out a deep exhale and scanned the forest behind her. "Okay, but not here. We need to get to the truck and get back." Rubbing his hands up and down her arms, he leveled her with a shadowed stare.

Olivia blinked out of her daze and looked around–her eyes adjusting to the dark, jagged lines of the forest. "Yeah, it's getting a little creepy out here."

"Let me take you back," Dawson said, clasping her hand in his.

"No, I'm not chickening out. Just realizing we should have been keeping our eyes peeled for critters out here."

Dawson lifted her hand and kissed her knuckles. The gentleness of his kiss mixed with the strength of his big hand in hers, creating a perfect storm. "You're the boss."

Good grief. If she was the boss, they were in trouble. She'd done nothing but make emotionally driven decisions since lunch, and she was walking a metaphorical tightrope.

Dawson picked up the flashlight and kept Olivia

close to his side as they walked to the truck. The path was easy enough to follow despite the dark, but nothing was about to tear her away from Dawson's side. The wilderness was spooky. Wilderness at night was going to leave her paranoid.

They reached the truck and Olivia went to the passenger's side while Dawson went to the other.

"Which side is it on?" Dawson asked.

"I don't remember." She opened the back door, but the cab light didn't come on. "Shine the light over here."

Dawson pushed through a few things on the other side of the truck and shone the light on the small space. "Is it in the front?"

"Must be." She reached for the door and started to close it, but Dawson grabbed for her other hand.

"What?"

"Get in the truck," he whispered. Any joking she expected from him was completely gone, replaced by a stern warning.

"Dawson?" she whispered.

"Get in the truck, and close the door behind you. Now." His attention was focused on something over her head.

Without hesitating, she got in the truck. She'd barely settled in before Dawson lunged across the back seat and grabbed her door, jerking it closed with a loud thud that filled the night.

Not even a second later, something hit the truck

on her side, rocking the full frame. There was a high-pitched whine following her scream.

Dawson turned to his door and shut it, closing them in the dark cab. He reached for her instantly, wrapping her in his arms.

When the tightness eased from around her throat, she dared to ask, "What was that?"

Dawson took two full breaths before answering. "Wolves."

21

DAWSON

Dawson could count on one hand the things he was afraid of, and tonight he'd tiptoed around two of the main ones.

First, being rejected by Olivia. Granted, he'd lived through a few minor ones–the kind that laughed off his attempt and promptly erased the moment from their history.

Then, he'd kissed her, and she hadn't backed away. Instead, she'd met his moves match for match, searing a brand on his heart. It was a kiss to top all kisses. The relief was immediate and incredible. Totally worth the ten-year wait.

The second fear–and the most intense–was anything happening to Olivia or his family.

If the wolves were still out there, he couldn't hear them over the roaring in his ears. He'd barely spotted the one behind her, and he'd almost dismissed it for a trick of the light.

Except the dim beam from his flashlight hadn't lied. The dark-gray predator had locked in on Olivia with hunger in its eyes.

Olivia's whole body shook in his arms as he tried and failed to comfort her. Maybe if he squeezed her hard enough, she'd forget about the brush with death.

No, neither of them would be forgetting anytime soon. The woman he loved enough to die for had almost been snatched from him by teeth and claws.

His chest rose and fell in deep waves, and if he let go of Olivia, he'd probably be shaking too.

Releasing Olivia from the rib-crushing hug wasn't happening anytime soon. Not until he could get that image of the wolf stalking her out of his head.

"Dawson?"

His name on her lips cracked just like his heart. Man, this woman had the ability to cut him open and lay his deepest, darkest secrets out for everyone to see.

"You're safe. I promise."

Promise. Swear. Vow. Guarantee. Mark it in stone. Write it in blood. He was certain she was safe as long as he was around. Nothing short of a direct hit by lightning would keep him from protecting her.

"Is it gone?" she asked, almost too quietly to be heard.

"I don't know, but I'm not taking any chances." He focused on lightening his tone. "I think we should just stay right here forever. Sound good? Good. We have beef jerky and water."

That earned him a little laugh, but he was kind of serious.

Well, as serious as someone could be about hiding out in a truck in the middle of the Wyoming wilderness for eternity. As crazy as it should have sounded, he'd do anything for Olivia, even become a hermit and give up Skittles.

Because spending a lifetime with Olivia was the stuff of dreams. It didn't matter where they were. As long as they were together, he was happy.

He brushed a hand over her hair and kissed her head. "You're safe. I promise." Maybe if he said the words enough she'd believe him. He'd protect her until the last beat of his heart.

She inhaled a deep, shuddering breath. "I think I'm okay now."

"Are you sure?" He didn't want to beg, but he'd hoped to hold her longer.

Lifting her head, she brushed back the hairs that had come loose from her ponytail. "Yeah. I'm okay. Thanks to you, I guess."

"If you'd like to call me your hero, my alter-ego is

known as Prince Charming. Please don't tell anyone. I don't enjoy taking photographs with strangers."

She laughed again, and his true superpower was at work. That sound had every atom in his body humming to life. It was as if she called to him at the most basic level.

Dawson glanced out the window, and his vision adjusted to the low light. The wolf was still out there, and he had friends.

"Looks like the pack wants to wait us out," Dawson said as he let his hands brush down her arms. He held onto one of her wrists, not ready to let go.

"Great. We're sitting ducks."

"Don't give up just yet." He lifted his hips in a cramped backseat and pulled his phone from his back pocket. "Let's call the others and tell them to be on guard."

"Don't ask them to come out here!" Olivia cried.

"No. I don't want anyone walking around in the dark. I'll just let them know where we are."

He pressed the button to call Lucas, but nothing happened. His phone was in emergency mode. "Shoot. I forgot there's no cell service out here."

Olivia pulled her phone out of her coat pocket. "None for me either." She let the phone fall to her lap. "Are we stuck here?"

Dawson brushed his hand up and down her arm. "Don't panic. I promise we'll be fine."

The tension in her shoulders slipped out of her. "I know. I trust you. If it wasn't for you, a wolf would be flossing his teeth with my tendons right now."

Dawson tried not to react to that disturbing visual. "Can we not talk about that?"

She picked up the flashlight from where it had fallen onto the floorboard. Pointing it straight up, it lit the cab, casting shadows all around. "Why aren't the cab lights on?"

He'd been asking himself that question, and he was not excited to know the answer. Mostly because he knew the reason, and he didn't like it. He reached up and pressed the interior light. Nothing.

"Don't tell me," Olivia whispered, staring up at the light as if she could will it to illuminate with her mind.

"Okay. I won't tell you."

"Dawson!" she whisper-screamed.

"You said you didn't want to know," he reminded her.

She huffed and shoved his shoulder. "Is the battery dead?"

"'Fraid so, my queen." He looked around the cab and located her purse. "Found it."

She took the purse and rummaged inside. A few seconds later, she pulled out a pill bottle and shook one out into her hand.

Dawson handed her a bottle of water from a six-pack he kept as an emergency stash in the truck. "Mission accomplished."

Olivia swallowed the pill and tightened the cap back on. "Now what? You think we can honk the horn and scare them off?"

"The battery is dead," Dawson reminded her.

She threw her head back and groaned. "Ugh. I forgot. Looks like we're not going anywhere."

Dawson turned off the flashlight and tried to count the eyes glowing in the muted moonlight. He had his gun on his hip, and he could use it if necessary. Though, he didn't pose the option since Olivia would shut it down faster than a bear trap could snap.

Olivia rested back against the seat and turned to him. He could barely make out the lines of her face in the dark, but he knew those features by heart. Long lashes covered the most beautiful hazel eyes he'd ever seen. The gold flecks in the center drew him in like a moth to a flame. Her cheeks were rounded and almost always lifted with her smile.

And that smile? Now that he knew how that smile tasted, he wanted more. He'd never get enough.

They were completely alone. No distractions. Nothing reminding them to keep their distance. Nothing standing between them. Even the forest hid them from the reality waiting just beyond its edges.

But for now, she was all his.

"Dawson?" His name on her soft breath was barely a whisper.

"Yeah?"

"We kissed."

A chuckle escaped before he had a chance to contain it. "Is that just now sinking in?"

Olivia covered her mouth with both hands, and the low moonlight reflected off her wide eyes. Her words were muffled by her hands. "I can't believe we did that. I'm freaking out a little."

Dawson tilted his head. "I'm not sure if I should be flattered or offended if you're more freaked out about our kiss than you are the pack of wolves we just escaped."

Olivia's hands fell from her mouth instantly, and she sat up straight. "I'm serious! What do you think about this?"

"'Bout time," Dawson said just as Olivia swatted his chest. "I'm serious. I've only wanted to kiss you for the last decade."

Olivia's breaths came in short gasps as she shifted her hands to frame her face. "I'm not supposed to want you like this. It's wrong."

So, she wanted him. That was the best news he'd heard in his life. He'd be playing those last words on repeat in his mind for the rest of his days.

Reaching out, Dawson rested his hands on her arms and rubbed his thumbs in small circles over her shoulders until her hands relaxed in her lap. "This is not wrong. It's right."

He leaned in and pressed a kiss to her cheek, then her temple. His hands slid over her shoulders to her neck and up to cradle her face.

Leaning his forehead against hers, he closed his eyes and stayed there until her breathing evened out. Slowly, she lifted her hands and pressed them on top of his.

When he was sure she wasn't in danger of hyperventilating, he brushed the side of his nose against hers before pressing their lips together.

Now he was the one losing his breath. Kissing Olivia was like crashing into the sun. It burned him on contact and left him lit up like a blue flame long after.

When he broke the kiss, he didn't pull away. "This is right," he whispered, praying she could sense the honesty in his words.

"But you don't understand. I–I don't even know what this is yet."

"Let me fill you in. You're my best friend, and while that friendship is one of the most prized relationships in my life, I want to be more than just your friend."

There. He'd laid it all out on the line, and now he just had to wait to see if she loved or hated this new development.

Olivia pressed her fingertips to her lips. "I have

feelings for you that are...more than friendly. On the one hand, I want more than friendship between us." She paused and looked at her hands in her lap. "But there are reasons we shouldn't."

"Reasons with an S? As in plural?" Dawson asked. Had she tallied up a defense against him, or was she just being cautious? "What are you talking about?"

She let out a deep sigh. "It's not just about us. There are reasons why we shouldn't..."

"You said that, but I don't know what these reasons are. Please, explain."

Olivia lifted her head, and he could have sworn there was a glint of the light in her eye. He brushed his thumb over her cheek where a tear had just escaped.

"Talk to me, Liv."

"There's someone in our lives who would be hurt if we were together."

Dawson stared into her eyes, hoping to find the answer to that vague revelation in their shadows. "Are you talking about Beau? Yeah, he's your brother, but he already knows I'd fight him and whoever else for you. So that's not an issue."

"What do you mean he already knows?" Olivia asked.

"He knows how I feel. He knows I'd do anything for you. I'd never hurt you."

Dawson almost let the word love slip out. While

it was entirely true, he didn't think Olivia would take it too well if he kissed her and threw his undying love on the table in the same night.

Olivia paused before saying, "I can't believe you told Beau."

"I would have told you too if you weren't so stubborn."

"I'm not stubborn." She said the words, but there wasn't a fire behind them.

"Yes, you are. But that's..." He'd almost let the L-word slip again. "That's a good thing."

Olivia lifted his hand and slipped her fingers in the spaces between his. That connection zipped all the way to his toes, and the longer their palms were pressed together, the harder it was to tell where he ended and she began.

"I wasn't talking about Beau," she whispered. "It's really not my place to tell."

"If it affects us, then I think we should talk about it."

Olivia sighed and lifted her chin. "It's Anna."

Dawson narrowed his eyes, hoping to get a better look at Olivia's expression in the darkness. "Um, why would she care?"

Olivia huffed. "You really have no idea. She likes you, and she's been dying for you to notice her for years."

Dawson straightened, waiting for the punchline that didn't come. "Are you serious? Anna Harris?"

Olivia only nodded.

Wow. That was unexpected. He'd known Anna all his life, but he'd never had more than friendly feelings for her. She was beautiful, but their personalities didn't match up.

He was the life of the party, and while Anna was usually smiling, it was more friendly than joking. She hardly ever responded to his humor.

That wasn't to say he didn't get along with her. He did. It was just easier in group situations.

Olivia fidgeted her fingers. "She's been hoping you'd notice her for a while. It's been tearing me up because I want her to be happy, and I felt terrible hoping you'd notice me too."

"Ha! Notice you? I am borderline obsessed with you, and you were the only one who didn't notice."

She chuckled. "I'm your friend, and we hang out a lot."

"Every wonder why I drop everything when you call? You're my queen because you have my loyalty, my protection, and my entire heart."

Olivia hung her head, covering her face with her hands.

Dawson reached for her, gently pulling her hands down. "Does this help?"

"It should, shouldn't it? We're on the same page, but I'm still an awful friend. I can't stand the thought of hurting her. I need to know if this is real or just a phase for you."

"Are you kidding me, woman?" He wanted to drop the word love and put her fears to rest, but he'd always been patient with Olivia, and he'd stick to that plan. "Don't take my word for it. I'll prove it to you. I've got nothing but time."

"So, you don't think I should tell Anna yet?"

"I'm not telling you what to do, but the whole Anna thing is a non-issue."

Olivia pressed her hand to her chest. "It is to me!"

"I didn't mean it like that. I'm saying nothing is ever going to happen with Anna and me. She's great, but she's not the one I want."

Dawson gripped Olivia's hand. "I admire your loyalty, but there are no feelings for Anna. You, on the other hand, have all of me. I could never belong to anyone else."

22

OLIVIA

Cloud nine was a dangerous place to be.

Dawson had stoked the flames of her feelings, assuring her that this wasn't an impulsive mistake. She'd known him enough to trust him completely. He wouldn't risk their friendship, as well as Olivia's friendship with her best and oldest friend, if this was a fling.

Despite the assurances, a knot settled in her gut. There was a mountain standing in front of her, and she had to cross it before things could be good for this new relationship.

Why did things have to change? She saw Dawson almost every day. They called and texted each other all the time. They helped and supported each other. They ran a farm together.

Well, they'd probably be kissing now. That was

definitely a new development. Anna would notice that change-up.

Dawson was laying it all on the line, and she wanted to soak it all in and wrap up in his words. She could almost forget the danger waiting just outside the truck.

Wolves and broken trust. Two equally vicious threats.

There was no way around it. Anna would be crushed, and Olivia couldn't imagine being the cause of that hurt.

Stay loyal and deny her feelings for Dawson, or seek her own desires and break the strongest loyalty of her life? It was an impossible situation.

There was still the secret of her possible infertility. The upcoming appointment with her doctor to discuss surgery options loomed over her head like a dark cloud, and she couldn't bring herself to mention it tonight. They had enough standing in their way already.

One step at a time.

Dawson rubbed circles over the back of her hand with his thumb. "What do you say? Can we give this a chance?"

It was the moment of truth. Except, only some truths were taken into account.

"I want to. I really do. I'm not ready to talk to Anna about this, so can we take things slow for now?"

Dawson tilted his head. She couldn't make out his expression in the dark, but the shadows gave her what little bravery she had to confess her feelings to him.

"I'm okay with taking things slow. Are you saying we shouldn't tell anyone yet?"

"That too, I guess. I don't want Anna to find out about us from someone else, but I need to figure out how to tell her."

"Okay, but I can kiss you, right?"

"Dawson!"

He leaned in and pressed his lips against hers. The world around them slowed as he stole her breath and heart. His voice was low and rough as he whispered, "I plan to kiss you a lot."

A thrill of excitement rushed up her spine. How long had she been waiting to kiss him? How long had she sat beside him wondering what it would be like to have his lips on hers?

Too long.

"Okay. Kissing is allowed," Olivia said. "I just need to figure this out with Anna."

"I don't know how to help you, but I'm here if you need anything."

She brushed a hand over his stubbled jaw. This sweet, protective, funny man was doing everything to ease her concerns. He understood her more than anyone else except Anna, and he had to know how difficult this was for her.

"Thank you. For understanding," she whispered.

"I wish you'd told me sooner. We could have pressed the play button on us a long time ago."

Olivia shook her head. "I don't think we were ready. I'm hoping we are now."

"Oh, I'm definitely ready," Dawson said.

She laughed and playfully shoved his arm. "On a more immediate note, how are we going to let our friends know we're okay? Won't they come looking for us?"

Dawson rubbed his jaw. "I hope not. I should have grabbed the sat phone before we came out here. I bet Lucas will come looking for us."

Olivia held her phone in the air and moved it around slowly, watching the screen like a hawk. "Mine isn't in emergency mode. Maybe I can get a signal."

"That doesn't mean they'll get it," Dawson reminded her.

"I don't need your negativity right now." She brought her phone down and typed up a message. "I'm at least going to try to send it."

"If nothing else, we'll sleep here and venture back out in the morning."

Olivia rounded on him, pinning him with a stare. "So we can see the wolves coming? No, thank you. I don't plan to meet death before I've brushed my teeth."

Okay, she sounded ridiculous, but she wasn't too

keen about going back out there knowing what was waiting for them.

Dawson lifted his hoodie and pulled his gun out of its holster. He opened the console and stashed the weapon inside. "I'm always prepared, and I can certainly try to take care of the problem tonight, but–"

"Nope. I don't think I can handle that," Olivia interjected.

"And I don't like shooting into the dark. If one of our friends did come looking for us, they might be out there."

"But they'll be unprotected!"

"Nope. I left my shotgun at the cabin, but I know Lucas has one too." Dawson rubbed the back of his neck, carefully avoiding eye-contact with her. "I always have my pistol on me, but I was a little distracted when we left camp or I would have brought the shotgun."

Olivia propped her elbows on her knees. "I was distracted too. Not that I would have been thinking about arming myself."

"Are you saying I'm eye candy?" Dawson asked.

Olivia threw her head back and groaned. "Stop it. You know you're hot stuff."

"Hot stuff. I'm putting that on my resume."

A laugh bubbled out of Olivia's chest, but it was quickly followed by a yawn. "I am exhausted. What time is it?"

"Dark-thirty," Dawson said without missing a beat.

Olivia yawned again. She was used to staying busy, but her bedtime was closer to nine than midnight. Add in the extra hiking she'd done in the afternoon, and sleep was calling her name.

Dawson nudged her arm. "Scoot over."

She did as she was told, and Dawson bent his tall frame as best he could to see under the back seat. A few seconds later, he pulled out a bulging plastic bag. "Blanket."

"Are you serious?" She'd worn an undershirt, a sweater, and a coat, but the night chill was starting to settle inside the truck.

"Best to be prepared."

"Look at that Boy Scout training paying off," Olivia jested.

"Eagle Scout. I'm an Eagle Scout, and that *is* on my resume."

She laughed, and silent tears crept from the corners of her eyes. Wiping them with the back of her hand, she huffed. "I'm so tired that everything sounds funny."

"You must be extremely tired because my Eagle Scout status is anything but funny. I worked so hard for that. It's like my greatest accomplishment."

"And Beau dropped out as soon as he hit high school," Olivia said, remembering her brother's grumbling about camping.

"Quitter," Dawson mumbled as he pulled out the blanket.

Shivering, Olivia reached for an end to spread it out over them. "If it was this cold, I completely understand why he quit."

"Don't worry. We won't freeze." Dawson handed her the blanket and braced his hands on the front seat headrests. "You think I can climb into the front seat?"

Laughter bubbled in her chest as she imagined the tall man beside her folding himself in the cramped space.

"You think this is so funny. Wait till it's your turn." With that, Dawson bent and turned, swinging his behind around to position it in the front passenger seat. Then his long legs swung over the seat until he was draped over the console.

"Shoot. Now what?"

Olivia's fit of giggles intensified. She gripped her chest, gasping for air as tears streamed from her eyes. "How...how are you going to..."

"I don't need your negativity right now," he said, throwing her words from earlier back at her. "I just need to figure this out."

She pointed as she tried to catch her breath. "Move the seat back."

He reached beside the seat and it started slowly creeping back. "Freedom!"

Olivia doubled over, wiping happy tears from her

eyes. "I'm glad this isn't a tiny truck. You would be in so much trouble."

"You wouldn't be much better off if you had to listen to my grumbling," Dawson reminded her.

Wrapping her arms around the seat to get to him, she rested her head against his, trying to stomp down her laughter. "I'm sorry I laughed at you."

"No you're not. You are having way too much fun." He turned his head and kissed her temple. "But it's your turn now, and I get to laugh."

Olivia raised her head and looked at him. "My turn?"

"Unless you want to sleep on that bench seat that's about a foot wide, you're sleeping up here with me." He opened his arms and smiled. "Plus, I promise body heat."

"We are not making friction in this truck tonight," Olivia said.

"Good grief, Liv. That's moving a little fast don't you think? No funny business. I just run hot." He pulled the collar of his hoodie to the side. "See?"

She slid her hand around the side of his neck, and the warmth tingled over her cold hand. "How are you that warm? It's freezing in here."

Dawson shrugged. "I'm always like that." He reached beside the seat again, and it started slowly reclining. "Come on."

"I can't believe we're doing this," Olivia mumbled so low Dawson probably didn't hear it. The thought of sleeping close to him was a little too exciting when she was supposed to be tempering her expectations.

Dawson guided her onto his lap, and she pulled the blanket over them. His arms wrapped around her, and she relaxed into his hold. With her head against his chest, the smell she'd come to associate with Dawson mingling with the lingering scent of the campfire filled her senses.

He squirmed a little, shifting her around in his arms. "You comfy?"

"Mmhm," she hummed as her eyes drifted closed.

Problems waited for them outside, but tonight, she'd sleep safely in Dawson's arms.

23

DAWSON

Dawson crept out of a deep sleep only to sink back in. Everything was warm and cozy–perfect conditions for sleeping.

Three knocks from somewhere nearby had his brow furrowing. *Not ready to adult today, thank you.*

Something moved against him, and he tightened his hold.

Louder knocks jerked him out of the slumber, and his eyes flew open. The dawn light was faint in the forest, shining into the cab of his truck as he blinked back the remnants of sleep.

Olivia shifted in his arms, and the events of the night came back to him. Camping, wolves, Olivia.

Olivia.

"Dude!"

Dawson tightened his hold on Olivia and met Beau's accusing stare out the window.

Uh-oh.

Beau threw his hands in the air, clearly irritated.

Dawson pressed the button to lower the window, but it didn't budge.

Oh yeah. Dead battery. He held up a finger to Beau and tried to shift Olivia's back away from the door.

She lifted her head and wiped at her eye.

"Good morning, my queen."

"Morning," she whispered.

"Your brother is here, and he wants an explanation."

Her head popped up at that. "What?" She turned around in Dawson's lap to find Beau waiting with his arms crossed over his chest.

"Shoot. What time is it?" she asked.

"Time for a reckoning."

Olivia opened the door and didn't bother to smile at her brother. "Hey."

"You decide to have a party for two?" Beau asked, looking back and forth between Dawson and Olivia.

Dawson kept an arm around Olivia's waist, hoping she'd relax. "Where to start?"

"We got trapped by wolves," Olivia said. Her ponytail was hanging to one side, and she had red marks on her face from sleeping against him.

Beau made a show of looking left then right before facing his sister again. "Wolves?"

"Yeah. We came back to the truck to get my medicine, and there was a pack of wolves."

"And my truck battery is dead. Any chance I could get a jump?" Dawson asked.

Beau shook his head and headed back toward his truck. Two mattresses wrapped in plastic rested in the truck bed.

Olivia pressed her hands to the sides of her head. "I can't believe he saw us cuddling."

"I know. It's awful," Dawson said with all the sarcasm he could muster.

"I mean, we haven't even figured out what this is yet, and he's going to think things." She gestured with both hands to where Beau had been standing.

"He's not going to think anything bad. Come on, Liv. He knows both of us. It's not like we're hooking up in my truck."

The wrinkle between her brows smoothed, and she looked at him like he was the source of her happiness. The darkness had hidden everything last night, and seeing that smile drove all his doubts away.

"We're in this together," he reminded her. It didn't really matter what problems came their way. He'd stand beside her through anything. This woman could drive him to the edge and make him jump, and he'd do it all with a smile on his face.

She snuggled back into his lap, burrowing her face in the crook of his neck. It was a moment he'd imagined millions of times, but no dream could ever touch this reality.

Olivia was in his arms, and he was never letting her go.

Beau's truck pulled up beside Dawson's, and Olivia crawled out of his lap. "Time to face the other wolf," she announced.

Her brother didn't really fit the description of a wolf, but he was snarly a lot of the time. Still, he'd face any predator if necessary.

Dawson stretched his aching muscles as he followed Olivia out of the truck. So it hadn't been the most comfortable sleep of his life the way he'd imagined a few minutes ago. His right leg was numb, and his back was protesting all movement.

"What are you doing here so early?" Olivia asked Beau as she stretched her back from side to side.

"Delivering the mattresses. I thought I was going to have to walk to camp to get some extra hands, but I guess the two of you will work."

Olivia held up a hand. "I'm all yours, but I need to use the ladies' room first."

Dawson spread his arms out. "The forest is yours."

She chuckled and pointed to a spot behind the other trucks. "I'll be that way."

Dawson slid an arm around her as she walked past and pressed a kiss to her cheek. "Morning."

She wrapped her arms around his neck and squeezed. "Morning."

Man, he could get used to this.

"Open the hood, lover boy," Beau said.

Dawson walked around and popped the hood of his truck.

"So, I take it things changed?" Beau asked.

Dawson clicked behind his teeth. "I never took you for the girl talk type."

Beau grumbled. "Is this an official thing?"

"Yes, it's official. As official as it can get without a ring."

Beau stopped, and his eyes widened.

"Okay. Not that official. Though, I wouldn't be against it."

"Liv isn't as impulsive as you are," Beau reminded him.

"I know. I know. I'm not asking her to marry me tomorrow, but let's be real. That's where this is heading if I have anything to say about it."

"Liv isn't–"

"I know what you're saying," Dawson interrupted. "I know her. I know her better than I know anyone in this world, including you. I've been patient, and I'll continue to be patient. I've got this."

Beau had no way of knowing, but Dawson had gone over every scenario of how things could go when he finally got the nerve to lay it all on the line for Olivia. He'd predicted at least a little of her freak-out, and they'd come through that with flying colors. Gold stars for both of them.

Dawson had been taking Olivia's thoughts and feelings into consideration for longer than he'd been legally driving, so he kinda had a handle on it by now.

Beau turned back to the battery under the hood and clamped the cables to it. "I won't say another thing about it."

Good. Now that the big brother talk was behind them, they could get to work.

Olivia walked around the side of Dawson's truck and leaned on the frame. "What can I do?"

Dawson tossed her his keys, and she caught them in the air. "Can you start it up?"

She slid into the driver's seat and started the truck. The engine roared to life as she revved it. She let out a whoop that scared more of the woodland creatures than the roaring of the engine.

"Looks like we're back in business," Dawson said. He turned to Beau and slapped a hand on his shoulder. "Thanks, man."

"No problem." Beau jerked his thumb at the truck. "Leave that running for a little bit."

"Thanks for the jump too, but that's not what I meant," Dawson said lower.

Beau nodded and scratched his jaw. "I know you'll be good to her."

"You better believe it. If she's giving me a chance, I'm not gonna waste it."

Olivia stepped out of the truck and pushed her hands into her back pocket. "Listen, Beau. Can you maybe not–"

Beau held up a hand, carefully not meeting his sister's eyes. "I won't say a word."

A grin lit up her face, and she let her hands fall to her sides. "Thanks. I haven't figured out how to explain it to...everyone yet."

Dawson would be freaking out a little bit if he didn't know about Anna's feelings. But he knew Olivia wasn't really trying to hide their relationship. It was okay if most people knew, but it would be too easy for word to get back around to Anna if everyone was in on it.

Beau pointed toward the back of his truck. "Grab an end."

Dawson snagged his gun from the console, turned off the truck, and turned to Olivia. "You have everything you need?"

"Yep." She pointed to her coat pocket where she'd stashed her medicine.

"Let's roll." He pressed another kiss to her head and met Beau at the back of his truck.

"Liv, can you guide us?" Beau asked.

"Sure. I'll be your eyes for the next half hour."

Carrying a mattress through the woods was an event, but Olivia was great about letting them know if fallen trees or holes were coming up. Lucas had created a bridge across the creek, so that obstacle was easy.

When they reached the rise leading to the camp, Olivia ran ahead to make sure the cabins were open. Maddie and Lauren darted out of the women's cabin and ran straight for Olivia.

"We were so worried!" Lauren said as she wrapped Olivia up. "Lucas got a call out on the satellite phone last night, and search and rescue was ready to deploy this morning."

"We need to let them know we're okay," Olivia said. "We made it to the truck, but wolves surrounded us and we couldn't get back to camp."

Maddie shuddered. "Lucas has a bad history with wolves. I'm glad he didn't go out there."

Olivia rubbed a hand on Maddie's back. "Me too. We were so worried you'd venture out and run into the pack."

Dawson repositioned the mattress in his hands to look over his shoulder toward the women. "Which cabin?"

Maddie sprinted toward the first one and propped the door open. Dawson and Beau guided the mattress inside and rested it on the box springs.

Lucas jogged into the cabin as soon as they had the mattress positioned. "I'm sure glad to see you," he said, slapping a hand on Dawson's shoulder.

"Glad to be back in one piece. We got cornered by some wolves."

Lucas's eyes widened, but he contained some of his shock. "Wolves?"

Everyone in town knew Lucas's cousin, Hunter, had been attacked by wild dogs when they were younger. The scar on his face was hard to miss. I guess an event like that left a mark on everyone around.

"We hid out in the truck until Beau showed up this morning."

Lucas shook his head slightly and turned to Beau. "Thanks for bringing these. I don't think Lauren and Maddie enjoyed the air mattress too much last night."

"No problem," Beau said. "We'll go get the other one after breakfast. I'm starving."

Lucas hooked a thumb over his shoulder. "Lauren is working on some sausage and eggs. It smells like it's almost ready."

Dawson rubbed his hands together. "You don't have to tell me twice. I hope she made extra."

"Aaron and Noah are on their way, so I'm sure there's plenty," Lucas said.

Maddie and Olivia burst into the small cabin with their arms overflowing with sheets and pillows.

"Get out of the way, boys. We've got work to do," Maddie commanded.

Dawson held up his hands and headed for the door. "I'm out."

Betsy bounded up the steps, meeting him on the porch with Levi on her heels.

"Dawson! You're back!"

Betsy jumped into Dawson's arms, and he barely had time to shift the dog to the side as Levi crashed into him.

"I thought you were a goner," Levi mumbled against Dawson's shirt.

Patting Levi's back, he swallowed the lump in his throat before speaking. "It'll take more than a pack of wolves to get me down."

"Wolves!" Levi shouted, looking up at Dawson with wide eyes.

Yikes. Probably shouldn't have mentioned that to the kid. "They didn't hurt us. We stayed in the truck. And they won't venture into the campsite. We're a little too loud for their tastes."

Levi looked over his shoulder and scanned the tree line. "You sure?"

"Pretty sure. Plus, you've got us. We'll protect you."

Levi straightened. "I can protect us too."

"Maybe don't venture out of the camp area. Just to be safe."

"Yeah. I won't. Trust me."

The terrified look on the kid's face said he

wouldn't be anywhere near the trees for the rest of the trip.

After they ate breakfast, Dawson and Beau brought in the other mattress with Levi's help this time. By mid-morning, the cabins were cleaned and spotless. Dawson and Lucas had a wood-chopping competition that served as the after-lunch entertainment. Aaron and Noah showed up just before dinner and started cleaning up the brush that had crept into the clearing.

Dawson did an excellent job keeping his hands and lips off Olivia, but she had all of his attention. Every time a cabin door opened, he had to see if it was Olivia. It was easy to keep tabs on where she was in the camp because he felt her. There was a radar that pulsed from her, drawing him toward her at all times.

Having mountains of chores to do helped him stay on track, but his focus was divided. It was day one of life with Olivia 2.0, and ideally they'd be cuddled up by a fireplace kissing the day away.

He'd always gotten a good dose of satisfaction about a job well done. He was usually the first to volunteer to help if someone needed a hand. But as much as he loved working, nothing could hold his attention like Olivia.

As soon as the sun started dipping below the trees, Lucas and Maddie started cooking up supper, and everyone else headed to the creek to wash up.

Dawson walked carefully behind Olivia, watching her movements more than his own as they made their way down the hill.

Olivia stepped, and her heel slid on the wet leaves. Dawson reached out and grabbed her arm before she went down.

As he wrapped her in his arms, all thoughts of keeping his distance in front of people flew out the window. "You okay?"

"Yeah. Just slipped." She turned to look over her shoulder at the incline ahead of them. "That would have been a bad fall."

Dawson held her tighter, unwilling to let thoughts like that take up any space in his head. "Do I need to carry you?"

Olivia laughed and slapped his chest as she straightened. "Thanks, but I can walk."

She might have thought it was a joke, but he was more than willing to wrap her up if it meant protecting her from harm.

He kept a hold on her hand as they continued toward the creek. He was careful with every footstep as he led them down the slope. Was she moving slower than usual?

He stopped and turned to look up at her. She was standing higher on the hill, and he pulled her to his chest until they were face-to-face "Hey, you okay? Did we work too hard today?"

She pressed a quick kiss to his lips, then rested

her head on his chest. "No, I'm fine. Maybe just tired."

He brushed her hair away from her face and whispered, "Good news. A bed is waiting at the campsite."

She chuckled, but the sound was cut short. "I'm ready for it."

"Let's get you cleaned up, and you can eat a quick bite before catching some Zs."

"Sounds like a good idea." She took his hand and walked the rest of the way to the creek by his side. Dawson loosened his hold as they caught up with everyone else, and she let their hands fall.

"You okay, Liv?" Lauren asked.

"Yeah. Just tired."

Lauren grinned. "Oh? Didn't sleep much in Dawson's truck last night?"

Olivia laughed but didn't look up at their friend. At least she wasn't acting like she'd never be caught dead snuggled up to him in the passenger seat of his truck.

They washed up and made the trek back to the campsite. The burgers smelled amazing, and everyone practically licked their plates clean, including Levi and Betsy.

The group moved to the campfire where they toasted marshmallows and talked. Dawson was all too aware of Olivia sitting beside him–too far away for his taste. She made little movements like she was uncomfortable–stretching her neck to the side, rubbing her temples, and hunching her shoulders. He'd done more than a little staring as the sparks from the fire matched the ones in her eyes.

Levi was telling everyone about something Baby Annie had done, and Olivia stood up.

Dawson was on his feet in an instant. "What's wrong?"

Olivia shook her head, but the shadow from the fire revealed a deep crease between her brows. "I'm going to the restroom."

"I'll come with you."

Lauren laughed beside them. "'Fraid she doesn't want an audience, Dawson."

"I just meant to the tree line," Dawson said. "I want to be close-by in case she needs something."

"Sit back down on your nest, mother hen," Beau said without taking his eyes off the marshmallow he rotated on the end of a stick.

Olivia chuckled. "I'll be right back. I'll take Betsy with me. I'm sure she'd love to walk around."

Olivia waved for the dog to follow, and Dawson swallowed a comment about Betsy's inability to protect a shoe much less a grown woman.

Dawson sat back down on the log by the fire, but he watched as Olivia and Betsy disappeared into the darkness.

"Are you in love?" Lauren whispered beside him.

Dawson whipped his attention back to Lauren. Sure enough, she was looking at him.

"I'm not blind," Lauren said.

"Um, yeah. I don't think Olivia is there yet though." He held up a finger in front of his lips, asking her to keep a secret.

Lauren nodded. "I won't tell anyone."

He knew she wouldn't. Lauren wasn't the gossiping type. If anything, she'd probably get Olivia talking about it and hopefully they'd work through how to tell Anna. If that was the only thing holding Olivia back, he wanted it cleared up as soon as possible.

Betsy ran up to Dawson, propping her front paws on his leg and barking rapidly. He looked up to find Olivia lagging a few steps behind with her head hanging.

He'd known something was wrong. Having Betsy call for help was all the confirmation he needed.

24

OLIVIA

The migraine hit full force as Olivia stepped out of the woods. The pressure had been building for hours, and she'd waited too long to take her medicine. Hopefully, it would kick in soon and she'd get some relief.

Betsy's sharp barks pounded in Olivia's head. She pressed the heel of her hand against her temple.

Dawson stood as she approached the campfire. His arm wrapped around her waist, anchoring her as her world swayed. He always found her, no matter the size of the crowd.

"What's wrong?" his deep voice penetrated the crushing fog surrounding her.

"Migraine." It was all she could do to push the word out with the invisible knives stabbing into her skull.

Dawson sat back down and gently maneuvered

her between his knees before guiding her to sit on his thigh. The warmth of his arm around her back was the only awareness that stood out amongst the pain.

Her head was too heavy, falling to one side, then the other.

"Is she okay?" Maddie asked from somewhere nearby.

Dawson wrapped his other arm around her, guiding her head to rest against his shoulder. "She said it's a migraine."

"I'll get her some water." The sounds were farther away now–too muffled for Olivia to tell who was speaking.

"What do you need?" Dawson whispered against her hair. The vibrations of his deep words reverberated through his chest and into her body.

"I've got water!" Lauren said.

"Water." Olivia lifted her head slowly, pushing against the crushing weight.

Dawson's big hand lifted hers and pressed the water into her hand. She didn't even have to open her eyes as the bottle lifted to her lips. She flinched at the freezing water as it slid down her throat.

Pulling away, she slowly shook her head. Pressure built at the nape of her neck, and the dinner she'd just eaten bubbled in her gut.

"It looks like she can't drink any more," Maddie said.

"Sick," Olivia mumbled as her head lolled again. She'd experienced a wide variety of migraine symptoms before, and vomiting was her least favorite.

Dawson wrapped his arm tight around her back and shifted to hook his arm behind her knees. "Let's get you to bed."

"I'll take care of Betsy," Levi said.

She was thankful for Levi's help but couldn't voice the words. Taking care of herself was more than she could manage.

"Thanks, buddy. You're a big help," Dawson said as he stood and started walking.

"Is she gonna be okay?" Levi asked, trailing along behind them.

"Don't you worry. I'm going to take good care of her."

"I know. Like Dad does for Mom when she's sick," Levi said.

"Just like that. Can you get the door?" Dawson asked.

Levi's footsteps pounded against the wooden porch. "Got it!"

"Shh," Dawson whispered. "Miss Olivia's head hurts really bad."

"Oh, sorry," Levi said lower.

"Can you grab her water and find a bucket?"

"Be right back." The kid's quick steps retreated, leaving only the rumble of Dawson's breaths beneath her ear where it rested on his shoulder.

"You still with me, Liv?"

"Yeah," she whispered, thankful for every movement Dawson made for her.

He stopped and lowered her to the bed. When the fluffy mattress cradled her back, she released her hold on his neck and let her body sink into the bed.

Olivia opened her eyes, thankful for the low light of the lantern. Dawson hovered over her, shielding her from the entire world.

Hadn't he been doing that for a while without her asking? Dawson was her first line of defense–a sturdy mountain that couldn't be moved unless he allowed it.

"What can I do?" he whispered. The sweet words warring with the formidable man protecting her from unseen enemies.

His brows pinched together, and his lips pressed into a flat line. When his hand brushed over her forehead, then her hair, there was a moment of relief before the pressure returned.

"I took some medicine. It needs half an hour to kick in."

Dawson reached for the blanket at the foot of the bed and spread it over her. The fuzzy softness was brand new, and the freshness calmed her as she breathed it in.

"Got the stuff," Levi said as he tiptoed into the cabin.

Dawson turned and took the things from Levi. "Thanks, buddy."

Levi let his arms fall to his sides with a slap. "What else can I do?"

Olivia did her best to smile as she reached for the kid. "Nothing. Thanks so much for your help."

"Are you gonna be okay?" Levi didn't even try to mask the worry in his words.

"I'll be okay really soon. I'll probably feel better before you go to bed tonight."

"Really?"

Olivia nodded slowly. "Really."

Dawson clapped a hand down on Levi's small shoulder. "Can you go tell everybody what Olivia said? Tell them not to worry."

"Okay." Levi darted out of the cabin, closing the door behind him with enough force to rock the old cabin walls.

As soon as they were alone, Dawson walked to the door and toed his boots off. Seconds later, he was crawling onto the other side of the bed.

"You don't have to stay. I'll be fine in a little bit."

"I'm not leaving you."

He settled onto his side, and she turned to face him. Pulling her knees to her chest, she bunched the blanket in her fists and tucked it under her chin.

Dawson gently skimmed the pad of his thumb over her temple before rubbing over her hair. The touch forced her eyes to close, and any willpower she had to open them again dissipated.

Dawson started talking, but the words were barely more than a whisper. She wasn't sure when he stopped, but the next time she opened her eyes, the morning sun streaked through the windows, filling the small cabin.

She lay on her other side facing the room and blinked until her eyes adjusted to the light. The pounding in her head was gone. The air mattress was inflated on the floor beside the bed, but the blankets were neatly folded on top of it.

"You okay, Liv?" Lauren asked softly.

Olivia rolled over to where her friend lay in the spot where Dawson had been the night before.

"I'm much better." She stretched her arms above her head and yawned. "What time is it?"

"Barely daylight. Maddie got up about half an hour ago."

Olivia searched the room, but there was no sign of Dawson. When had he left? How long had he laid beside her?

His sweetness from the night before had more than butterflies fluttering in her middle. He'd carried her to bed and given her everything she needed to wait out the storm of a migraine.

She loved helping others. Working for her community fed her soul and filled her cup, but she wasn't usually the one on the receiving end of the kindness.

Did anyone appreciate it when she helped them out like this? Gratefulness swelled inside her and pushed against the walls of her chest until she was afraid she'd burst open.

"Liv? What's wrong?"

Moisture stung behind Olivia's eyes, and she covered her trembling chin with her hand.

Lauren rubbed Olivia's shoulder. "What do you need?"

"Just...Thank you."

Lauren chuckled. "I just got you some water."

"And Dawson?"

Smiling, Lauren propped her arm up and rested her head on her hand. "He stayed with you a while. We switched places when it was time for bed."

Olivia swallowed, getting a grip on her raging emotions. "You think he's awake yet?"

"Yep. He texted me for an update on you about five minutes ago."

Olivia rubbed her eyes, trying to brush away the last of the deep sleep. "I'll go find him."

"He's a good one, you know," Lauren said. "He cares about you so much."

"I care about him too. We're just...It's all really new."

Lauren nodded. "And there's Anna."

Anna's feelings for Dawson weren't exactly a

secret within their friend group. There'd always been an unspoken rule not to mention it to him or their guy friends, but it was obvious Anna wanted Dawson to notice her.

Olivia fidgeted with the hem of the blanket. "I don't know how to tell her. Or what to tell her. Where do I start?"

"I wish I could tell you it'll be easy to just share the truth, but I don't think it'll go over well. At least not at first. Anna is a little blind with a crush."

"It's not a crush," Olivia corrected.

"It *is* a crush. Anna might not agree right now, but it's not love. You and Dawson are compliments. You understand each other. You work well together. There are dozens of reasons why you two make a better pair than Dawson and Anna. She's stuck in a fantasy that she's created. It isn't real."

Olivia groaned. "I want to believe that, but I've heard her talk about how she feels about him."

"I have too. She truly believes it, but there isn't a foundation. That's all made up. What you and Dawson have is real. There's a huge difference, but she won't see that easily."

"I know. She's going to be crushed. I don't even know a way to ease into the conversation."

Lauren clicked her tongue behind her teeth. "I don't know the answer, but I'll be praying you can find the words."

Prayer. Olivia was always first to pray for

someone else, but she'd forgotten to pray for guidance in her own life.

"Thank you. I appreciate it."

Lauren smiled and rubbed Olivia's shoulder. "You'll figure it out. We're adults, and we'll all get through this."

"Not without a broken heart–one I care about."

With a heavy sigh, Lauren rested her head against Olivia's shoulder. "She's strong. She's intent on finding true love. I just think she's trying to force something that's not meant to be."

"You're a good friend," Olivia whispered.

"I try my best." Lauren lifted her head and sat up in the bed, stretching her back from one side to the other. "Now, go find Dawson and give him proof of life. He's probably pacing outside the door waiting for you to get up."

Olivia kicked the covers off. "Thanks for the pep talk."

"Anytime."

Grabbing her toothbrush, toothpaste, and hairbrush, Olivia darted out into the cool morning. She didn't spot Dawson as she grabbed a bottle of water from the cooler and headed for the creek. Navigating the hill was much easier in the daylight without a migraine threatening to crush her.

Continually scanning the creek bed around her for dangers like the wolves, she brushed her teeth and hair in record time. After splashing some water on her face and pulling her hair up into a ponytail, she trudged back up the hill toward camp.

She spotted Dawson the moment she crested the top of the hill. He had his back to her where he stood by the picnic table he was building with Aaron.

Dawson turned and locked eyes with her as she took her second step into the clearing. A boyish smile stretched over his lips, and a dark shadow of stubble covered his jaw, giving him an air of maturity that almost stopped her in her tracks.

What would Dawson be like in ten years? Twenty? Would she get to see that older, wiser man? Would they still be friends? Would they be married with kids?

Kids. The thought crashed into her chest like a freight train, knocking the breath out of her.

No. She didn't want to allow anything to steal this moment when he was finally hers–when she gave in and let the joy have free rein.

Her feet were moving before she knew what she was doing. She picked up speed as she ran toward him.

Dawson opened his arms, as she barreled into his waiting embrace, entwining her arms and legs around him.

All air left her body in a rush as they collided. She buried her face in his neck and breathed him in. Every bit of the campfire smoke, sawdust, and the basic smell that was simply Dawson filled her up, seeping into every crack in her heart until it was whole and perfect again.

His strong arms wove around her, crushing her to him. His deep whisper tingled against the shell of her ear.

"Good morning, my queen."

Those words crumbled every wall around her heart. Yesterday, she belonged to herself. Today, she was his.

25

OLIVIA

Olivia settled into the front seat of Lyric's car and scooted it all the way back. Opening her arms, she turned to her friend. "Okay, lay it on me."

Shaking her head, Lyric handed over a six-tier stack of trays full of canned spaghetti. "This is an awful idea. Asa will lose his cool if he finds out we did this."

"Look at you being a rule follower. I love it," Olivia joked.

"I'm serious, Liv. We'll get a lecture about vehicular safety. It could go on and on."

"I forgot you married a goody-two-shoes."

Lyric huffed and added another tray to the stack in Olivia's lap. "Says the woman dating Barney Fife!"

"Okay, I think that's enough for my lap. This is getting heavy."

Lyric grabbed another tray and stacked it on top. "If we're doing this, we're going all the way."

"That's my girl!" Olivia said.

"One more. Do it for the kids."

Olivia adjusted the stack on her lap. "Oof. I don't need circulation in my legs. It's fine."

"That's everything. I can't believe we stuffed all of it into one car."

A few churches in the area got together once a month to pack bags for the Fish and Loaves ministry. They delivered bags of food for some of the kids from low-income families to take home over the weekends.

Lyric's packed car was only a portion of the food they'd distribute this month. Olivia's stomach twisted every time she thought about what those kids would do if they didn't get meals sent home from school with them every weekend.

Lyric slid into the driver's seat and started the car. "You okay?"

Olivia wiggled beneath the stack of canned goods. "Five minutes. I can do this."

"I'll make it four," Lyric said as she merged onto the main road.

Olivia pushed a breath out. The stack was close to crushing her legs, but she'd done enough complaining already. "So, how's married life?"

Lyric's eyes lit up like a Christmas tree as she

kept her attention on the road ahead. "Absolute perfection."

"I'm so happy for you. Asa is an awesome guy."

"I can't believe this is my life. I married Asa, but I also got his whole family. Jacob is the best kid, and Betty is like..."

"The Mom you've been missing?" Olivia finished.

Lyric nodded. "But I'm glad my own parents are back in the picture. They're head-over-heels for Jacob, and it's just...I didn't think I'd have all these people in my life."

Olivia reached over and rubbed her friend's arm. Lyric had made a ton of mistakes in her life, and she was living, breathing proof that God's grace knew no bounds.

"Believe it, sister. It's real."

Lyric sniffed and placed a hand over Olivia's. "I couldn't be happier."

"How's it going at work?"

Lyric's new job as a police dispatcher allowed her to work with her new husband sometimes, which also meant she saw a lot of Dawson.

Everything seemed to find its way around to him these days. Olivia couldn't go to the grocery store without thinking about Dawson's favorite foods. She couldn't look at her chickens without seeing his goats. His Instagram videos always popped up first on her feed.

Not that she minded. She'd been running

around like a cat on catnip since the camping trip, but her thoughts were always on Dawson.

"Work is great. I think I've got the hang of things now, and tomorrow is my first day on my own."

"That's awesome. Do you like what you're doing?"

"I do! It's difficult at times, but I love connecting people to the help they need. I know I'm not doing anything groundbreaking, but I love it when the dust settles and things work out."

There was no way on God's green earth Olivia was going to bring up the times when things didn't work out. She probably wouldn't make a good police dispatcher because she'd have a really hard time compartmentalizing the calls that didn't have a happy ending.

Lyric cleared her throat. "I'm really glad you and Dawson are giving it a shot. He's such a good guy."

There it was. The casual mention of the man who had her completely wrapped up in an all-consuming love.

They'd been official for less than a week, and she was already positively in love. The realization wasn't really a quick one. She'd loved him as a friend for half of her life, but opening her heart to his full affection was like turning on a light. Dawson was as much a part of her heart as her family, and that would never change.

It was love, plain and simple. Dawson made it easy.

"You have no idea. He's so good to me, but I think I love it more when I see him being good to others. That's weird, isn't it?"

"Not at all. I feel that way about Asa too. I think seeing him be a good dad is the most attractive thing I've ever witnessed."

Olivia's grip on the stack of food in her lap tightened. What was she doing? Dawson had no idea that he might be trading kids for a relationship with her, and she didn't know how to tell him.

The ride was silent until they parked in the church parking lot. Lyric rounded the car and started lifting trays.

"You okay?" Lyric asked.

"I'm fine. Why?" That was a stretch of the truth, but Olivia was getting used to impersonating a vault when it came to talking about the problems she and Dawson had in front of them.

Lyric shrugged. "You just looked a little green. Are you sure you're not getting sick?"

"Positive."

When only a few trays remained on her lap, Olivia stood with the last of the load and stretched. They still had the entire back seat and trunk to unload, and volunteers would be arriving soon.

She walked inside to put down the trays when her phone rang. Hurrying to the table filled with food items, she put the trays down and pulled her phone out of her pocket.

Anna Banana.

Why did her gut have to roil whenever her friend called? It wasn't supposed to be this way. They were sisters–on the same team.

Not anymore. At least Anna wouldn't think that after Olivia gathered the courage to have the talk with her.

Olivia answered the call and pressed it between her ear and shoulder. "Hey."

"Hey." The greeting was flat and lifeless. "Have you seen Dawson's latest post on Instagram?"

Olivia raised her chin and looked around. The church dining hall was packed. The whole place buzzed with volunteers. She was the only one standing still, and she couldn't make her legs move for all the money in the world. She swallowed the burning in her throat and croaked out a hoarse, "No."

"It's a reel," Anna said. "He's asking the goats if they think TheChickenChick should give him a chance."

No. No, no, no. Olivia hadn't seen the reel, and she wasn't prepared for this confrontation. "I–I–"

"It has almost a million views," Anna added.

Olivia gasped. A million? He had to have posted it today because she hadn't seen it earlier.

"I didn't know about it. I've been picking up food

for Fish and Loaves this afternoon, and I just haven't–"

Anna sighed. "I know you didn't have anything to do with it. I just saw it, and the internet is going crazy over it. Women are begging him to be their baby's daddy in the comments like he's the last man on earth."

Olivia stared at the blank wall in front of her. Comments like that weren't uncommon on his Instagram posts, but a million views on a video that connected them in a romantic way?

Lyric stepped back inside with her arms full of food. She stopped when she saw Olivia standing dumbstruck.

Anna laughed. "I know he's hot, but wow. I can't imagine throwing myself at someone like that. And publicly!"

Olivia took a half-breath. Anna was laughing. That was a good sign. "Um, yeah. Some of the comments he gets are wild."

Anna continued laughing. All of the hesitancy from a moment ago had dissipated like a vapor. "It really is funny. Some of the comments are tagging you and saying you're crazy if you don't take him up on it."

Great. Now she was having true chest pain. The thought of telling Anna the truth and being the cause of her heartbreak was enough to make Olivia's lunch revolt in her gut.

"And I know it's just farm stuff," Anna went on. "People really love those goats and chickens."

Olivia's week had been packed from beginning to end. She hadn't had a second to wash her hair, much less have a friendship-breaking conversation. She definitely wasn't prepared to spill the toxic beans over the phone and with an audience.

Julia Letterman stepped to the front of the room and clapped her hands. "Okay, everyone. Let's pray before we get started!"

"Do you have to go?" Anna asked. "I'll talk to you later. Love you."

"Love you too."

The hollow words hung in the air as Anna disconnected the call.

Lyric stepped in front of Olivia with her brows pinched together and lifted. "Liv, what's wrong?"

Blinking past the paralyzing fear of the conversation that hadn't actually happened yet, Olivia rubbed the side of her face. Had they already finished the prayer? "It was Anna. She said Dawson had a reel go viral today. About us."

Lyric's eyes widened. "Did he say you were together?"

Olivia shook her head. "No, but apparently he was asking if I should give him a chance."

Sucking in air through her teeth, Lyric rubbed the back of her neck. "Oh, that's not good."

"Not good is an understatement. She sounded upset at first, then she was laughing."

"So she thinks it wasn't serious."

"But it kind of is. What if she'd found out that way? How am I going to tell her?" Olivia's voice was rising with her panic. "I'm not ready. I don't know what to do. I am terrified of her finding out from me or otherwise."

Lyric rested her hands on Olivia's shoulders. "Shh. Calm down. We'll figure this out, but right now we need to focus on what we're doing here."

Olivia looked around at the people working–doing what they were here to do. After a few deep breaths, the storm in her mind began to clear. She needed to be working anyway. It would distract her from the crippling fact that she was betraying her best friend.

"You're right," Olivia whispered.

Lyric pressed a hand to Olivia's back and gently nudged her toward the front of the room. "Grab a bag and forget about this. You'll have time to talk to her later."

Later. How much later could it be? The truth of their relationship was disguised as a joke and running rampant over the internet.

The phone in her pocket vibrated, and she pulled it out. Dawson's name and a photo of him holding Henry filled the screen.

Her chest heaved, and she silenced the call. They had plenty to talk about, but it would have to wait until later.

26

DAWSON

Deep twilight fell over the woods behind Beau's garage as Dawson pulled up. Overtime was usually his friend, but he'd grumbled through the extra hours this week. Granted, it wasn't as if Olivia had extra time either. They'd spent the last few days just missing each other at every hour.

He pulled out his phone and checked the time. She'd be working at the church for the next hour and a half.

Impulse had him pressing her name on the screen. The steady rings dragged on and on. His hand fisted and flexed where it was propped on the steering wheel of his truck.

"Hey, you've reached Olivia. I can't answer the phone right now."

Even her recorded voice had his shoulders lifting, but he ended the call quickly. On any other day, he'd leave her a funny message.

Not today. Today, he missed her so badly he could barely breathe. She'd been number one in his life for years, but he'd only experienced a day and a half of bliss before they both went back to the real world.

But the time they'd spent together at the campsite? It was epic. Those days would forever live at the top of his list of favorite memories. They'd finally given up on acting like they weren't together and just told their friends not to tell anyone.

Dawson took full advantage of their time after that. He'd been so wrapped up in Olivia he couldn't see straight. He'd barely been able to work–the reason they were camping in the first place.

Now, he was having Olivia withdrawals. He fired off a text message asking if they could meet up later tonight. Another night without seeing her sounded like torture.

A few extra trucks were parked in front of the garage. He'd expected to see Asa here, but Olivia's dad and Asher Harding were a surprise.

Gage Howard's beat-up truck stayed parked at the garage lately. Nothing about that guy sat well with Dawson, but he'd been doing a good job of keeping his eyes and ears open when Gage was around. You don't earn a rap sheet like his without logging a whole bunch of hours for the dark side.

Dawson wove in through the open garage bay, but the shop was empty. It was suppertime, and just the thought of food had his mouth watering. He stepped through the back door and turned down the small hallway where voices drifted out of the break room.

Five men sat at the table, leaving only one empty chair. Beau and Asher took up one side with Jacob and Asa across from them and Mr. Lawrence at the head of the table.

"Evenin', gentlemen," Dawson said as he made his way around the table shaking hands and slapping backs.

"Good to see you, man," Asher said as he stood to shake Dawson's hand. "How are you?"

"Any better, and I'd be you. What brings you out here?"

"Just getting the tires changed on Haley's truck. She drives like the law is after her twenty-four-seven."

"We keep a close eye on her," Asa said.

Asher laughed, but the smile on his face was nothing but pure, gushy love for his feisty wife. "Then you're smarter than you look."

"Olivia isn't here," Jacob said.

The room erupted into laughter, and Dawson joined. "Buddy, you'll understand one day."

"Not today, though," Asa added.

Jacob shrugged like he wasn't sure he cared to understand why Dawson followed Olivia around like a lost puppy. "Where is she?"

Dawson picked up a paper bowl and started filling it with chili. "Church. They're packing for the Fish and Loaves ministry tonight."

Jacob turned to his dad. "Oh, I want to do that too. Can I go next time?"

Asa nodded until he finished chewing the bite in his mouth. "Sure. Lyric is there now. I didn't know you wanted in on it."

"I do," Jacob said quickly. "I've heard Lyric and Olivia talk about it before."

Dawson added a pile of cheese to the chili and took the last seat at the table. "Then consider yourself volunteered. Liv would love to see more kids helping out."

"How's Liv doing?" Mr. Lawrence asked. "I haven't seen her all week."

Dawson didn't run into Mr. Lawrence nearly as often as he did Beau and Olivia, despite the goats living on the old man's farm. Mr. Lawrence lived a quiet life since his wife's death, though Olivia constantly pushed him to get out of the house.

For the first time in a while, Dawson noted the extra gray hairs on the man's head and the sagging skin under his jaw. Mr. Lawrence was Dawson's hero growing up–a man who worked hard, loved the

Lord, and made sure his family was fed and clothed.

Everything Dawson's dad wasn't. He couldn't imagine Jerry Lawrence bailing on his family. What made a man do that anyway?

He looked back at Jerry. For once, the giant of Dawson's childhood looked tired. "She's good I guess. I haven't seen her much this week either. She's been busy."

"She came by earlier and dropped off the chili," Beau said without looking up from his bowl.

Mr. Lawrence shook his head, but the grin on his face said he was proud. "That girl is something else."

Dawson often had trouble explaining his unwavering attraction to Olivia. Not because of her looks, but the way she compelled him toward her without a single word. She radiated kindness and love. Who wouldn't want to be around that?

But Dawson couldn't break free of that bond, and he hadn't tried. He wanted to stay stuck in Olivia's orbit his entire life.

"How are things going with you two?" Asa asked.

Jacob's chin lifted, zeroing in on Dawson like he was about to spout off the answers to the questions on his next test.

"Awesome. Well, I'm sure it would be better if I'd seen her this week, but things are good."

For someone with a lot of doubts hanging

around like hungry buzzards, he sure could pull off the aloof act when pressured.

Dawson's phone dinged in his chest pocket, and he pulled it out. A text from Lyric had the last few bites of chili threatening to revolt in his stomach.

Lyric: Warning. Liv is freaking out a little bit about the reel that went viral.

Dawson flipped over to the Instagram app to see thousands of unread messages and comments.

"Son of a tater tot," he whispered as he spotted the number of views on the reel. He'd posted it earlier on a whim while he'd been missing Olivia like crazy.

"Oh, tater tots would go great with chili," Jacob said.

"What's wrong?" Asa asked.

Dawson typed out a quick message.

Dawson: Does she want me to delete it?

He switched back over to the Instagram app. The number of likes and views on the reel kept climbing. Dawson gripped the phone in his hand, willing it to slow down. "I posted a reel on Instagram this morning, and it's taking on a mind of its own."

Beau scoffed. "You take your shirt off again?"

A reply came in from Lyric.

Lyric: No. But I think she got a little freaked out after Anna called.

Dawson dropped the phone on the table and covered his face with his hands. "I messed up."

"What'd ya do?" Jacob asked.

"I kinda implied that Olivia and I should get together."

"And... that's bad?" Jacob looked back and forth between his dad and Dawson.

"It's not bad, but it's not great because Olivia wasn't ready to tell everyone we're dating."

Jacob tilted his head, clearly confused. "But you are dating. And we know. Why wouldn't you tell everyone?"

Asa clapped a hand on his son's shoulder. "Grownups don't always know what they're doing."

Jacob's shoulders sank. "Aw man. I was hoping I'd know everything when I hit twenty."

Asher had just taken a drink, and he covered his mouth to contain the spit as he choked on a laugh.

Dawson pointed his spoon at Jacob. "One thing I do know is that you do whatever your woman says to do. That also means I might have just made a big mess."

"What kinda mess?" Jacob asked.

Gage Howard walked into the kitchen, and Dawson watched him carefully. The guy had grease from his bearded face to his boots and wore the same Black Sabbath T-shirt he'd worn for one of his mugshots.

Yeah, Dawson had brushed up on some records when Beau hired the guy. He didn't love the idea of

Gage working in the place where Olivia, Lyric, and Jacob liked to hang out.

Gage opened the refrigerator and pulled out a bottle of water. He turned around to prop his back against the counter and crossed his ankles.

Dawson leveled him with a warning glare.

"Don't stop now," Asher said. "I'm invested in this story like it's my retirement plan."

Gage took a sip of water and stared around the room. "Don't mind me," he whispered.

No one said a word, and Dawson wasn't about to talk about Olivia with Gage around. He took a breath and turned his attention back to his chili. Beau needed the help, and running off the only guy in town who knew the difference between a crescent wrench and a pipe wrench wasn't going to help anyone.

Still, that didn't mean Dawson had to befriend the guy.

"Like I was saying," Dawson continued, "I just don't know if I should wear the green shirt that matches my shoelaces or the gold shirt that brings out the flecks of amber in my eyes."

Gage pushed off the counter and headed for the door without looking back.

Beau glared at Dawson when Gage was out of earshot. "Dude, lay off."

"I know he works here now, but you won't catch

me braiding his hair and going fishing with him anytime soon."

Asa pinched the bridge of his nose. "I don't like him being here either, but Beau needs the help."

"I know. I know. I'll behave, but I can't let down my guard around him."

"I get it. I wish I had other choices too, but the guy knows cars and he gets the job done," Beau said.

"So things are working out? No issues?" Dawson asked.

"Fine so far."

Asher cleared his throat. "As much as I love dancing around our feelings for Gage, can we hear more about your budding relationship with Olivia? Haley is going to want all the details when I get home."

"We're not telling anyone yet. Well, a lot of people know, but we want to keep it sort of secret until Olivia gets to talk to...someone."

Asher propped his elbows on the table and steepled his fingers. "That's not vague and curious at all. Who are we not telling?"

"Anna Harris."

Asher nodded. "I won't tell. Well, except Haley, of course. You know, Haley and I kept things a secret for a while too."

Asa leaned back in his chair and crossed his arms over his chest. "I remember that. She dated Micah first."

Dawson laughed. "Love triangle plus brothers equals disaster."

Asher rubbed the back of his neck. "Could'a been. Thankfully, it all worked out."

Jacob held up a hand. "Wait, are you saying Haley and Micah dated? I didn't know that."

"They didn't really date," Asher explained. "They were talking on a dating app, and when she came to surprise him with a visit, she thought I was him."

"And planted a big kiss on him before realizing she'd smooched the wrong brother." Dawson slapped the table as another laugh bubbled out of him. "Those were good times."

"Happy to be your comedic relief today," Asher said. "Yeah, it was a mess for a hot minute, but we got things worked out. You and Olivia will too."

Dawson pushed around the chili he'd barely eaten. The gnawing in his gut about the viral reel was still too fresh. "I think you're right, but I need things with Olivia and Anna to smooth over before I'll sleep easy at night."

Mr. Lawrence shifted in his chair and propped his elbows on the table, leveling Dawson with the fatherly look he'd seen the man give his own kids hundreds of times over the years. "The Lord has someone for all of us, and if it's meant to be with Olivia, things will work out at the right time."

"I hope so, sir. I'm trying to be patient, but I've been hung up on Olivia for a decade."

The older man's beard twitched to one side, and a smile crinkled the lines on the outsides of his eyes. "Did I ever tell you about how I got together with Martha?"

A wave of reverence relaxed Dawson's shoulders. Mr. Lawrence hardly ever talked about his late wife. "No, sir."

Mr. Lawrence blinked down at the table as he composed himself. Or maybe he was traveling back down memory lane.

"We went to school together. I'd known her all my life. Martha was always quiet, and she might as well have been another faceless person in my class all those years.

"But one day, I woke up. She walked into Deano's with her friends, and I immediately noticed her. I stopped hearing anything my buddies said and walked right up to Martha and asked her if I could buy her breakfast."

"I bet she liked that," Jacob said.

Mr. Lawrence chuckled. "She did not."

"What?" Jacob's wide eyes moved from one man at the table to the next, trying to understand why a woman would turn down a free meal.

"Because she wasn't interested in one meal. Martha knew what she wanted and what she didn't want, and she wasn't about to get our wires crossed over a plate of biscuits and gravy."

Jacob scratched his head. "But you two got married," he pointed out.

"We did, but it wasn't easy. She was a stubborn one. She had her own thoughts about me before she got to know me, and I had a long row to hoe when it came to convincing her things with us could be more than just a flash in the pan."

"I don't know what that means," Jacob said.

Asa patted his son's shoulder. "She wanted a commitment, and she was afraid he only wanted a fling."

The kid nodded. "Oh, okay. That makes sense."

Mr. Lawrence stared down at his empty dinner bowl. The man probably had a million memories running through his head. Losing the woman you love had to be torture of the worst kind.

"She was beautiful, but that's not why I noticed her. It had nothing to do with Aquanet or that smile that lit up a room. No, it was all about that woman's heart. It was because she helped someone."

Shoot. Dawson's throat was threatening to close. There wasn't anything as gut-wrenching as watching a man relive true happiness while realizing he'd never have it again.

Mr. Lawrence sighed. "There was an old man at the checkout counter at Deano's. He'd stopped by the diner for breakfast, but he noticed his wallet was missing after placing his breakfast order.

"I knew enough about Martha to know her family was just as poor as the rest of us. She probably only had enough money with her to buy her own meal that day. I had to beg her to let me buy her breakfast, but I think I bought every meal she ate after that one."

Olivia's heart was just like her mother's. She couldn't sleep at night knowing she hadn't done something for someone else, and she never asked for payment. She just worked extra hours to cover the costs.

Dawson had plenty of friends, but at that moment, he understood Olivia's dad as if they shared the same mind.

"I was drawn to her goodness," Mr. Lawrence said. "She made me a better man every single day."

Nodding, Dawson met the man's stare. "It's the same with Olivia."

"She picked up right where her mother left off. She needs a man who will support her like that."

"You don't have anything to worry about, sir. I'm behind her one hundred percent."

Mr. Lawrence's mustache crinkled. "I know you are, son. You two will figure it out."

"Yeah, I think it'll be okay too once the storm blows over," Asa said.

Storm. That was a good way to describe what was coming. It definitely wouldn't be peaceful, but if Anna was half the friend Dawson thought she was, she'd see Olivia's heart and be happy for them.

In a perfect world.

Asa stood and started stacking empty bowls. "You two are the home team. We've been rootin' for you since day one."

Dawson's phone dinged, and he pulled it out. A text from Olivia waited.

Olivia: Tonight sounds good. Your place?

Dawson pocketed the phone and picked up his empty bowl. "You're right. We'll figure it out."

They had to. Losing wasn't an option.

27

OLIVIA

Olivia parked in front of Dawson's place and turned off the car. Her heart wasn't beating like a war drum in her chest anymore, but she shook out her sweaty hands.

The Fish and Loaves packing had taken her mind off the call with Anna, but now the task in front of her was focusing in her mind's eye again.

She got out and blinked to adjust her night vision. Dawson's porch light was on, and her headlights hadn't turned off yet. Still, there was a chill in the September air that had her jogging for the house.

She reached for the door and opened it without knocking. After being cornered by wolves, leaving her back exposed to the night was a big no-go.

"Dawson!" she shouted as she tossed her purse onto a cornflower-blue recliner in the living room. A fire crackled in the fireplace, and *NYPD Blue* played on the muted TV.

The moment her word died in the air, a heavy stomping bounded down the hallway. Dawson jogged into the living room and straight toward her. Within a second, she was twirling through the air in his arms. Wrapping her legs around him, she clung to him as if her life depended on him. After the evening she'd had, Dawson was a lifeboat to her sinking ship.

"I missed you like crazy, my queen," Dawson whispered against her ear.

"I missed you too." Why did it feel like a wall was crumbling inside her chest? Why did Dawson Keller have the ability to absolutely crush her with just a few words?

Dawson kissed her forehead before pressing his lips to hers. The contact breathed life into her entire body, and she kissed him back with everything she had. They'd waited so long for these stolen moments, and it was as if everything she'd felt for Dawson over the years was continuously rising and spilling over the dam. Nothing could contain it.

Olivia threaded her fingers in his hair, preventing him from pulling away as she kissed him long and wanting. Every brush of his mouth against hers whispered silent promises.

Dawson continued kissing her as he turned and walked to the couch. Sitting down, she settled in his lap as the force of their kiss calmed from a thunderstorm to a gentle rain.

Dawson peppered small kisses on her lips, then her cheeks, before moving to her temple and forehead. He rested his head against hers and inhaled a deep breath. "I want to hear all about your day," he whispered. "Your whole week. Tell me everything."

Olivia rested her head against his shoulder. "Can we just stay like this for a minute?"

His arms caged her in, holding her up in more ways than one.

"As long as you need."

She tightened her hold around his neck. "I'm terrified of telling her," she whispered.

Brushing a hand over her hair, he whispered, "Don't worry, my queen. We'll figure this out."

"How?" Olivia lifted her head to face him. "She was upset when she called me about the reel, and I had no words. None. I was paralyzed with fear."

Dawson brushed her hair from her face. "That's a good thing."

Olivia jerked back, caught off-guard by his response. "Are you crazy? That's not good."

"It means you care, which tells me that no matter what, we're going to get through this. You care about us, and you care about Anna too. You're a good friend. You realize that's where all this comes from, right? You're worried about hurting someone else, and it's hurting you."

Olivia's shoulders slumped. She carried exhaustion like a pile of firewood on her back. "I can't hurt her," she whispered. The words slicing through her throat left it burning and stinging.

"You won't."

Olivia swiped the back of her hand under her nose. "Can we talk about that video? How has it had over a million and a half views?"

"I have no idea. I didn't know it would cause a problem with Anna before I posted it. I just had you on my mind and wanted the world to know."

That longing in her own heart recognized the need in him. Hadn't she been fighting against the same urge to shout about her feelings? It was the biggest, most exciting news of her life, and she couldn't openly show her happiness. Hiding it from the world felt wrong.

Dawson cradled her face, directing her attention to his hazy blue eyes. His massive hands only reminded her of his size. Dawson was tall and lean but every inch of him was carefully corded with muscle. The strong hands on her cheeks belonged to the gentle giant who fought off the screaming doubts in her mind with a whisper.

"This isn't going away, Liv." He swallowed hard and locked his steel-blue eyes on her. "I love you."

Her small gasp was immediate, but all surprise dissipated in the next instant. Those three little words were amazing and familiar. So much had changed between them recently, but so much was still the same.

It wasn't love, was it?

It was. The asking revealed the answer in her own heart.

Dawson's smile grew as his gaze brushed over her. "I've loved you in so many stages of your life. I've loved you through days and weeks and years. I've loved you through thousands of yesterdays and tomorrows. I've loved you as long as I can remember, and I'll love you until the very end. Whatever happens, we'll make it through together."

Olivia wrapped her arms around his neck and squeezed. Every doubt and every worry slipped away in the wake of Dawson's love. It was the piece of the puzzle she'd been afraid to place, but it fit perfectly into the life they were building together. "I love you too."

"Really? I thought it would take you at least a month or two," Dawson said.

Olivia laughed through silent tears. "You've only been my best friend for two decades."

"Are you saying it's about time? 'Cause that's what I was thinking."

She sat up in his lap and wiped the tears from her eyes. "I know you're right. I just had a rough day, and I still haven't figured out how to tell her."

"We can tell her together. Strength in numbers, right?"

Olivia shook her head. "She's leaving tomorrow for a trial in Casper. She'll be gone for at least a week. It's a big one."

"Then let's relax for a week."

A spicy scent tickled her nose, and she sniffed. "What's that smell?"

Dawson's eyes widened and he stood, carrying her toward the kitchen with her legs and arms still locked around him. "Oh shoot. I forgot I made you dinner."

"Really? I'm starving."

"Steak and potatoes for my queen," Dawson said as he set her on the kitchen counter by the sink. He lifted the cover off a plate revealing what looked like a juicy T-bone.

"There's only one," she said.

"I ate the chili you dropped off at the garage earlier, but I figured you'd be hungry after working at the church."

She reached for him, wrapping her arms around his neck and squeezing hard. When she let him go, he let out a series of coughs.

Oh no, she'd squeezed the life out of him. She couldn't have a boyfriend for a week without proving to be a danger to his health. "I'm sorry. I'm so sorry."

Dawson coughed again and shook his head. His voice was hoarse when he spoke. "I'm not complaining. Death by being overloved by you would be a good way to go."

She rolled her eyes, but he probably didn't even notice the exaggeration. Dawson lived in a world of all or nothing. He wasn't a lukewarm kinda guy.

That was exactly why she could trust every word he said. He loved her, and it wasn't a surprise. Everything he did reflected that confession. He didn't just speak love, he lived it. He thought of her when they were apart. He checked on her when she got home in the evenings. He took care of her in little moments throughout their life without even telling her.

Dawson was love in action. In a world of black and white, he was vibrant color.

He stepped to the side and moved her plate to the table. "What can I get you to drink?"

"Water would be great." She hopped off the counter and took her seat at the table.

Dawson had a glass of ice water sitting in front of her within seconds and took the seat beside her. "You want me to pray?"

Olivia nodded and bowed her head. No one but Dawson would be that excited to pray a blessing over someone else's food. The selflessness of the moment stuck in her throat as he thanked the Lord for everything from breath in their lungs to the grocery store that butchered the meat.

Dawson filled her in on things at work while she ate. He mostly told her about how Lyric was settling into her dispatch job. Then he moved on to the restoration he was working on at Beau's garage.

When she finished eating, she pulled out her phone and checked the few messages she'd skipped over throughout the day. One was a reminder about an upcoming appointment with her doctor.

The date in the text message ticked like a clock. She'd forgotten all about the appointment. Life had been coming up roses, but now the frost was coming full-force to kill the beautiful moment.

"Liv?"

Olivia looked up at Dawson. He stood beside her with a hand extended.

"You okay?"

She took his hand and stood, sliding the phone back into her pocket. "Yeah." Her throat threatened to close, but she had to get the words out before she lost her nerve. "We need to talk."

28

DAWSON

Talking was good. Talking was normal and fine. It was a casual thing he did with Olivia every day.

But "We need to talk" referenced a conversation that would probably chew him up and spit him out.

"Um, okay. What do you want to talk about? I've already thought about our couple name. I prefer Olison over Dalivia."

Olivia chuckled, which was a good sign. She still looked happy behind her tired eyes. "It's not necessarily...awful, but it's definitely a serious conversation that impacts our relationship."

"More than this stuff with Anna? Come on, Liv, there can't be that many things standing in our way."

When Olivia didn't outright agree with him, he reached for her, pulling her to rest against his chest where she belonged. "I love you. We can get through anything."

"If we both *want* to, that is."

Dawson took a step back so he could see her face. "What does that mean? I always want this. I want us. More than anything."

She swallowed hard and nodded. Her easygoing attitude from earlier was gone, replaced by a nervous humming that radiated from her entire body. "I know you do. I do too. But let's go sit on the couch."

She threaded her fingers in his and led him into the living room. This was one of those times when he wanted to dig in his heels and run away from whatever trouble Olivia was about to reveal.

But if it was her problem, then it was his problem now too. They would do everything together from here on out, and what better time to start than right now?

She settled onto the couch with her legs tucked underneath her before she patted the seat beside her.

Not liking the idea of any space between them when they needed to be a united front, Dawson sat beside her, lifting her knees until they rested on top of his thigh.

Olivia took a deep breath and faced him. Red splotches crept up her neck as she swiped her hands down her thigh.

Dawson covered her hand with his. "Let's play a game."

"This isn't a game," she whispered mournfully, as if she'd give anything to participate in something as simple as a game when this revelation was causing her to break out in hives.

"Do you trust me?" he asked.

"Of course I do."

"Then humor me. Let's tell secrets."

Olivia huffed a small breath. The golden flecks in her hazel eyes blended with the brown and green as they turned glassy. "Yeah. I guess that's what we're doing anyway."

Dawson rubbed lazy circles over the back of her hand. If he could convince her that he wasn't worried, maybe she'd calm down too. "One good secret and one that's...not so good. I'll go first."

She rested the side of her head against the back of the couch and grinned, but the expression was somber. "Okay."

"First, I don't know if you know this, but I've been thinking about applying for a job."

That got her attention. She lifted her head and squeezed his hand. "What? What kind of job?"

"Sergeant."

There. He said it. Now, what would she do with it? He'd been kicking the idea around for months, but actually telling someone was bigger than he'd expected.

Love for a Lifetime

"Sergeant? Really? That's amazing. It's exciting!"

Her joy lit him up from the inside out. Olivia sure knew how to supercharge his mood. "I've been talking to Chief about it. He thinks I'd be a good fit. I've been studying for the sergeant's exam."

Olivia slid her hand through her hair. Her mouth hung open for a few seconds before she clamped it closed. "I'm so excited for you. That's huge."

"For us." Dawson held up their linked hands. "This is about us. The pay is better. I don't need much, but if it's going to be the two of us, I want you to know I'll always provide for you. That means I intend to make sure you have all the money you need to volunteer and support all of the things you already do and more. I know how much it means to you."

Olivia's head tilted slightly, and a rogue wrinkle dipped between her brows. "You'd get a different job so I could..." She waved her hands in the air because she couldn't think of the words to describe her thoughts.

"So you can give more. I know how much you love it."

"I do, but I would never do more than we could afford. I mean... what are we even talking about? We're not married. Our finances aren't even combined yet."

"Whoa, whoa, whoa, whoa. It's not crazy to think about those things. That's where this is headed for me. You have to know I want the long-haul with you. This is the love of a lifetime, Liv. I know what I want, and it's this. You. Us."

Olivia sniffed and pulled her hand from his to wipe her cheek. "Dawson, we need to talk–"

"Wait, please. That was my good secret. Now I have a bad one to tell you."

She ducked her chin but gave him a small nod.

Putting it all on the line was his shot in the dark at making this whole game worth it. He had to prove to Olivia that they could share anything–the good and the bad. He had to show her that some things were tough, but since neither of them were perfect, they had to be a united front and face them together.

"I bumped into my dad a few months ago," Dawson said, hating the way his chest tightened at the mention of the man who'd abandoned him.

Not just him. Jared Keller had disappeared without a trace, leaving Dawson, his mom, and Jeremy to fend for themselves. Hadn't even looked back.

Years of resentment had clawed out a black hole in the deepest, darkest parts of Dawson's heart, and he did a good job of keeping his feelings about the man under wraps.

"Dawson, why didn't you tell me? What did he say? How did it go?"

Now, for the tricky part. The part that he didn't want to confess.

"He asked me to look him up if I was ever in Silver Falls."

Olivia covered her mouth, cutting off a gasp. "He's in Silver Falls? That's not far from here."

"Yeah. I was picking up a part for the Porsche when I ran into him on the sidewalk outside the shop. He has a family there. Apparently, there are more Kellers running around that Mom doesn't know about."

"Would she care? I mean, does she still have feelings for him?"

"Not a chance. He was dead to her as soon as he walked out, but I bet it would still hurt. He didn't want the family he had, but I guess the second time was the charm."

She reached out and grabbed his hand. "Dawson, you have to know it's not your fault. Or your mom's. If he left you, he missed out. You're a great man, and... I can't understand why he left you, but I'm proud of the man you've become."

Dawson twisted his fingers around hers, keeping their bond moving and fluid as the secrets poured out. "We held things together without him. Mom is a rock star, and she made sure we had everything we needed. I don't regret any of that. That's not the bad part."

He looked up at her and prepared for the disappointment he knew was coming. "He wanted to get to know me. He asked for a chance."

Olivia didn't say anything. She just kept her hold on his hand and his heart.

"I told him there wasn't anything in Silver Falls I cared about. Which is a total lie because some of my friends live there, but I wanted him to hurt. I wanted to stick just one knife underneath his armor and twist."

"That's kind of understandable, considering what he put you through," Olivia whispered.

"Yeah, but we both know it wasn't the right thing to do. I know I could have said worse things, but he actually looked hurt. Why do I even care if he's upset? I shouldn't."

"It's because you're a good person."

Dawson groaned. "Are you throwing my own words back at me? What is this about us caring too much about what other people think?"

"Life would be easier if we didn't care," she said.

Dawson leaned in and touched his forehead to hers, breathing her in like new rain on a summer's day. "Whatever you have to say, I care. It matters to me, and you don't have to be nervous."

"Okay," she whispered.

He raised his head but brushed a thumb over her cheek. She was brave. He'd known that for a long time. Would she trust him to stand by her?

"Start with the good," he reminded her.

She looked around as if she were searching the

room for the answer, tapping her fingertip against her chin. "A good secret."

"Good luck finding something I don't already know about you."

A soft chuckle reminded him that no matter what good she told him now, something bad that he truly didn't know was waiting to throw their carefully-held peace into chaos.

Olivia shifted in her seat. "Okay. Do you remember when we were little and used to ride bikes at North Park?"

"Yeah, that was only half of our childhood. Mom took us there every Friday after school."

"You and Beau hated that Jeremy and I had to tag along."

Dawson held up a finger. "Not true. I liked it when you were around. Jeremy, on the other hand–"

"Jeremy got you into so much trouble," she finished.

"I got blamed for all kinds of things I didn't even do!"

Olivia rolled her eyes, but a smile played on her lips. "He was just trying to get his big brother's attention."

"He succeeded. I couldn't relax around him my entire childhood."

"But you love him."

"Well, yeah. He's a twerp, but he's family."

"Exactly. Well, back to my secret. I think I was

about five when this started. I just remember that I still had training wheels."

"You had training wheels until you were almost eight. You were the worst driver I've ever seen."

That honesty earned him a true laugh. Olivia tilted her head back and let the sound bubble out of her. "I've been told that a time or two."

"Your mom used to tell me and Beau all the time to prepare ourselves because we'd be driving you around for half our lives."

"And she was right. I didn't pass my driver's test until I was almost seventeen."

"But you're a decent driver now."

"I'm better than a decent driver," she said, lifting her chin at his little jab.

"I think I recall pulling you over last month for speeding in a school zone."

Her smile faded, and he watched as the light dimmed in her eyes. "Do you remember when we used to race on our bikes?"

"Yeah."

Olivia lifted Dawson's hand and pressed her palm to his, studying the way his hand engulfed her small one. "I think I've loved you since then–when you used to let me have a head start."

The word love reached out and punched him in the chest. He'd loved Olivia so long she had seeped into his skin and threaded herself into his atoms.

But he'd always assumed she was slower to warm

up to the idea. His love had been a constant while hers was a seed that had barely broken ground.

At least, that's what he'd assumed.

"What are you talking about?" he asked.

"We would line up and you would say 'go,' but you never started when I did. You let me get ahead."

He remembered that. It wasn't anything he'd made a conscious decision to do, but he'd started holding Beau back to let her have a chance.

"A lot of good it did. Beau always jumped off the starting line and flew past you like a slingshot."

"But that didn't matter. I didn't even realize you were giving me a head start until years later. Do you have any idea how much that meant to me?"

He didn't. He hadn't even thought about it. Now, she'd brought him face-to-face with the memory, and love for the little girl she'd been welled up inside him. As much as he'd love a son to fish and hunt with, having a little girl who looked just like Olivia would absolutely overwhelm him.

She brushed a hair behind her ear before returning her hand to his. "I want you to know that this hasn't been one-sided. I've been terrified of loving you for a long time. It's taking some time to get used to…acting on it."

"I'm not rushing you. If it sounds like I'm moving too fast, just tell me."

Olivia shook her head. "It's not that. I have a doctor's appointment tomorrow, and…it's probably not going to go well. I haven't told you about it. Only a handful of people know."

The extra second it took him to respond jammed in his throat. He didn't want to push her to share something with him that she didn't want to, but knowing others knew things about her that he didn't was like a sucker punch.

"Why wouldn't it go well? Are you sick?" The mere idea of Olivia suffering through something alone made him want to scream.

"Not sick, but it's sort of like that. Remember when Levi was at the farm and I was hurting?"

"Yeah." That was a moment in time he'd rather not relive. Being helpless was the worst, and knowing he couldn't help her then was like having his hands tied behind his back.

"I have endometriosis. It's a condition some women have that can be painful. The gist of it is that sometimes endometrial tissue grows in places it shouldn't."

That didn't make a lot of sense, but he'd be doing his own research as soon as this conversation was over. "Is there a cure? Will it get worse? Will it go away?"

"Well, there's not a clear-cut answer. There isn't a pill that can cure it. It does get worse over time. It could go away, but it would take surgical intervention."

A wave of cold washed over his skin. Surgery

could be minor or major. Associating Olivia with that unknown danger turned his stomach. With or without surgery, she'd been living with this pain for a while, and she'd hidden it well.

"The appointment tomorrow is to talk about what type of surgery my doctor thinks I should have."

Dawson's nostrils flared as he tried to suck in enough air to calm his racing heart. "There are different kinds? What's the difference? Do these doctors know what they're doing?"

Olivia laughed quick and sharp. "Yeah, I think they know what they're doing. You can breathe. They're not really dangerous surgeries."

"Sorry. I'm panicking a little." That was an understatement. He was freaking out on the inside. Completely losing his cool. "Can you break it down in simple terms for me? What would these surgeries do?"

"The minor option is a procedure I've done before. They basically scrape out a lot of the tissue that's not where it's supposed to be. Cleaning things out. It could come back, like it has before."

She'd done this before? How had he not known?

"I kept it a secret. Stop overthinking it."

"I'm definitely overthinking it. I see you all the time."

"It was years ago."

"Still, I would have noticed."

"I told everyone I was sick. I rested and recovered quickly. I mentioned that it's pretty minor."

Dawson rubbed the back of his neck, feeling the sticky clamminess of his skin. "I can't believe I didn't notice. I could have been there for you. I could have–"

"I didn't want anyone to know. It's kind of a personal thing. No woman wants to explain to her neighbors and friends that she has a disease that's particular to the female reproductive system."

Dawson scanned back through their years together. When and how had she completely hidden this from him and everyone else?

"The other option is a form of a hysterectomy. It's a common surgery, but..." She shrugged and looked down at their linked hands. "But that means I can't have kids."

Dawson stared at her, waiting for some other information that would erase what she'd just said.

Olivia wouldn't be able to have kids.

He couldn't breathe–couldn't move. Everything in the room blurred except for Olivia's face as he focused on her.

Of all the things she could have told him, this was completely unexpected. He wanted kids. He knew *she* wanted kids. The magnitude of what she was dealing with choked him like unrelenting hands around his neck.

A sob broke from Olivia's chest. She pressed a hand to her mouth as her shoulders shook.

Dawson scooped her up in his arms and moved her to his lap. Her head pressed against his shoulder as she cried. A gut-wrenching cry that split him open.

He wrapped his arms around her, shielding her from the reality closing in around them.

"Can I go with you? Tomorrow?" he asked.

Olivia didn't answer. She wailed and cried until her frame rested limp against him.

When her tears slowed, he asked again. "Can I go with you?"

"I don't know." She wiped at her nose with her sleeve. "I–I don't know what this means for us. I know you want..." She sucked in a shaky breath. "I know you want kids."

"I know you want kids too, but if that isn't in the cards for us, then it isn't."

"How can you say that?" she asked with a wail. "This is a huge deal. If we get further into this and you decide you want kids, it'll just be harder for both of us."

Dawson leaned to the side and lifted her chin with a finger. "Olivia, I'm so far into this there's no going back. This is a shock, but I already told you there's nothing we can't get through together."

She heaved a fractured breath. "Just because this

is my fate doesn't mean it has to be yours. You'd make a great dad, and I can't..."

"If you're not going to be a mom, then I'm not going to be a dad. It's that simple, Liv. There are other ways. We could foster or adopt. Maybe you only need the other surgery."

She shook her head. "The other surgery leaves behind a lot of internal scarring. Even if I don't have the hysterectomy, it could still be hard for me to get pregnant."

He pulled her to him and breathed in the soft, comforting scent of her hair. With his eyes closed, the scent tingled in his nose and calmed his roaring thoughts enough to let him think.

Lord, I need You. I need words and wisdom, but Olivia needs strength, peace, and healing. I need understanding, but I bring it all to You. I know You have a plan, and I bow to it. Whatever the outcome, give us the strength to endure it.

Olivia's arms tightened around him. "Thank you," she said shakily.

He hadn't realized he was praying out loud, but he didn't want to keep anything from Olivia. If he was praying, she had a right to hear it.

"Liv, whatever happens, I'll be right here. I love you just as you are, and you won't ever be alone. This doesn't change anything."

"You'll resent me. If you can't have kids, you'll–"

"I won't. You have to trust me on this. I know you

think you know how I'll feel, but you don't. You have no idea how devoted I am to you. I fell in love with *you*. Everything else flows from that."

Dawson nudged his nose against hers and she looked up at him. Her eyes were swollen and pink with red splotches down her cheeks.

"Can I go with you tomorrow?"

"Why do you want to go? It's just a consultation."

"Because I'm worried sick about you, and I want to be there for you. I said you'll never have to do anything alone, and I meant it."

Olivia sniffed and wiped at her face. "You have to work tomorrow."

"That's the least of my worries. My queen needs me, and you better believe I know where to line up."

Olivia nodded, squeezing her eyes closed.

"Do you believe me?" Dawson asked.

She nodded again.

"I'm gonna need a verbal confirmation. Try 'Yes, Dawson. I know you're in this for the long haul, no matter what, cross my heart, no take-backsies, one hundred percent.'"

Her laugh was hoarse, but the sound had his aching heart lifting like a hot air balloon.

That understanding and peace he'd prayed for settled in, and Olivia's tears dried. The appointment would come with its own uncertainties, but tonight, he'd love her like there was no tomorrow.

29

DAWSON

Dawson walked into the station whistling a hit Country song from the 90s. Last night with Olivia was rough, but he'd woken up with a new outlook on life.

Everything was going to work out. He'd laid it all at the feet of Jesus and stepped back. Whatever happened at Olivia's appointment today, he'd trust that it was all for the good.

That's what Dawson was doing. Olivia? She'd still been nervous when he talked to her before his shift.

She was going to be a tough egg to crack, but who could blame her? The future she wanted was hanging in the balance.

He'd spent half the night sorting through his own worries about Olivia's health. His first thoughts were for her physical and mental state, but he'd thought just enough about her possible future with or without kids to know that *he* would be okay either way.

Would she?

Of course it was a big deal–a huge deal–but he hadn't lost hope when she first told him she might not be able to have kids. There was still a possibility, and he'd had a good feeling when he suggested fostering or adopting.

The station was bustling, but no one was stomping around or loudly popping off information. That was always a good sign. Asa stood beside Lyric's desk, looking down at her with a goofy grin on his face.

The guy was head over heels–totally drooling over his new wife.

Who could blame him? Dawson was finally getting the chance to love Olivia like he'd always wanted, and he'd been obnoxiously obsessed with all things Olivia the entire week. He couldn't go a minute without thinking about her, and he had zero intentions to change.

"Morning, ladies and gentlemen," Dawson said as he walked by them, tipping an imaginary hat.

"What are you doing here?" Lyric asked.

"Gotta write up a report before heading out for the rest of the day."

Asa propped his back against the wall by Lyric's desk. "Where are you going?"

He'd promised not to share about Olivia's problems, so he went with the closest thing that wasn't a lie. "I'm hanging out with Olivia this afternoon."

Lyric clasped her hands at her chest. "Aww. That's so sweet."

"Missing work already. You got it bad, man," Asa said.

Lyric swatted her husband's arm. "Stop it. It's cute, and Dawson never takes off days." She turned to Dawson with a smile. "I'm so happy for y'all."

"Not as happy as I am," Dawson said.

"Happy about what?"

Dawson turned at the question to find Olivia walking up. A pastel green headband that matched her sweater pushed back her long, dark hair, and she carried a big white bag with a Deano's logo on it.

Dawson was heading toward her before his feet knew what they were doing. He took the bag from her hands and moved it to the side as he pressed a kiss to her lips. It ended too quickly, and it took Olivia an extra second to open up her eyes.

"Hello, my queen. I thought we were meeting at the doctor's office," he whispered.

After a short hesitation and a longing look meant just for him, she said, "I left work a little early to change and grab some lunch." She tilted her head toward the bag he now held. "Want to eat before we go?"

"I will never say no to food, though you're the bigger and better surprise."

He held her close to his side as she scanned the room around them. At least a dozen people milled about, but he doubted anyone cared about their public displays of affection.

"What if someone sees us?" Olivia whispered.

"Anna is out of town. We have a few days before we have to worry about that," he reminded her.

"It's not just Anna. What if someone sees and tells her?"

Dawson released Olivia and gestured for her to head toward the break room. "Okay, I'll keep my hands to myself."

She pressed up onto her toes and whispered against his cheek, "Not that I mind. I've been thinking about kissing you all day."

Dawson's breaths deepened. That was one way to make his brain short circuit. Every sound in the room faded as he grabbed her hand and pulled her toward the break room.

Olivia giggled behind him. "What are you doing?"

"Praying for an empty room." He dragged her into the quiet room, put the bag on the counter, and twirled her around to face him.

He cut off her laugh with a kiss, tasting that sweet melody that hummed through his entire body.

Kissing Olivia was an otherworldly experience. It

was a give and take that balanced everything. They both gave their whole selves every time their lips slid against each other. His hold tightened around her waist with the need to crush her to him, eliminating all space that separated them.

Holding back the floodgates for over a decade had taken all of his self-control, and giving in was blissful and dangerous.

Olivia pulled back and hummed low in her throat. "As much as I'd love to keep doing this, we need to eat quickly if we're going to make it to the appointment on time."

The appointment. Nope. Dawson would not let that little ticking time bomb ruin this moment or any other.

"I don't need food. I need you." He pressed another quick kiss to her lips before pulling back to say, "I'll feed you on the drive over."

Olivia pushed against his chest with a hearty laugh. "I have a feeling that would break a few laws." She pointed to the bag of food. "Eat."

"What's on the menu?" He opened the bag and reached inside. "Skittles!"

Olivia snatched the bag from his hands. "That's for later. Food first."

"I thought being an adult meant I could eat dessert first."

She held up the candy bag and shook it, crinkling the packaging. "This is a distraction for the waiting room."

"Ah. Got it." He plucked the candy from her hand and stuffed it in his pocket. "Let's eat so we can make out in my truck."

Olivia laughed loudly, then covered her mouth.

He loved that. He loved that there was so much joy in her heart that it couldn't be contained, even right before a meeting they were both dreading.

"You two are just adorable," Lyric said as she walked into the kitchen with Asa right behind her.

"Guilty, and I have no regrets," Dawson said. As soon as he got the green light to talk about their new relationship, he'd be shouting it in the streets. How awesome would it be to tell the entire world that he'd found the one woman that he was made to love and support for his entire life?

Olivia opened the bag and started pulling out containers. "There's plenty for you two if you want chicken fingers."

Of course she brought extra. Olivia never did anything halfway. It was all or nothing. She took care of people without being asked. There were dozens of people who'd been blessed by Olivia's work who didn't even know her name. She never asked for fanfare, and she was happy doing anything for someone else.

Dawson could understand that dedication. He practiced it many times himself. What was the point of doing something if you weren't going to do it right?

His love for Olivia? It was everything. She was a perfect snapshot of each part of his life. She was the light in every second, and he couldn't wait to see all the things she'd do in the Lord's name.

When they'd finished lunch with Asa and Lyric, Olivia looked at her watch. Dawson stood and started cleaning up their mess. "Time to go?"

"Almost." The word came out defeated, and she kept her head down.

Dawson tossed their trash and stopped beside her. Offering his hand, he pulled her to her feet and lifted her chin. Those hazel eyes were tired and afraid, but he wasn't. Dawson knew that whatever the outcome, it would be good.

"I'm right here with you," he whispered. "Never leaving."

She pressed her lips together and nodded. It wasn't any kind of assurance, but she'd learn over time. The Lord would never leave her or forsake her, and neither would Dawson.

30

OLIVIA

Olivia stepped into the elevator in a fog. The appointment went well. She'd kept it together in the office, and she hadn't gotten the worst news imaginable.

They. The news belonged to Dawson too, not just herself. His future was twisted up in hers for as long as he allowed it.

What a tangled mess it was. They were finally moving forward with a relationship, and her baggage was stepping into the room and calling the shots. Stripping them of options they hadn't had the chance to consider yet.

Dawson entered the elevator behind her and pressed the button for the second floor. Soon, they'd be out in the real world again, and this building and its soul-crushing news would be their souvenir–

something to carry around and remember their time here.

Time was a fickle thing measured in seconds and minutes, but it was more of a bartering tool. You get what you put in, right?

Wrong. She worked hard, loved others, and gave of herself as much as possible. What was she getting in return?

Stop. She pressed her eyes closed, shutting out the anger and doubts. It was wrong to think things like that.

Dawson wrapped his arms around her before the elevator doors closed. She let the rough planes of his uniform press against her face and body as she embraced him.

"It was good news," Dawson reminded her.

She disagreed, but they had enough problems gunning for them right now. They didn't need her negativity piled on top.

He rubbed a steadying hand up and down her back as the elevator took them farther away from the office. The doors opened on the second floor, revealing the concrete parking deck.

Dawson left one arm draped behind her as he guided her toward his truck. The stale air in the parking deck squeezed her lungs into the stone prison. A faint light shone through the openings in the outer walls, but the shadows lay claim to more than half the vehicles.

The barriers were closing in, slowing her steps and stealing her air. Or was it just the smell of oil and metal clogging her airways that had her gasping for breath.

"Liv?" Dawson's question was soft and far away, like a whisper on the wind.

"Liv, you okay?" he asked again.

He stopped and curled his arm in, dragging her back to his chest.

"I'm fine. I just need air."

She stayed pressed to his side as he led them into the open-air part of the level where they'd parked. His red truck was like a waving finish-line flag in the bright midday sun.

Dawson opened the passenger side door for her, and she slid into the cab. Seconds later, he was in his seat beside her, leaning over the console between them.

"What do you need?"

Olivia sucked in deep pulls of air. "I'm okay. Just a little shaky."

Dawson wrapped her hand in both of his and bowed his head over them. "Father, thank You for the doctor's patience as she took the time to study Olivia's condition and give us sound advice. I pray now that You would give us understanding as we go forward. Also, Olivia needs peace. I do too, but Lord, we need the constant reminder that You are here with us every step of the way. You are the Great

Physician, and we know healing and mercy comes from You. Help us to keep our focus always on You. In Jesus' name we pray. Amen."

He pressed a kiss to her knuckles and looked up at her. His soft brown eyes held an assurance she lacked but desperately wanted.

"Thank you," she whispered.

"Always. You're always in my prayers. And trust me, I talk to the Boss a lot."

The confidence in his voice steeled her spine. His faith was breathing new life into her, reminding her of all the things she'd let fall to the side in her internal spiral.

He released her hand to start the truck and back out of the parking spot. Once they were on the road back toward Blackwater, he claimed her hand again.

They had gotten good news. At least, as good as they could have hoped for. Her doctor was adamant that a hysterectomy was premature at this point. Her endometriosis was moderate and usually manageable, and Dr. Barnes was quick to assure them that kids were still a possibility at this point.

Her doctor's prayer had calmed some of the storm in her heart. She couldn't imagine battling through this journey with a doctor who thought their medical miracles happened at their own hands.

They didn't talk much on the way back. Dawson was probably going through the same emotional overload as her, and she'd almost drifted off to sleep when they passed the Welcome to Blackwater sign.

"Can we go to the farm? I need my chickies."

"Anything for you, my queen."

A few minutes later, they pulled up in front of her dad's house. His truck was gone, and he was probably helping out at Blackwater Ranch. Her dad had been spending more and more time with the Hardings since her mom died.

She couldn't blame him. She'd sought out people everywhere after her mom passed. Being alone left her too raw and susceptible to the memories.

Dawson rounded the truck as she stepped out onto the land she'd grown up on. The sun was sinking to the west, setting the tops of the trees on fire with its orange glow. Her childhood home stood steadfast and comforting like an old friend, but they walked past it with their hands linked.

Their steps weren't in sync, and she watched them with rapt attention as Dawson's longer stride beckoned her to move quicker.

Don't overthink it. You may not walk the same way, but that doesn't mean you aren't in this together.

Even her silly attempts to distract her mind were failing–crumbling as they walked in silence that threatened to crush her.

When they reached Cluckingham Palace, Olivia went straight to the hideous rusted pink chair by the chicnic table. Dawson had picked it up at a garage sale five years ago, and she couldn't bring herself to throw it out.

She wanted things to hang on to while her hope was crumbling. Her dreams for the future were falling through the gaps in her fingers like dry sand.

Dawson squatted in front of her, demanding her attention. He still wore his uniform, but the tenderness in his eyes was a stark contrast to the stiffness of the outfit.

His hands slid up the outside of her thighs and wound around her where he threaded his fingers together at the small of her back. "We got good news today, Liv."

Olivia scoffed. "Good news?"

"The surgery is minimally invasive, and the recovery time is short. Plus, you won't be in as much pain after. Yeah, sounds like great news to me."

Her shoulders sank. How could he be optimistic all the time? It was exhausting.

"Baby, I'm here for you. I will wait on you hand and foot until you're back to one hundred percent. You're not doing any of this alone."

He stood to press a kiss to her forehead before returning to his crouch before her. His smile had her own cheeks lifting. This man had the whole town wrapped around his finger. He was the best friend anyone could ask for, he was loyal and dependable, he was too handsome for his own good, and he was sitting before her promising better days were ahead of them.

"I'm sorry," she whispered. "I'm sorry I didn't tell you. I was just so scared of how you'd look at me."

"I don't know what you mean. This doesn't make me look at you differently."

"It should." Her breaths were coming quicker now, racing against her heartbeats. "You need to decide if you want this baggage."

"You are not baggage. You are my queen. I'll gladly sit at your feet for the rest of my life. Trust me to help carry your burdens, Liv. I don't know why this would change my feelings for you."

She swiped at her eyes and stared at her folded hands in her lap. "I've kind of been a drama queen about it."

Dawson laughed. "That's not the kind of queen I mean."

"It's true. Do you remember the school nurse when we were in high school?"

Dawson squinted one eye. "Maybe? Why?"

"I had to go to her office quite a few times in high school. This was before I had the surgery the first time or even had a diagnosis. At least once a month, I would hide out in the bathroom until a teacher would send someone to check on me. Then I'd show up in Nurse Joy's office and she'd give me the lecture about taking advantage of her time and send me back to class."

Dawson's jaw set tight as he stared at her. Man, she hated being thought of as a slacker who just wanted to get out of doing schoolwork. She loved school and always did well.

"So I didn't tell anyone because I didn't want the attention. I wanted to be invisible and blend in like everyone else. I didn't want people to think I was making excuses."

"Liv, it's killing me to know you were in pain and suffered alone. Please tell me you told your mom at least."

"I did. Finally. She took me to the doctor where they found out what was causing the pain. Mom was my biggest supporter. She was there for me and helped me through everything, and she didn't treat me like a helpless baby."

"I loved your mom. I don't think I've said that enough."

Olivia brushed a hand under her nose. "You tell me that a lot."

"Good. She was an amazing woman, and you're so much like her. You're a rockstar, Liv. Until a few weeks ago, I had no idea you'd been suffering in silence, and that's saying something since we're always together and you never let on that you were in pain."

"I'm sorry. I just didn't want to live in a snow globe where everyone could watch me get shaken up and dumped on."

Dawson's strong hands spread over the small of her back, supporting her and comforting her the way only his presence could.

"I get it. You like your privacy. I can protect that."

With his words, the dam holding back her tears crumbled. A sob snuck out before she could clamp her hand over her mouth.

She hated crying. Hated the sting in her throat and the tingling in her eyes. She hated the wetness and the heat in her cheeks.

Dawson stood and scooped her up before turning to take the rickety seat with her in his lap. She let the worst fears of the day leak out, creating room for something new inside of her.

Dawson's hand brushed over her hair as he whispered, "Let it all out. Break apart if you have to. I'll always help you put the pieces back together. And no one has to know."

After a few minutes, her tears slowed. The rush of anger and fear was gone, and she actually felt better–stronger.

When she caught her breath, she lifted her head and wiped her face. "I don't know what the future looks like."

"Are we supposed to know that? Darn, I knew I missed something important when I got my tonsils removed in second grade."

Olivia chuckled. "I remember that. You were pitiful."

"Hey, it was the anesthesia. The nurse said it could have that effect on people."

"Yes, crying about the loss of 'the only body part you ever loved' is probably a side effect."

Dawson huffed and reached for his chest pocket where he kept his phone. "You know what? I'm going to look it up. I'll show you–"

Olivia grabbed his hand. "Stop, I'm joking with you."

"You're never going to let me forget that! I was eight. I didn't know what a tonsil was, and I was afraid they'd removed a toe or something else I needed."

She brushed the short hair away from his forehead and framed his face with her hands. This man was special, and she couldn't fathom why he would possibly want her. "I don't know what the future looks like," she repeated softly.

"Me either, but I don't care what comes next as long as I'm with you. You're the only thing I need. I'd be happy with a few fiery sunsets and clear starry nights too, but those are optional."

Shoot. Why were her eyes trying to leak again? Loving Dawson was too much and not enough all at the same time.

Dawson adjusted his arms around her and propped his chin on her shoulder. "You're the first to remind everyone to bring their hardships to the Lord so you can pray for them too, but have you shared this problem with anyone so they can pray for you?"

Olivia shook her head, and the old memory of being scolded by her dad for leaving the back door open one night and letting a raccoon in drifted back to the surface. She knew what Dawson was getting at, and it was never fun getting taught a lesson in real-time.

"Jesus is in the boat with you, Liv. Why are you afraid of the storm? He knows you need help, so why are you afraid to sit at His feet? It's like you don't trust Him to take care of you."

"I do," she whispered.

"Good. He hears your prayers," Dawson whispered. "But He could be hearing your name in a hundred prayers."

Olivia nodded. "You're right. I've been so scared of God's answer to this problem that I hid it from everyone. If I talk about it, it's like it makes it real, and I'm scared of the plan He might have for me."

Dawson pressed a sweet kiss to her temple. "You're the strongest person I know, but you're not facing anything alone. No matter what path the Lord has in store for you, I know you'll do more than just survive. You'll thrive because you have faith. It's okay to be scared, but don't stay there. Get up and remember who stands beside you."

Hope filled her heart and made a home, settled down and planted roots right in the dirt Dawson had plowed with his words. He turned her world upside down, but now it was how it was meant to be. She wasn't an army of one, and that was what she'd been missing all along.

"I know you'll always be beside me," she said.

"And?" Dawson coaxed.

"The Lord."

"That's right, my queen. He'll never leave you."

She wrapped her arms around his neck and relaxed into his hold. God knew she needed help, and He sent her the perfect man to walk beside her through the toughest times in her life.

No matter what happened, they'd face it together.

"I have an idea," she whispered.

"I like ideas. Do tell."

Olivia leaned back and watched the chickens roaming the yard, then the goats hanging around the barn. "Want to make a video with me?"

31

OLIVIA

Olivia cuddled Henrietta and showed her the new chickie fountain. It was an elaborate fake-stone fountain with gently flowing water. "This is your new bath. You're going to love it."

Dawson had just turned it on, and some of the other hens ambled over to check it out. They'd spent the afternoon playing with the chickens and goats and making a ridiculous amount of photos and videos. It was exactly what she'd needed, and now that she'd had time away from her intrusive thoughts, all of Dawson's advice hit home.

Letting Henrietta investigate the new playground equipment, Olivia brushed her hands off on her jeans and met Dawson by the feed shed where he'd been watching her play with the hens.

They'd both laughed more over the last few

hours, and the appointment from earlier seemed like a lifetime ago. The shadows and dread weren't hanging over them anymore.

She slid her arms around his waist and tilted her head up to look at him. His arm wrapped around her, and the intensity in his eyes raked over her like a warm touch.

She took a deep breath and said, matter-of-factly, "I love you. I thought I couldn't love you more, but I was wrong. You're teaching me things I didn't know I needed to learn."

Dawson chuckled. "Not exactly what I was going for, but I'll take it."

"I'm serious. You're right about the way I've been looking at this whole thing. I was being selfish, and I wasn't trusting God. If I was, I would have gone to others for help. I would have put my fate in God's hands and trusted Him. You made me see that."

His strong hands cradled her face as he pressed a kiss to her forehead. Her eyes drifted closed, and she cataloged the moment.

"You're a wise woman. You would have figured it out on your own eventually."

Olivia shrugged. "Maybe, but I wasn't even close. It's so freeing to tell you about it."

"Feel free to share other things. You know, if you've secretly thought about our wedding or where we'll go on our honeymoon."

She laughed and pressed her forehead to his chest. "I may have thought about those things."

"Really? You think we'll spend a couple of weeks on a beach in the Pacific or cruising the Mediterranean?"

"Hmm. What about the French countryside or a tour of Spain?"

Dawson hummed deep in his chest. "Sounds perfect."

Pressing her eyes closed, Olivia tried not to read too much into how easily they'd slid into the conversation of marriage. Dawson had already hinted that he hoped their relationship would end in marriage.

Not end. Begin. It would only be the beginning. They hadn't even scratched the surface of the life waiting before them.

Olivia tilted her head up, propping her chin on his chest. "Though, I wouldn't say no to the beach."

"You just want to see me shirtless," Dawson said, pecking a small kiss on her forehead.

"Not gonna lie. That would be a selling point."

It was all just a fantasy, wasn't it? They'd barely begun to truly date, and Dawson would have them married by the end of the year.

He hadn't even asked her to marry him, but he talked about their future as if it were already decided. As far as she was concerned, it was.

"Are you thinking winter or summer?" he asked.

"For what?"

"Our wedding. Isn't that what we're talking about?"

Laughter bubbled out of Olivia's chest as she stepped back, pushing playfully against his chest. "Stop it. You're getting ahead of yourself."

Dawson pursued her and reached out for her hand as her footsteps quickened. When he missed her again, he picked up his pace.

"Then let's iron out the details over dinner. I'm starving."

Her feet barely touched the ground as she dodged his advance. She faked to the right before darting left, but he anticipated the move and folded her into his capturing arms.

Her high-pitched laugh split the air as he buried his face in the crook of her neck and kissed along the sensitive skin. She opened her eyes just as Anna walked around the side of the feed shed.

A hard kick hit Olivia in the chest as she scrambled out of Dawson's grasp. What felt like a ten-ton weight fell in her gut.

The look on Anna's face said she wasn't faring any better. Her blonde hair was twisted back in a tight bun, and she wore a navy suit jacket and matching pencil skirt above nude heels.

"Anna, I–I thought you were still in Casper."

Anna didn't move. Her mouth didn't even open as she stared at Olivia.

No, not like this. Anna wasn't supposed to find

out this way. Olivia and Dawson had spent a good portion of the afternoon going over what they would say to Anna when she got back in town.

Those plans had all been carefully-crafted words. Anna wasn't meant to see one of the private moments that had become the only times when they could be themselves.

Anna wasn't meant to see them so happy and in love.

Dawson took a step toward Anna, holding out a hand as if approaching a wild animal. "Anna, can we talk?"

His words seemed to spark the life back into Anna, breaking her stare from Olivia. "I'm sorry. I didn't mean to interrupt."

There wasn't any bite in her words, but they held so much hurt–hurt Anna was trying so desperately to disguise. She took a quick step back, then another before repeating, "I'm sorry."

"Anna, please." Olivia was begging, but she didn't care. She'd crawl on her knees if Anna would stay.

Holding up a hand, Anna ducked her chin. "I'm sorry." Then, she turned and ran back through the yard toward her car.

"Anna, stop!" Olivia broke into a sprint as she chased Anna, who could run in heels better than most women could run in sneakers.

Olivia caught up to Anna as she reached her car and opened the door. Grabbing it, Olivia held it open as she gasped for breath. "Please... wait," she panted.

"I'm sorry. I didn't know. I shouldn't have come. I'm sorry," Anna fired off the apologies and regrets faster than punches in a mixed martial arts match.

"Stop apologizing. I'm the one who needs to apologize. Please let me explain."

Anna grabbed the steering wheel with both hands and stared out the windshield. Her chest heaved with deep swells with hiccups at the beginning of every inhale. "I need to go."

There was no emotion in that robotic voice. No humanity or care or anger.

There was nothing behind the words, but they cut Olivia's heart wide open. She'd been properly gutted and fried in the fire before Anna looked up at her.

"I need to go," she repeated.

"Anna, please. Please just talk to me."

"Get out of the way."

The demand left no room for negotiation, and the stab in Anna's words had Olivia stepping back.

Olivia covered her burning face with her hands as Anna slammed the door and backed up, slinging gravel as she peeled out of the driveway.

DAWSON

Dawson stared blankly at the TV screen as Bugs Bunny tricked Elmer Fudd into thinking he'd missed rabbit season. *Looney Tunes* was usually a surefire way to lighten Dawson's mood, but the cartoons failed to take his mind off Olivia.

He checked his watch and stared at his front door. She was going to try to talk to Anna again today. Was it a good sign or a bad sign that he hadn't heard from her yet?

Half an hour. He'd give her half an hour before he called to check on her. Maybe she hadn't showed up yet because she and Anna were having a long talk and patching things up.

Fat chance. Anna hadn't answered Olivia's calls or texts all week, and knocking on her door hadn't gotten her an invitation inside either.

All of Olivia's and his good intentions blew up like an ACME bomb when Anna caught them at the farm. He'd known the second he laid eyes on her that she was hurt.

Olivia hadn't fared well either. She'd barely eaten or slept, and the only thing she could think about was Anna.

Dawson muted the TV and turned his recliner to face the door. Crossing his arms over his chest, he settled in to stare at the space where he desperately needed Olivia to appear.

Intermittent glances at the TV told him half an hour had passed, and he unlocked his phone and called Olivia.

"I'm almost there," she said in answer.

Her voice gave nothing away other than she wasn't crying.

At the moment.

"I love you." His constant reminder had done little to cheer Olivia up lately, but he wouldn't give up.

"I love you too."

Less than five minutes later, her engine rumbled outside, sending Dawson to his feet.

He met her on the porch and held the door open for her. She walked through it without lifting her chin from where it sat on her chest.

Well, that was as much of an answer as he needed.

"How'd it go?" he asked as he closed the door behind him.

Olivia looked up wide-eyed as if she'd just realized he was there. "I'm sorry." She slid her arms around him and tilted her chin up to press a kiss to his lips. It ended all too soon as she stretched the fakest smile he'd ever seen and asked, "How was your day?"

"Peachy. How was yours?"

She tilted her head from side to side. "Could'a been better."

Dawson brushed a hair from her face before letting his thumb trail down and over the darkness under her eyes. He hated those shadows. "How'd it go with Anna?"

"Not great. She said she didn't want to talk about it yet."

"Yet? That's a new word. Is that hope I hear?"

Olivia let her forehead rest on his chest. "I don't know. All I know is I can't keep doing this to her."

"Doing what to her? You didn't do anything wrong. We were going to tell her. She just found out first. We didn't even know she was back in town."

"The way she saw us together." Olivia huffed and shook her head. "She must be so mad at me."

Dawson tilted her chin up. "Once again, we intended to tell her. We can't help our feelings. Even if you and I weren't together, I wouldn't be with Anna. She's nice, but we have nothing in common."

"Oh, like the dozens of things we have in common," Olivia muttered.

"We've been friends since we were kids. We take care of a farm together. We go to the same church and do pretty much everything together. That counts for a lot, Liv. And how was I supposed to spend any amount of time with you and not fall in love with you?"

Olivia's chuckle brought some life back into the stale air before she sighed. "I can't hurt my friend," she whispered.

"And I can't live without you."

Olivia's head whipped up, and she sucked in a deep breath. "I'm the one holding the knife here. I'm hurting everyone around me. I was keeping things from you. Then I was keeping things from Anna. Now my best friend won't talk to me."

"Second best friend," Dawson corrected. "I'm number one."

"I'm sorry."

"And you're forgiven. You had reasons for not telling me those things, even though you should have known you could trust me and we'd figure it out together."

"And I'm glad I did," she added. "Can we have a fun night? I just need to take my mind off things."

"Barn Sour?" Dawson asked as he lifted her hand above her head, coaxing her to twirl. "We can dance the night away."

"That sounds perfect, but I need food before dancing," Olivia said. The light was already gleaming in her eyes again.

"You read my mind. I could go for a ton of totchos right now."

Olivia closed her eyes and hummed. "And a cheeseburger."

Dawson tilted her chin up and kissed her. Every movement was soft and sweet, reminding her to savor the moments when everything was right in the world. "Your wish is my command, my queen."

DAWSON PARKED his truck in front of the church on Sunday morning. Only four other vehicles sat in the parking lot. One belonged to the pastor, one belonged to Lyric, and the other belonged to Anna.

It was the second Sunday since the run-in with Anna, and Dawson wasn't about to let the Lord's day pass without the lines clearing up. Olivia loved going to church, and seeing her unease last night at the mention of the mid-morning service was where he put his foot down.

He said another prayer for the right words as he walked through the front doors of the church. Lyric waited in the entryway, dressed in a brown-and-gold dress that reflected the fall weather, pacing with her fingernails between her teeth.

When she spotted him, she dropped her hands and lifted her shoulders. "I can't believe I lied to get someone to church."

Dawson chuckled. "I'm sure God will forgive you. It's for a good cause."

"I know. I hate to see Olivia and Anna like this. It breaks my heart."

"And that's why we needed to do this."

Lyric shook out her hands and nodded. "You're right. Let's go."

Dawson took his place beside Lyric and followed her to the dining hall. "What did you tell her?" he asked.

"I told her I needed help with Baking Blessings."

"Nice one," Dawson said.

Lyric swatted his arm. "Shut up. I'm still not happy about lying."

If everything worked out this morning, Dawson would buy Lyric a cake this week for her trouble. He'd probably have the baker write "Thanks for lying" on it just to make her laugh about it.

They stepped into the dining hall, and Anna looked up from her phone. As soon as she spotted him, she lowered her phone to the counter beside her and looked from one side to the other like a cornered animal.

Lyric held up her hands and walked straight to Anna. "I'm sorry. I don't need help with Baking

Blessings. Dawson asked me to get you here so he could talk to you."

Anna averted her gaze and inhaled a deep breath. "I get it."

Lyric threw her arms around Anna's neck. Lyric's dark hair contrasted with Anna's blonde hair as the women embraced.

"I love you," Lyric whispered. "Olivia does too."

Anna just nodded and stepped back. Her expression was resigned as she let go of her friend.

Lyric looked between Dawson and Anna. "I'm going to let you two talk." With a wink at Anna, Lyric stepped out of the dining hall, her heels clicking on the tile floor.

Dawson leaned back, resting his hands against the counter behind him. "Don't be upset at Lyric. She means well."

"I know. I've just been running from reality," Anna admitted. Her voice had almost no inflection, as if she were resigned to defeat.

"Olivia and I didn't mean to hurt you. In fact, I had no idea you were even interested in me."

Anna huffed. "And that was the way I liked it. It was just a…" She waved her hand above her head. "An infatuation or something. Nothing real. I just want to find a guy that treats me well, and I saw how good you always are to women. I kind of latched onto that."

"So, you're not interested in me, just a guy who is nice like me."

"Basically. It took me all week to figure that out though."

"You deserve a man who will treat you well. Don't ever settle."

Anna scoffed. "Have you seen the options out there lately? I'm creeping toward my thirties, and I haven't met a decent man in...a while."

"That's not true. There are lots of good guys around here. Still, I get that it's hard to find someone you're compatible with, attracted to, and who loves you back. Dating isn't meant to be easy. Figuring out who you're meant to walk through life with is a big decision."

Anna fidgeted with her fingers. "You and Olivia sure made it look easy."

Dawson held up a halting finger. "Wait a minute. You saw us for about point-two seconds. That's not an accurate representation of our relationship."

Straightening and propping her hands on her hips, Anna looked up at him. "You're telling me that your relationship isn't perfect?"

Okay, he really couldn't deny that claim. "It's only been a couple of weeks. Give us some time, and I'm sure we'll have a disagreement over...something."

In truth, he couldn't imagine opposing anything Olivia said or believed, but he was right when he said they would eventually have to face-off over something. Especially if they spent the rest of their lives together the way Dawson intended.

"Maybe you will, but..." Anna tucked her chin and shook her head. "I was so stupid."

That was unexpected. "Stupid how?"

"I had no idea Olivia had feelings for you. Real feelings. Not the silly ones I made into a big deal. I mean, how long has she been interested in you? I steamrolled over her with my own petty crush, and I never thought to ask about her. I'm the worst kind of friend."

Dawson held up his hands. "Whoa, whoa, whoa. No one thinks you're a bad friend. In fact, Olivia is torn up over this. She's heartbroken that she might have ruined the best friendship she's ever had."

"If the two of you ever have an argument, she's supposed to come to me–her best friend–for girl talk. How can she do that when she can't even talk to me? I mean, she didn't feel comfortable enough to share her feelings with me. I'm supposed to be the one she runs to when a man breaks her heart. I failed her."

"You didn't. And for the record, she's never getting her heart broken. She wants a chance to apologize. We were going to tell you soon, but Olivia was terrified of what you might think. She respects you, and she cares about you. Also, she's going to need a lot of support in the next few weeks."

Anna sniffed and jerked her head up. "Why?"

Anna was one of the few who knew about Olivia's battle with endometriosis, and until Olivia was ready to share it with the world, Anna would be the one she looked to for support.

"She's having surgery in a few weeks for endometriosis."

"Again? I guess I should have expected that. It's been a while since her last one." Anna's brows pinched as she looked up. "Wait. She told you?"

"Finally. She didn't want to." He'd gotten past that little secret, realizing all of Olivia's reasons for hiding it.

"That's a big step," Anna said, biting her lips to conceal a smile. "I'm glad she told you."

"You and me both. I'm glad she's had you by her side all this time."

Anna brushed a hand over her blonde hair and sighed. "I'm so embarrassed."

"About what?"

"She probably liked you this entire time. If I hadn't been so mouthy about my perceived feelings for you, the two of you could have been together for a long time–getting engaged, married, and having..."

The color drained from Anna's face as she realized her poor choice of words. "I'm sorry. I know that must be a tough subject."

"It is, but I'm confident we'll make it through."

Anna's eyes went glassy as she smiled. "I know you two will figure it out. I'm so happy for you.

Truly." Blinking back the moisture in her eyes, she squared her shoulders. "I have to find her."

Dawson checked his watch. "She should be arriving any minute."

Anna clicked past him in her heels before turning back to face him. "Thanks again for forcing my hand. I was planning to call her today, but I'm glad you came to me sooner."

Dawson tipped an imaginary hat. "My pleasure."

With that, Anna bustled out of the dining hall and toward the church entrance. Dawson followed her quick steps and rounded the corner just in time to see Anna barrel into Olivia and wrap her up in a hug that probably cut off her air supply.

"I'm so sorry. Can you ever forgive me?" Anna asked, pressing her face into Olivia's dark, flowing hair.

Olivia caught sight of him over Anna's shoulder, and her eyes widened. Dawson gave her a big ol' smile and two thumbs-up.

"What are you even talking about?" Olivia asked. "I'm the one who needs to apologize."

Anna leaned back and shook her head hard enough to swing her hair from side to side. "No. We have a lot to talk about. Can we have lunch after the service?"

Olivia glanced at Dawson, and he gave her two more thumbs-up. He'd made lunch plans with Olivia already, but his hope had been to reserve her time in case things went well with Anna this morning.

"I'd love that," Olivia said, locking Anna in a rib-crushing hug.

Dawson had taken a leap of faith when he set up the meeting with Anna this morning, but everything had worked out for the good. Olivia had her friend back, and Dawson had a smiling girlfriend again.

33

OLIVIA

Olivia ordered a reuben and a lime soda before scooting to the side so Anna could order her usual cranberry walnut salad with water. Sticky Sweet's Bakery was always packed on Sunday afternoons, but Tracy ran an efficient business and handed out gourmet sandwiches quicker than the nearest fast-food restaurant.

Moving to the side to wait for their food, Olivia scanned the crowded restaurant. She spotted lots of people she knew, including Lucas and Maddie Harding. The pair waved at Anna and Olivia, and she appreciated the couple's discretion, considering they'd known about her relationship with Dawson for about two and a half weeks without telling anyone.

Now, she could finally talk about it with her best friend, and judging from the way Anna hadn't left her side as if they were stuck together with super glue, the conversation was bound to be a good one.

"Olivia!" Tracy shouted from behind the counter. She handed the tray over and called out, "Anna!" half a minute later.

The two picked up silverware and napkins before heading to a recently vacated table near the back of the restaurant. Olivia slid in on one side, and Anna took the other.

"Let's pray first," Anna said as she bowed her head. "Dear Lord, thank You for this food, and thank You for this friendship. Help us to always be supportive and lift each other up no matter what comes our way."

Olivia almost opened her eyes at Anna's surprising prayer, but she kept her stance, appreciating the good news all too much.

When they lifted their heads, Anna's expression was clouded in concern. "I'm so sorry, Liv. First, I want you to know that I don't have any wild ideas about having feelings for Dawson."

Olivia's traitorous eyes widened without her permission. "You don't?"

"No, and I'm sorry it took me so long to see that. I just want to find a man who cares about me...the way Dawson cares about you. I want an all-consuming, forever love."

Olivia turned her attention to the sandwich in

front of her. "I don't ever want to hurt you. You know that."

Anna reached across the table, covering Olivia's hand with hers. "I do. Trust me, I do. You're such a good friend. I kinda don't want to know how long you've had feelings for him because I already feel horrible about keeping you two apart."

"You weren't the only thing keeping us from acting on our feelings," Olivia admitted. Despite the issue with Anna being completely cleared up, Olivia and Dawson probably had years of important discussions ahead of them when it came to family planning.

Anna squeezed Olivia's hand, and the gesture of solidarity had Olivia's throat constricting.

"I know you'll figure it out. Don't give up hope. Maybe you can still have kids."

Olivia shrugged. "Maybe. I guess it's all up to the Lord."

Anna released Olivia's hand and sat up straight. "Amen. Leave it in His hands."

She didn't have much of a choice, but no one would be getting a hard and fast answer to the will-they won't-they when it came to having children.

Anna picked up her fork and moved the lettuce in her salad around. "Dawson said you're having another surgery."

"I guess I am. The doctor recommended it."

"Just say when. I'll take some time off work like last time."

"No way. You were just a clerk last time. You just got your own cases, and you don't need to take time off."

"But I will," Anna said as she shoved the first bite of salad into her mouth.

"I know you would, but please don't. Dad said I can stay with him for a few days, and if I need anything, he can get it for me."

Anna scrunched her nose. "No. Dads are great and all, but you need a woman by your side after this kind of surgery."

Not for the first time this week or even today, Olivia's eyes stung at the thought of her mother. She missed her mom continuously, but sometimes, the longing was enough to leave her speechless.

Pointing her fork at Olivia, Anna said, "I know that face. You're thinking about your mom. For the record, she'd be absolutely thrilled to know you and Dawson are together. She always loved him."

Oh no, tears were pooling in Olivia's eyes, and she grabbed a napkin from the table. "Yeah, she did."

"I know you miss her, and no one else can replace her. Just try to remember that you're never alone. You have so many people who care about you."

Olivia dabbed at her eyes before the tears were

able to mess up her makeup. "Actually, I've been thinking a lot about that. I've decided to...tell people."

"About your endo?" Anna said, a bit too loud for secrecy.

"Yeah. I'm ready for the people in my life to know about it. I've been doing a lot of hiding and lying to keep it a secret. I hate the thought of letting someone down because I can't handle my responsibilities. I don't want it to be an excuse, but I've had to use other excuses that weren't always the truth when I had to cancel things at the last minute. I don't want to do that anymore."

"Amen! You won't regret this. Everyone will understand."

"I know they will. Dawson thinks I should share about it on Instagram too."

Anna gasped and let her mouth hang open an extra second. "That's an amazing idea. You already have a huge following and tons of people who care about you, even if they've never met you. You're so genuine and friendly. I bet you'll have prayers and support from all over the world before you know it."

Olivia sucked in a big breath and let it out in a whoosh. "No pressure."

"There isn't any pressure. Just be yourself. I always thought you could inspire the world."

Olivia laughed. "That's a bit of an exaggeration."

"Not really. You're tough, but you needed to figure out that being tough doesn't mean suffering in silence. We're called to help each other, and I'm glad you're going to let us now."

Ugh. Olivia did not want to cry in public, but the waterworks were already turned on. "I love you," she choked out before the first sob.

Anna stood and pulled Olivia to her feet. Leaning into the embrace, she let her overabundance of love pour out. God gave her a challenge, but He also gave her plenty of help.

"I love you too, Liv. I always will," Anna whispered against Olivia's hair.

A minute later, she lifted her head and wiped her tears. Thankfully, the other people in Sticky Sweet's weren't interested in their exchange.

Olivia wiped her face just as Dawson rounded the corner with a tray in his hands loaded down with a cheeseburger, fries, a milkshake, and one of Tracy's fudge brownies.

He stopped when he saw her and flashed her the smile that always sent her heart racing. "Fancy meeting you here."

Anna turned around, wiped her eyes, and laughed. "We can't blame you for craving one of Tracy's cheeseburgers."

Beau walked around the corner and almost bumped his tray of food into Dawson's back. "Hey, keep it movin', man." He noticed what the hold-up was all about and looked back and forth between Olivia and Anna as they wiped their teary faces. "What'd I miss?"

34

DAWSON

Dawson strolled around the sanctuary nervously fisting and flexing his hands. The Wednesday night church service had just ended, but most of the attendees were still in their seats.

Just waiting on the guest of honor.

His plan could go one of two ways.

Olivia would either be thrilled and thankful or disappointed and embarrassed.

The latter scenario made Dawson want to hurl. Hopefully, she'd see his good intentions.

You know what they say about good intentions.

Asa walked into the sanctuary followed by Lyric and his son, Jacob. Lyric gave Dawson a thumbs-up and mouthed, "She's coming."

Asa flipped to a blank page in the notebook

Dawson had asked him to bring and clicked his pen. "Ready to get this party rollin'?"

"Did you bring the directory?" Dawson asked.

Asa held up the packet of papers stapled together on the left side. "Got it. Not sure how updated it is."

"Let's not mention that to Olivia or she'll put it on her to-do list."

"If her to-do list is as long as you say, she can't add a single thing to it. There might be a riot at the end of the evening."

"Nah. Many hands make light work, right?" At least that was the philosophy Dawson was banking this entire meeting on tonight.

The double doors at the church entrance opened, and two kids ran inside giggling, followed by a laughing and heaving Olivia. Her dark hair was down and flowing around her heart-shaped face.

But those eyes. Those beautiful eyes captured him, body and soul. They drew him to her, over and over, like a moth to a flame.

He'd known her for the better part of his life and loved her for almost as long. How many more years would he get to love her?

It would never be enough, but he'd settle for whatever the Lord allowed. He would cherish every moment and hold onto every second of happiness, storing them up like a kid collecting seashells on the beach.

When the kids ran into the waiting arms of their parents, Olivia spotted him at the front. Her head tilted slightly in confusion, but she gave him a small wave and took a seat beside Lauren.

In that moment, every jittery nerve in Dawson's body calmed, responding to her presence like water rolling over hot coals–she cooled the fire inside him. He took his place behind the small podium from one of the classrooms while Asa stepped behind the pulpit.

Dawson clapped his hands and said, "Thanks for coming tonight. I know you're all ready to start decorating the church for fall, and we'll do that after this quick meeting."

No one in the congregation batted an eye except Olivia, who was now looking around and whispering to Lauren.

"You all know that Olivia Lawrence does more work for this church and our community than one person should do alone. In case you haven't heard the news this week, Olivia needs to have surgery soon. It's supposed to be a minor surgery, but she will need to take some time to rest and recover for a few days after."

Wow. Avoiding eye contact with Olivia in a room full of people was tougher than Dawson had expected.

"I think we all want Olivia to take all the time she needs to get well, but she's a little stubborn and likes to help out a lot. I'm hoping that between us, we can lift some of those responsibilities off her plate so she doesn't try to do something crazy, like work at the soup kitchen the day after her surgery."

A chorus of "Amen" and "Of course" spread throughout the crowd.

Dawson made the long-awaited eye contact with Olivia and raised his hand to beckon her. "Liv, can you come up here, please?"

Olivia stood and stepped out into the aisle. She kept her chin tucked a little, but her eyes darted around the room, greeting friends and neighbors as she walked to the front.

When she was by Dawson's side, he reached for her hand and squeezed it before bending to whisper in her ear. "Are you mad?"

"The jury's still out. What are you doing?" she whispered back.

"Helping. I hope." It was the plain, honest truth. Olivia needed help if she was going to do all of the wonderful things she wanted done in their church and community, and what better place to ask for help than from the church.

Dawson lifted his chin to the expectant faces. A humming of anticipation had everyone slightly squirming in their seats.

"Love is an action, and Olivia Lawrence knows what she's doing. We could all learn a lot from her. This is our chance to step out of our comfort zones and give some of our time and efforts where they're needed."

"Amen!" Anita Harding shouted. Her hearty acceptance was followed by a dozen more agreements.

Dawson guided Olivia to stand by the pulpit where Asa waited with his pen and paper.

"Olivia is the only one who knows about all the things she does, so I'd like for her to tell us where she needs help. As she mentions tasks and dates, feel free to raise your hand and volunteer wherever you can. We'll also be checking your contact information against the latest directory so I can keep in touch with everyone about details. No need to call Olivia while she's recovering."

A low chatter spread throughout the room as Dawson pulled a microphone off its stand and handed it to Olivia. She stared up at him with a wide-eyed look of wonder that he couldn't quite read.

"You okay?" he asked.

"I think so. This is...a surprise."

"Hopefully a good one."

She blinked rapidly as she looked out at the sea of people waiting to help her and others in Blackwater. "A really good one."

He covered the microphone with his hand and whispered, "You don't have to stop doing what you love, but it's okay to ask for help. Now, all you have to do is delegate."

She nodded, stepped up beside Asa, and lifted the microphone. "Thank you all for being willing to help. To be honest, I was a little nervous about how I was going to do all the things I had committed to without letting anyone down. Sometimes, my brain forgets what's already on my to-do list."

There were a few chuckles as Olivia wiped her eyes. "I guess we can start with the monthly tasks."

Dawson watched and prayed as Olivia explained the causes and hands shot into the air. Most people were excited about some of the things they'd volunteered to do, and Olivia spoke quicker as her own excitement built.

By the time Olivia stepped down from the pulpit, joy radiated from her smile. A bunch of people flocked to her side to chat about things they'd been assigned and offer prayers for her surgery. She glowed when she talked about her passion for service.

When the crowd thinned and groups moved off to gather decorations from the attic or storage shed, Olivia turned to him and covered her mouth with her hands.

"Feeling better about things now?" Dawson asked as he reached for her.

"I can't believe you did this. It's amazing!" she exclaimed as she barreled into his arms.

"I can't believe all the things you have your hand in. In case you haven't figured it out yet, you've been doing the work of an entire community."

Olivia pushed her hair behind her ear and grinned. "You're kinda right. I didn't realize how much it is until we went through the list tonight."

Dawson wrapped his arm around her and pressed a kiss to her forehead. "It's okay to rely on others sometimes and trust that the Lord will provide."

"That's certainly the truth tonight."

Jerry Lawrence walked in carrying a tote that read "Harvest" on the front in big black marker. He rested the tote on the front pew and walked up beside Dawson and Olivia.

"You two seem to have everything figured out," he said with a wink at his daughter.

Olivia wrapped her arm around Dawson's back and rested her head on his shoulder. "Not everything, but at least some."

This was where she belonged. This was where Dawson belonged–standing beside Olivia, helping her accomplish her dreams for the rest of their lives.

Jerry extended a hand to Dawson, and they shook. Olivia's dad had always been the father figure he'd never had in his own home, and making sure Jerry liked him was in his top five things to do for the rest of his life.

"Looks like you're taking care of my baby girl," Jerry said.

"Every minute, sir."

Every minute. Every second. Every breath for the rest of his life. All of it was in service to the Lord, then Olivia.

Jerry looked at his daughter who released her hold on Dawson to hug her dad.

"Love you, Dad."

"Love looks good on you, sweetie."

Yeah, it did. And Dawson intended to keep it that way forever.

EPILOGUE
OLIVIA

Herbert the goat kept his attention fixated on Olivia as he munched on hay. The intense stare was getting a little weird, but she was in his territory now.

Sitting in the barn beside Dawson should have been her territory too since it was her family farm, but she was getting creeped out by present company.

She cradled Genella to her chest. "I promise I'm not going to hurt her. She likes me," she told Herbert.

Herbert and Genella had an unexplainable goat-chicken bond, and they looked after each other in strange ways.

"Dawson, Herbert is staring at me again," Olivia said over her shoulder.

Dawson didn't look up from the phone in his hands. "He's harmless. Just worried about his chick."

"Let's go hang out at Cluckingham Palace. I don't think he likes me."

Dawson looked up from his phone and pressed a sweet kiss to Olivia's cheek. "He likes you. He just likes his lady more."

Olivia eyed the protective goat at her feet. "If you say so."

"I think it's ready," Dawson said as he turned the phone so she could see it.

An Instagram Reel played showing Dawson and Herbert as Genella strutted over. Seconds later, Olivia entered the scene, and Dawson stood as his full attention shifted to her. He pulled her into his arms and pressed a quick kiss to her lips just as Betsy bounded to their side. The words on the video read, "The Goat Guy's got a chick (and a dog)!"

"And cue the hate comments," Olivia said.

"Those are few and far between. I bet more people will be happy for us."

"Tell that to Herbert," Olivia said with a jerk of her head toward the goat.

"I think more people are going to be surprised you've befriended a dog than they are about our dating announcement."

Dawson looked around. "Where is she?"

"Hanging out in the sunroom with the hens. She's not a fan of the cold weather."

Dawson pulled up another video and showed Olivia. "I still think we should use this one."

He played the alternate video they'd made last week of him bench pressing her. Olivia rolled her eyes. "You just want to show off your muscles."

"My queen," he corrected. "I want to show off my queen."

Olivia's cheeks heated, despite the early October chill in the air. Dawson hadn't been quiet about their relationship, proudly telling everyone that Olivia had finally given him a chance.

As if she hadn't been as giddy as a schoolgirl about their new relationship too. She'd been getting congratulated by everyone in town for weeks, and it wasn't getting old.

Olivia stood and set Genella on her feet. "Are you sure it's a good idea to make it this public? What if something happens?"

Dawson rose and pocketed his phone. "Nothing is going to happen. There's no way in this world I'd let anything mess this up."

Tracing the lines of her cheek and jaw, Dawson's gaze roamed over her face. Years of love and commitment washed over her. He was right. Nothing could take this happiness from them.

Their love could slip through time. One minute, she was ten and running behind him and her brother on the farm. The next, she was twenty-eight and crashing into his waiting arms where his love swallowed her whole.

Dawson tilted her chin up and lightly brushed

his lips against hers, taking his time as he adored her. Seconds later, his kiss turned urgent and eager.

She knew that hunger. The promise of a lifetime of happiness sat waiting before them while the present consumed her, reminding her to bask in every second of his love.

He pulled back and breathed in a contented sigh. "I love you, my queen."

"I love you too, future husband."

The blue in Dawson's eyes darkened. "I know I promised I wouldn't get ahead of myself, but does that mean–"

Olivia pressed a fingertip to his lips. "It means we probably don't need to get engaged when we've only been together a month, but you have me, heart and soul."

Dawson groaned and kissed her again, crushing her body to his as he sealed their futures together.

BONUS EPILOGUE
GAGE

Gage rested his back against the counter in the break room and crossed his arms over his chest. A dozen people dressed in suits and dresses crowded into the small area, and excited whispers filled the air. Most everyone had just come from a wedding.

Everyone except Gage.

He was here to fix what was broken and get a paycheck, not schmooze and chit-chat, and being pulled away from a transmission overhaul for this pow-wow was tanking his mood.

The job at Blackwater Automotive hadn't come with enough warnings.

Tapping the heel of his boot on the floor, he eyed the door. He could slip out and no one would notice.

"Don't even think about it," a feminine voice said beside him.

Gage turned to find Lyric wearing an orange dress and looking up at him with one eyebrow raised and a manicured finger pointed at him.

"I'm not thinking about anything."

Expectations were the key to acing life. If everyone assumed he was worthless, no one could claim to be disappointed when he screwed up.

Lyric narrowed her eyes at him, and the look reminded him of one his sister used to give him. Thea was a couple years younger, but she had always been the responsible one.

Until he shipped her off to who knows where. The old memory tugged at parts of his past he didn't want to revisit.

Gage tensed his jaw and looked away. Most people got the hint when he stonewalled them.

"I see you, and I know what you're doing." Lyric's whisper held an edge he hadn't heard from her before.

Granted, he kept his interaction with her and everyone else to a minimum. So he knew as much about her as he knew about the vegetation on the Rock of Gibraltar.

Nothing. And he didn't care to know either.

Without looking at her, he whispered, "I know what you're doing too, and I'm not interested."

"Who isn't interested in friends?" Lyric whisper-screamed.

Gage turned slowly, and Lyric met his disgruntled look with one of her own.

She had guts, he'd give her that.

"Me. Now go pester someone else."

Lyric folded her arms and straightened her shoulders. "No one else needs pestering. You, on the other hand, need a kick in the pants."

"Watch your language. There are kids around." Gage jerked his chin toward Jacob, who was getting licked on by Olivia's little ankle-biter. It had an old lady name that Gage could never remember.

"I've bent over backward trying to include you in things for months, and I haven't heard a thank you."

"Why am I thanking you?" Gage asked.

Lyric took a moment to compose herself before huffing. "You'll get it one day. You'll see what you're missing here, and you'll thank me. Until then, can you at least fix your face so that scowl isn't memorialized forever in the photos?"

"I'll talk to my plastic surgeon about it as soon as possible," Gage snapped back.

Lyric didn't back down like he'd expected. Instead, she held his gaze a little longer. "There has to be something you care about."

"What makes you think that?" Gage asked.

"Because everyone cares about something. Or someone."

"You're right. I do care about something. What is up with the prices at Sticky Sweet's? A cupcake–a *single* cupcake–is two dollars. Sometimes, a man just wants to enjoy a tiny cake without having to take out a second mortgage."

Lyric checked her phone, completely unfazed by his off-the-wall rambling. "She's here." Turning around, she announced to the room, "She's here!"

Everyone in the room started moving around. The buzz of excitement hummed in the air.

Gage slowly moved away from the door. After Lyric's warning about photos, he wanted to be as far away from the paparazzi as possible.

Everything quieted as they waited for Olivia. Gage ducked his chin as the click of heels tapped up the hallway.

"Surprise!" The whole room erupted into a shout as Olivia jerked back and pressed a hand to her chest.

"What are you doing? It's not my birthday!"

Dawson Keller, wearing a suit without the jacket, stepped forward and knelt in front of Olivia. She gasped and covered her mouth as she stared wide-eyed at the cupcake Dawson held.

Gage caught a glimpse of it before the room got crowded. A tiny crown was squashed into the pink icing with a diamond ring resting in the middle. He'd overheard Lauren talking to someone about it. Apparently, it was a princess cut.

How precious.

Dawson wasn't Gage's favorite person in the

world, but he was mildly tolerable as long as Olivia was around. At least the guy didn't glare at Gage as much when she was present.

Did it count for nothing that Gage had been on his best behavior since he started working at the garage five months ago? No, not to Dawson, at least.

"Olivia Mae Lawrence, you'll always be my queen, but would you do me the honor of letting me be your husband?"

Good grief, this guy could lay it on thick.

"Yes!" Olivia exclaimed, and everyone in the room erupted into a chorus of cheers.

Everyone except Gage. He had nothing to celebrate, and he never would.

A few minutes in, and Gage's head was beginning to throb from the noise. He pushed off the wall and skirted the perimeter of the room. He'd made it all the way to the last wall before Jacob jerked to a stop in front of him.

"She said yes!" Jacob threw his arms around Gage's middle and gave a quick squeeze before running off to tell someone else the news. He'd probably had way too much sugar between the wedding and this little party.

Okay, Jacob wasn't so bad. He liked to talk about cars, and he didn't look at Gage like he was a rubber band ready to snap.

Gage slipped out into the hallway and headed toward the garage. He didn't like standing around when there was work to be done. Two vehicles waited for tire changes, and half a dozen of the others promised more difficult mechanical problems.

Maybe Lyric was right. Gage could probably put cars on the list of things he cared about.

But what else was there? Was he the only person on earth who didn't have someone he cared about? Aside from his mom–the one heading into a later-stage of bone cancer.

Nope. Don't go down that road. Gage had been failing everyone around him his entire life, and it kinda sucked that he hadn't even done something good for the only person in the world who deserved his loyalty. He wasn't the "I'll make you proud" kid. That could have been Thea.

Gage tensed his jaw as he pushed out memories of his sister. He'd sent her away because she had a target on her back. It was the best thing for her to get out of his town and as far away from the people who hated them enough to spill blood.

"Hey, man."

Gage looked up from the beat-up Chevy Malibu when Beau came into view. The guy had a handful of years on Gage, and he'd been a good boss...so far.

He hadn't fired Gage yet, and that counted for something.

Beau propped his hands on the vehicle, careful not to grease up his white shirt and black pants. He tilted his head toward the party going on in the break room. "Thanks for showing up for a few minutes."

Gage nodded once and turned his attention back to the vehicle. "Welcome."

"We're heading to Barn Sour in a little bit."

"More celebration?" Gage asked.

"Yeah, it's not my idea of fun either, but Olivia is pretty convincing."

"Pushy is the word you're looking for."

Beau let out a single huff of a laugh. "True, but I'd do anything for my sister."

Gage looked up and studied Beau. Everyone in town knew Gage's family tree, and it wasn't a secret that he had a sister–one who disappeared five years ago.

But how much did Beau know about Thea?

"You coming?" Beau asked.

It was easy to say no. Gage had gotten good at it over the years.

Shoot. Lyric's little speech was actually gaining traction. What was wrong with him?

The phone in Gage's pocket rang, and he wiped his hands on the grease rag. He pulled it out to see his mom's name on the screen. "I need to take this."

"Sure. Just meet us there if you want," Beau said before waving over his shoulder as he walked off.

Gage answered the phone with a hushed, "Hey."

"Gage, she's back," his mom's breathy voice said in greeting.

The blood in his veins ran cold. There was only one girl who had left, and only one person in the world whose appearance could upset his mom like this. "What?"

"It's Thea. She's back."

OTHER BOOKS BY MANDI BLAKE

Blackwater Ranch Series

Complete Contemporary Western Romance Series

Remembering the Cowboy

Charmed by the Cowboy

Mistaking the Cowboy

Protected by the Cowboy

Keeping the Cowboy

Redeeming the Cowboy

Blackwater Ranch Series Box Set 1-3

Blackwater Ranch Series Box Set 4-6

Blackwater Ranch Complete Series Box Set

Wolf Creek Ranch Series

Complete Contemporary Western Romance Series

Truth is a Whisper

Almost Everything

The Only Exception

Better Together

The Other Side

Forever After All

Love in Blackwater Series

Small Town Series

Love in the Storm

Love for a Lifetime

Love in the Wild

Unfailing Love Series

Complete Small-Town Christian Romance Series

A Thousand Words

Just as I Am

Never Say Goodbye

Living Hope

Beautiful Storm

All the Stars

What if I Loved You

Unfailing Love Series Box Set 1-3

Unfailing Love Series Box Set 4-6

Unfailing Love Complete Series Box Set

Heroes of Freedom Ridge Series

Multi-Author Christmas Series

Rescued by the Hero

Guarded by the Hero

Hope for the Hero

Christmas in Redemption Ridge Series

Multi-Author Christmas Series

Dreaming About Forever

Blushing Brides Series

Multi-Author Series

The Billionaire's Destined Bride

ABOUT THE AUTHOR

Mandi Blake was born and raised in Alabama where she lives with her husband and daughter, but her southern heart loves to travel. Reading has been her favorite hobby for as long as she can remember, but writing is her passion. She loves a good happily ever after in her sweet Christian romance books and loves to see her characters' relationships grow closer to God and each other.

LOVE IN THE WILD
LOVE IN BLACKWATER BOOK 3

It's all fun and games until the fake relationship puts their lives on the line.

Gage Howard's last name is a legacy, and not a good one. The Howards and the Pattons have been rivals for half a century, but his sister's actions have branded her a traitor. Now, his own loyalty is divided.

Hadley Morgan has no clue how bloody the family feud between the Howards and the Pattons is when she volunteers to help her new roommate get information to Gage. A fake relationship with her roommate's brother is a simple solution to stay below the radar.

Gage is guarded and stoic, while Hadley is full of hope. As they carefully navigate their arrangement, they find unexpected connection in the tragedies of their past.

Hadley is determined to show Gage a God of forgiveness as he is constantly reminded of his dark past. Alliances are drawn and betrayals can put a target on anyone's back. Together, they'll have to strive to keep the Howards and Pattons from destroying each other while fighting for the new love that could be the way to healing for both of them.

Made in the USA
Coppell, TX
05 June 2024